Children of the Pride

Prideland Series: Book 3

Theo Mann

Invisible Publishing Company

Prideland Series

Contents

Chapter 1

A shout made Dina look up from the tub of water she was using to wash clothes. A ripple of tension went through the people around her and voices called back and forth from house to house.

"There's movement in the trees—right over there!" one man yelled.

"Arm the walls!" another bellowed through the canton. "Stand the watch and defend the walls!"

Armed men rushed from all sides, charged to the fence surrounding the canton, and clambered onto the rails to aim bows and arrows over the top.

Another six men grabbed the heavy sliding gate and started to haul it closed to blockade the canton. No one would be able to get in or out once they lashed it shut.

Dina dropped the shirt she was washing, wiped her wet hands on the seat of her pants, grabbed the axe leaning against her house, and rushed to the fence, too. She stepped onto the lower log rail and pulled herself up so she could see out into the jungle beyond.

The Riverbend canton had been constructed much differently than either of the other two cantons Dina had seen. This village had been built so it would be as defensible as possible from any attack, especially an attack by cats.

The canton occupied a protected position against high stone cliffs that surrounded it on three sides.

Those cliffs towered two hundred feet above the houses situated behind the fence. Even a cat would be foolhardy to drop from that height.

The cliffs angled forward to form a hollow between them. The fence covered a hundred feet of space across the front of this hollow. The sentries and guards only had to face one direction. They didn't have to worry about guarding the canton's rear and sides.

Guard towers had been constructed across the whole run of fence line so the sentries could see out into the jungle, including into the canopy.

A huge waterfall pounded off the cliffs right outside the fence. The spray fell into a pool and then twisted into the river that provided the canton's water supply.

The waterfall's constant beat made it impossible for anyone to hear if cats might be sneaking up on the village. That was a small price to pay for the cliffs' protection and the close proximity to such a pristine water source.

Cats could sneak up on the village silently anyway, so the sentries and guards relied instead on keeping an around-the-clock watch for movement in the surrounding jungle.

Whoever might be sneaking up on the village right now didn't even try to hide what they were doing. They crashed and tumbled through the branches. Dina could hear them even over the waterfall noise.

"Did you see them?" a man to her left asked. His name was Goss and he lived two houses away from Dina's.

"I didn't see them, but there are a lot of them," another man replied. "They're covering the territory in a hurry. They started over there and they made it all the way over there in a matter of seconds."

"Get ready in case they change directions," Richard Shriver ordered. "Get ready to put them down so they don't get over the fence."

"They aren't here to attack the village," Dina cut in. "They're Children. Isn't that obvious?"

"You don't know that," Goss countered. "We can't take the chance that they might be cats."

Dina compressed her lips. She resisted the urge to roll her eyes and gasp in exasperation. "The Children have been gone for three days and now they're back. That's why they aren't trying to conceal themselves."

"They are concealed," Richard pointed out. "We haven't confirmed whether they're cats or Children."

"They're the only ones who would come so close to the village—and they aren't even coming toward us. They're moving away." Dina stepped down from the rail and headed for the fence. "I'm going out there to bring them in. Open the gate."

She rested her axe against the fence inside the gate. She didn't want to approach the Children with a weapon. She didn't want to give the Children the wrong idea. After living at Riverbend canton for a year, she'd learned never to do anything threatening toward the Children.

"You can't go out there!" Goss insisted. "It's too dangerous! If they are cats, they could attack you and we wouldn't be able to defend you."

"They aren't cats!" Dina spat. "Wake up. They're our Children. Now open the gate."

"You're putting the whole village in danger, Dina," Richard snapped. "I can't let you do this."

"I'm not putting anyone in danger because you guys will still be here guarding the fence after I'm gone. Now, unless I'm mistaken, I'm still free to come and go from this village whenever I please. Unless you plan to hold me as a prisoner, you'll open the gate and let me out."

Just then, Meredith Fellows and Nicholas Lockerby happened to walk by. They heard the argument and came over. "What's going on?" Meredith asked.

"Apparently, the canton is keeping its members as prisoners now," Dina spat.

"We saw movement in the trees," Richard interjected. "Dina assumes it's Children and she wants to go out there to find them."

"You can't go out there, Dina," Nicholas told her. "You could be wrong. It might be cats."

"It would be my decision if I went out there even if it was cats," Dina fired back. "If you're all too afraid of your own Children to set foot outside the fence, that's your problem."

"We aren't afraid of our own Children," Meredith countered.

"Oh, really? They can climb, jump, fight, and run as fast and as well as any cat and the Children get faster and more agile every day. They can outrun, outclimb, and outfight any human."

"You're right about that," Nicholas replied. "They grow up so fast and they're so different from human children."

"That's the problem," Meredith pointed out. "No one can stop the Children from doing exactly as they please. *You* might let your Children run and climb and explore as much as they want, Dina, but some of us still have to discipline our Children when they step out of line."

"What you call stepping out of line is just their natural instincts to run and climb and explore," Dina countered. "If you let them push themselves the way they need to, you wouldn't have to discipline them and their abilities wouldn't cause you so many problems."

"It isn't just their abilities," Richard chimed in from the side. "The Children get more independence, determined, and even outright belligerence every day, too. They're so headstrong and stubborn. They don't care about doing anything but what they choose. It's bound to cause problems for anyone who tries to restrain them."

"Then stop trying to restrain them," Dina countered. "These aren't human Children. You can't expect them to act like they are. They need to test their strength and ability, explore wherever they want to explore, and push themselves against their environment. Surely any of you can see that. They thrive on it. You can see that in my Children. I give them all the independence they need and they don't give me any trouble."

"You raise your Children your way, Dina," Meredith told her. "The rest of us have different ideas about how to handle our Children. They might only be a year old, but they're still too young to live without parental supervision."

"They need families, too," Richard added. "They need to learn the value of community and belonging to a social structure."

"Maybe their instincts are telling them something different," Dina pointed out. "Maybe they need a social structure the village can't give them."

"They do spend more and more time away from the village," Nicholas pointed out. "Dina's right about that. They stay away longer and longer. They hardly come home at all anymore."

Dina turned away for the last time. "I'm going out there unless you plan to tie me up and throw me in the basement. If I see any of your Children out there, I'll tell them you want them to come in, too. Open the gate."

The three parents glared at her and then Richard gave a curt nod to the men at the gate. They hauled it open a few feet and Dina scrambled out.

Dina set off down the river to the tree line. The dense jungle canopy blocked the light and she moved into the cool shadows.

She didn't have to search for the Children. They made so much noise that she went right to them.

Getting near them was a different matter. They leapt from branch to branch moving fast through the upper story.

A boy launched himself off the trunk of one tree, soared thirty feet through the air, landed on another branch, and when it bowed under his weight, he used its motion to propel himself another forty feet to a different tree.

He landed in a crouch on the branch and she saw him clearly. He would have looked about ten years old if he'd been a normal human boy, but he wasn't a normal human boy.

Mottled grey, brown, and tan patches covered the tortoise-shell fur on his face, arms, legs, and body. It darkened the parts of him not covered by his clothes.

He wore almost no clothes at all. A pair of torn pants covered him from his waist to his thighs. He would have been naked other than that if he didn't have fur to cover him.

Claws curved from his fingers and toes to grip the bark. He could curl and bend his toes to flex his feet like a cat's and his ears came to a point at the top. Other than that and his fur, the rest of his body followed the same pattern as any normal human boy.

His nose lay flatter against his face to give his features a more feline appearance, but in every other way, the Children appeared human.

Their furred faces made it all too obvious that they weren't human and their appearance unsettled people almost as much as their behavior.

The boy cocked his head to one side in a very catlike way and then scampered down his branch on his hands and feet, slithered his body around the tree trunk, darted out onto another branch, and rocketed away.

Children streaked all over the place up there. Their shouts and laughter drifted to the ground and the boy met up with three more Children all racing through the canopy just as fast.

"Dexter!" Dina called up. "Dexter—hey, wait! I want to talk to you!"

The tortoise-shell boy stopped where he was, peered down at her, and cocked his head the other way. "What are you doing out here, Dina?" he asked.

"I just told you. I want to talk to you." She glanced at the Children around her. "Is everyone here? Are Adrian and Iona with you?"

"They're here," a small, white-furred girl replied in a high, childish voice. "I think they're over there somewhere."

She pointed behind Dina in the direction of the waterfall. The girl had fluffy, silky white fur and petite, delicate features. She posed a stark contrast to the much larger boy next to her.

Midnight black fur covered every particle of his skin, which was also black. Even his eyes were deep, velvet black and they were so large that they seemed to obliterate the white part of his eyes.

He glared down at Dina and then cast a flinty glance toward the village. "Why are the sentries arming? Do they plan to attack us?"

"They don't know it's you," Dina replied. "They think you're cats."

He snorted. "Don't they know any better by now? They should be able to see and hear that we aren't cats."

"You can't blame the sentries for taking precautions, Karim. You've been gone for three days. Now come down and come inside before someone gets the wrong idea." Dina surveyed the surrounding trees.

The other Children had gathered around to listen, but they didn't come down to the ground. They hunched on their branches or clung to the tree trunks with their claws.

All the Children angled their heads from side to side, cocked their ears to listen, and pierced Dina with sharp, hard, watchful eyes.

She'd gotten used to the Children's strange ways and she knew every Child here intimately. She didn't feel threatened by them and they couldn't possibly feel threatened by her.

She opened her mouth to tell them again to come back to the village, but right then, a different boy rocketed out of the canopy moving impossibly fast. He bounded from branch to branch covering the distance in seconds.

He came from far away closer to the waterfall. He must have started much farther away than the others, but he caught up in no time.

He hurtled across the area, over Dina's head, and pelted toward the girl with the white fur. The boy laughed out loud, whooped, and barely avoided colliding with her. "Come on, Naia! What are you waiting for? Come on, Dexter. We're going down the gorge to go hunting."

"Dina is here," Dexter told him. "She wants us to go back to the village."

The other boy hit a different tree trunk, blasted off it, and hit another tree. He scampered up the bark to a sturdy branch and stopped to crouch in the crook where the branch met the trunk.

Dina didn't get a good look at him until he stopped moving. He was bigger than Dexter and more muscular than Karim.

This boy had orange-gold fur with white streaks running outward from his face in a star pattern. It gave his features a distinctly tiger-like appearance.

Dina's stomach turned a somersault when she realized for the hundredth time how much her son Adrian looked like his father, Renfroe.

"What are you doing out here, Dina?" Adrian asked. "You know it's dangerous for humans in the jungle."

Dina tried to keep the resentment out of her voice, but it might have snuck in anyway. "How else was I supposed to talk to you? I haven't seen any of you for days. Come back to the village."

"We don't want to," another boy replied from a different tree. "We want to go hunting."

"You can go hunting anytime," Dina countered. "If I had to guess, I'd say you've been doing almost nothing else in the days since you've been gone. Go on and admit it. You know I'm right."

No one answered. Thirty Children peered down at her from the canopy.

"I've never stopped you from spending as much time as you want in the jungle," she went on. "I'm one of the few parents who let you come and go as you please, but I never get to see you anymore. You only have one mother. At least come inside and spend the night with us. You can come back out here tomorrow if you really want to."

Karim, Dexter, the white-furred girl, and practically everyone else glanced over at Adrian. He didn't look around at anyone. He kept his gaze locked on Dina.

"All right," he finally agreed. "We'll come inside, but not now. We'll come when it starts to get dark."

Dina made a decision not to argue. "All right. Just make sure you come.....and bring Dion, Salvatore, and Elio with you—and anyone else who's out here. Their parents are worried about them."

"No one is worried about us," Karim growled. "They're worried about themselves."

"Well, I'm not worried about myself and I'm not worried about you," Dina countered. "I just want to see you and talk to you sometimes. Is that asking too much?"

"We'll come later." Adrian took another flying leap off his branch, and in a second, he bounded away into the canopy again. "Come on, Naia!"

The other Children hesitated and then they all sprinted away into the canopy to follow him. Naia waited a little longer before she left. "We will come, Dina. I promise. We want to see you, too."

Dina had to smile up at her. "It's okay, sweetie. You go have fun. I'll see you all later."

Naia burst into a bright grin and dashed off into the trees. The others streaked away in no time and vanished out of sight.

They left the jungle too quiet and Dina's heart sank. She really wished they would come around more often and not spend so much time away from the village.

That would never work, though. The Children's natural behavior conflicted with natural human behavior. The Children didn't behave in what their parents thought was normal human interaction. It was bound to lead to conflicts.

Dina stared after the Children, but they were already long gone. Part of her wished she could go with them, but she never would have been able to keep up with them.

Part of her also wished they *wouldn't* come back to the village. Her lenience in letting her Children run freely made them by far the unruliest of any in the village—or out of it, for that matter.

She finally tore herself away, but when she turned back to the village, she discovered one girl who'd stayed behind. She was the same age as the others with pale, yellow-white fur.

Darker golden stripes radiated outward from her face the same way Adrian's did, but this girl had much more delicate features than her brother.

Dina took a few steps nearer. "Iona—sweetheart!" Dina frowned. "Are you okay? Don't you want to go hunting with the others?"

Iona shrugged and glanced in the direction the others had just gone. "You're right. We always hunt. We can do that anytime." Iona's dark brown eyes snapped back to Dina's. "We never see you anymore."

"It's all right. I understand." Dina crossed the last few feet to the girl's side and ran her fingertips through Iona's hair. It blended into the fur on her face and hung down her back in shimmering pale blonde tresses. "You don't have to go out with them if you don't want to. You can come back to the house with me now if you want to."

"I do want to go with them.....but I want to see you, too."

"You will see me. You'll see me tonight when you come home to the house."

"I guess so."

Dina studied her daughter more closely. Iona had grown up so fast. Dina never got a chance to enjoy her Children being Children. Now she sensed them leaving home after only one year.

She put her arm around Iona's shoulder, hugged the girl against her body, and kissed the top of Iona's forehead.

Dina tried not to notice Iona stiffen at the touch. That was another thing about the Children. They didn't like physical affection—not that kind. They instinctively guarded themselves against it.

It would have bothered Dina that her own Children shunned her affection, but she'd come to understand that as part of their nature, too.

Her Children tolerated it from her, but she did her best to keep it short and sweet.

She let Iona go, stepped back, and smiled down at her daughter again. "You should go if you want to go. You won't be happy coming to the village now. You would only wish you'd gone with the others."

"You're right," Iona replied. "I would."

Dina indulged in stroking her daughter's cheek one more time. "Go have fun. I'll see you tonight."

Iona burst into a grin, too, rose on her tiptoes, and gave Dina one quick kiss on the cheek before Iona burst away into a run. "Thanks, Dina!" Iona called over her shoulder and she leapt off the ground.

She vaulted into the lowest branches, propelled herself into the high canopy, and disappeared to catch up with the other Children.

Chapter 2

Dina stayed where she was under the trees and listened to the silence. The Children disappeared so fast. They crashed through the treetops and made the branches sway, but in a minute, the noise and movement stopped, too. Nothing remained but the usual jungle sounds of tree lizards and insects buzzing around.

Dina sighed and turned back to return to the village. She wasn't looking forward to the reception she got when she met up with the other parents.

Her lenient attitude toward her Children's catlike nature didn't sit well with the parents who wanted their Children to act more normally—normally in human terms.

A bunch of archers in the watchtowers took aim at her when stepped out of the trees. She raised her hands and kept on walking toward the gate.

The men pulled it back to let her in as she approached, but before she could enter, a different man broke out of the undergrowth to her left. He carried a fell deer carcass slung over his muscular shoulders and his powerful legs braced into the forest floor with every step as he labored under his load.

Link Randall burst into a grin when he saw Dina standing there. She had to smile back at him and she stopped to wait for him. The burden of worry and tension lifted off her, now that he was back.

She entered the canton first and the guards shut the gate behind Link. He bent down and kissed her in front of all the sentries, but before he could say anything, Meredith and Nicholas came over to her again. Troy Engel happened to be standing near the gate and heard their conversation.

"Well?" Meredith asked. "Where are they? You said you would bring them in."

"I said I would talk to them and I did," Dina countered. "They're going hunting right now and they agreed to come in when the sun goes down."

"That isn't good enough," Richard interjected. "We can't let them run wild through the jungle like animals. You should have brought them in, Dina."

"I'm not going to drag my Children or anyone else's Children back here by the scruffs of their necks," she fired back. "You try it if you like your chances."

"What's going on?" Link asked.

This time, Dina found it impossible not to roll her eyes and gasp in exasperation. "Nothing that hasn't been going on for months."

"You're setting a bad example for the rest of *our* Children by letting yours run wild," Meredith went on. "You let your own Children call you by your first name....."

"I've already explained more than once why I do that," Dina replied. "I do it so I'm not throwing it in my adoptive Children's faces every minute of the day that Adrian and Iona are different from them or that my adoptive Children have a different relationship with me. How I relate to my Children is none of your business. If you were in my situation, you would do the same thing—or I hope you would. I hope you would have enough consideration for these Children's feelings to see why I have to do it this way."

"That isn't the point," Troy interjected. "Our Children see you letting your Children do whatever they want and our Children think they can do the same thing. Admit it. Our Children were running around with Adrian and Iona just now."

"How do you plan to stop them?" Link interjected. "You've tried that before and it never ends well. If you try to lock up your Children, they'll just run off."

"And don't you dare put this on Adrian and Iona," Dina spat. "All the Children are running around together out there. If Adrian and Iona weren't there, your Children would go running around with someone else. When are you going to see reason? The Children have their own social structure and that's the way it should be."

"They aren't cats," Richard countered. "They aren't wild animals that should be running around in the jungle with no rules or order in their lives."

"They aren't human, either," Dina argued. "These Children have never existed any-where in history before. It only makes sense that they would have to come up with their own society and their own way of doing things. I can't be the only person in this whole village who sees that."

"You aren't," Link interrupted and took her hand. "Come on. We're going home."

He pulled her away from the others. They glared after her and she turned her back on them. This same argument was becoming a daily occurrence.

Link climbed the steps to the house they shared with their Children—or that they used to share with their Children. The house had been empty for days and this wasn't the first time the Children had gone off on their own.

"Are you okay?" Link asked over his shoulder.

Dina sighed and passed her hand across her eyes. "Yeah, I'm all right. The Children are coming in tonight—and I guess that means all of them."

"It's a good thing I brought this, then." He dropped the fell deer carcass on the floor in the main room, squatted down, and started skinning it right there in the middle of the house.

Link's and Dina's house wasn't a typical canton house. It had no furniture in the main room and only one bed in Links' and Dina's bedroom. The rest of the house was completely empty. It always had been.

Link and Dina had become accustomed to this after raising more than thirty Children in this house. They never slept in beds. They preferred to sleep curled up on the floor with each other to keep them warm.

"What do you think I should do about the other parents?" she asked him while he worked.

"Nothing," he replied without looking up. "Let them raise their Children their way and we'll keep raising ours our way."

"We hardly raise them at all anymore," Dina murmured. "They aren't even a year old."

"You've said yourself that cats reach maturity by one year. Why would the Children be any different?"

"They aren't mature. They're still Children. They can't be more than ten in equivalent human years."

"Ten-year-old human children still play and explore as much as our Children do," Link countered. "I don't see our Children doing anything abnormal....and neither do you. You're just letting the other parents get inside your head."

Dina sighed again and turned to the open house door. "I know. You're right."

She gazed through the door at the canton outside. It looked and sounded peaceful, but only on the surface. An undercurrent of tension ran through the place and not because of the constant arguments between Dina and the other parents.

That tension would have been here even if Link, Dina, and their Children left the canton. The bigger conflict kept simmering between the other parents and their Children.

The parents' desire to restrain, civilize, and discipline their Children threatened to boil over into hostility. The fact that only Link agreed with Dina's point of view really started to get to her. Did they misread the situation? What if the other parents were right and she and Link were wrong?

The Children didn't return. A few women approached the gate and asked the sentries to open it so the women could bring in water from the river.

The men opened the gate, and when the women returned, the men left the gate open. Life returned to normal and the noise in the village settled to a steady hum of regular activity.

Link flipped the carcass over onto its other side. The thump on the floorboards brought Dina back to her senses. "You better get busy if the Children are coming to stay here tonight," Link told her.

Dina turned away from the doorway. "You're right. They stay away so much that I'm starting to get used to not having them around."

"They're good kids," he muttered under his breath while he worked. "There's nothing wrong with them. They're just being kids."

She let the subject drop. She, Link, and the other parents went around and around with this debate all the time.

She got to work and pulled a bunch of rough woven blankets out of the cupboards built into the walls. She left the blankets lying on the floor. The Children didn't need or want any other bedding.

They'd slept with Dina when they were babies, but that ended soon enough when the Children got older and more mobile. They preferred to just crawl or run around all day and then flop wherever they happened to be when they wanted to sleep.

She brought in buckets of water and started heating them on the fire. Link hauled his deer carcass to the front door, hung it up from the doorpost, and gutted it there.

Dina was just passing him with another bucket of water when he nodded past her shoulder. "Here they come."

She turned around to look. The sentries on watch all stiffened and some raised their weapons, only to lower them when the Children stepped out of the trees.

Adrian, Karim, and Karim's two brothers, Kaiser and Kenji, let the mob of more than fifty Children. Each Child had distinctive patterns to their fur, pointed ears, and hooked claws on their fingers and toes.

They walked upright this time, but they didn't always.

They'd divided themselves into groups with siblings gathered together. Tania Barnes's three sons from Khalid stood out from the rest.

The three brothers' satin black fur erased their features and even their eyes. The fur made Karim, Kaiser, and Kenji look even more feline than the rest of the Children.

Naia, another tiny, slender girl, and two equally miniature boys crowded together on the other side of the group. Their fine white fur made them blend in with each other.

The girls' high-pitched giggles bubbled over a tide of conversation and laughter coming from all over the group.

Dexter and four others with matching tortoise-shell fur patterns followed Adrian and the three brothers. Osiris's Children always stayed close to Adrian, but never as close as Karim, Kaiser, and Kenji. Those three never let Adrian out of their sight.

Six Children with golden fur occupied the center of the group. The Auroras were all older than everyone else as were Link's five nieces and nephews.

Four boys brought up the rear. Riggs, Rex, Rey, and Rome had all inherited Fallon's orange fur and his piercing orange eyes. They'd also inherited his ferocious nature, short temper, and merciless attitude toward anyone who got in their way.

The sight of those four boys made Dina send up another prayer of relief and gratitude that Amaryllis had given Anoushka to Dina to take care of instead of giving her to someone else.

Any other parent in this canton would have tried to rein in Fallon's four boys. That was the worst thing anyone could have done and it would have made them even more aggressive than they already were.

Spending a lot of time out in the jungle and running around with Adrian, Karim, and the others seemed to calm the boys down. It calmed all the Children down and made them less explosively violent.

That was the thing the other parents didn't seem to understand. Restraining the Children and trying to civilize them only made them wilder, more explosive, and more vicious when they did lash out.

Twenty other Children accompanied Dina's Children back to the village, including Troy Engle's five Children, Meredith's two sons and two daughters, and a whole crowd of others.

"We got trouble," Link murmured in Dina's ear. "Look."

He nodded to the other side of the village. Meredith, Troy, Nicholas, and three other parents left their work and converged on the gate as the Children approached.

"Great," Dina muttered. "I better go out there and....."

She broke off when Adrian and the three brothers got nearer, but when they turned to enter the gate, another shout echoed down the fence line. "Intruders approaching!" someone yelled. "Arm the fence! Shut the gate!"

Dina froze as a bunch of other Children broke out of the trees across the river. These Children didn't belong to the canton. Dina had never seen these Children before. They halted there and eyed the mob standing outside the fence.

One of the sentries dove across the gap, grabbed Adrian by the arm, and tried to pull him inside. "Get in here!" the man snapped. "We need to shut the gate and defend ourselves!"

Adrian shook him off. "Get your hands off me! They're our friends. Come on, Black. Come with me. The rest of you stay here. We don't want them to think we're threatening them."

He turned around and crossed the open ground to advance on the strange Children. Karim, Kaiser, and Kenji shadowed Adrian all the way.

The other Children parted to let the four boys through. No one said a word or moved out of position at Adrian's command.

Everyone inside the canton froze, too. The sentries forgot to shut the gate and all the Children turned around to watch Adrian approach these strangers.

Link startled Dina out of her trance. "Come on. Let's go down there."

He led the way outside, crossed the canton, and approached the gate from the inside. None of the Children saw him. They all had their backs to the entrance.

Dina hurried to catch up with him and everyone watched in rapt fascination as Adrian advanced on the strange Children. He talked to them for a minute and pointed in different directions. They nodded and then slipped back into the trees.

Adrian watched them out of sight and then he and the three brothers walked back to the group the way they left it.

"Who are they?" Riggs asked as soon as the four boys came back.

"They come from Hardship canton," Adrian replied. "They want us to come visit them." He halted there in the middle of the group. "The Black went last time. You Manx can go this time."

Riggs pumped his fist. "Yes!" He spun around and his brothers mobbed him. They grabbed each other and practically jumped up and down celebrating.

Adrian turned to the rest of the group. "Auroras, you can go scout out Northfall. If any of you comes across any other canton, let me know. We need to send out representatives to all of them."

He strode through the group getting closer to the gate....and came face to face with Link and Dina.

"You're visiting other cantons?" she blurted out.

"Do you have a problem with that?" Adrian countered. "They're our own people. Why shouldn't we visit them?"

Dina shut her mouth. "I don't have a problem with it. I just didn't know you were doing it."

He waited for her to say something else, and in that moment of silence, Link stepped forward. "It's good to have you all back. We missed you. Come inside. I have a deer carcass for you at the house."

"Hey, Link!" Dexter exclaimed and rushed him.

The other Children crowded around and everybody started talking at once. The Children told Link all about the ox they'd caught down the river. They related every detail of how they'd chased it down, surrounded it, and brought it down.

He beamed at them all. "That's wonderful! You're all getting to be fantastic hunters."

He turned around to escort them all inside when Troy came forward and grabbed one of his sons by the arm. "Where have you all been? We've all been worried sick about you. Come home right now, Leroy—you, too, Devon. We need to talk."

The boy tugged his arm out of his father's grasp. "I'm not going home. I'm going with Adrian and the others."

"You aren't going anywhere except straight home," Meredith interrupted and drew her own Children out of the crowd. "You've spent too much time out already."

More Children started to protest. "I'm going to Dina's house," Meredith's son Dion declared. "You can't stop me."

"I'm still your mother," Meredith countered. "If I say you're coming home, that's what you'll do."

"If I can't go with Adrian and the others, I'll go straight back out into the jungle," Dion snapped back. "You don't tell me what to do."

"You can't come to my house against your parents' wishes," Dina interjected. "As long as you're in the village, you have to do things their way. If they say you can't come, then that's the final word."

"Thank you, Dina," Meredith replied.

"Then I'll go back out into the jungle and I'll stay there," Dion yanked his arm out of Meredith's grasp again. "You can't stop me."

"You have to let him come, Dina!" Adrian cut in. "You have to let them all come. You can't turn them away."

"I'm sorry, sweetheart," Dina replied. "I don't like it any better than you do, but I have to live in this village with these people."

"You heard your mother," Link chimed in. "The rest of you go home to your parents. You'll catch up with Adrian and the others when you go back out into the jungle. You can spend one night behind walls just to satisfy your parents, can't you?"

Silence fell over the group and then a few Children grumbled under their breath. They shifted their weight and then turned away to accompany their parents back to their houses.

Everyone else's Children split away and drifted off in different directions. That left Adrian, Iona, Tania's three boys, Elyse's four Children, Osiris's five, Fallon's four sons, Link's nieces and nephews, and the Auroras standing just inside the gate.

"You shouldn't have let them take the Children away," Adrian growled under his breath.

"I don't let anyone do anything with their own Children," Dina told him. "Besides, if things go the way I think they will tonight, the Children won't be spending tonight behind walls anyway. These things never turn out the way the parents want them to."

"Let's not talk about that." Link pushed his way into the group and hugged the Children one after the other. "I missed you all so much! Come home! We have so much to talk about."

Chapter 3

Link led the way back to the house. The Children talked his ear off while he unstrung the deer carcass from the doorway.

He laid it on the bare floor in the middle of the room and the Children gathered around. They tore into the meat with their sharp teeth while Dina brought over a clay pot full of burning coals.

She set it next to the carcass, sliced off strips of the meat, and skewered them to roast over the embers for herself and Link.

The Children ate the meat raw and Dina found herself watching them with new eyes. The Children's eating style had seemed normal when they lived at home all the time.

The other parents reacted with disgust and horror when they saw the way Dina let her Children eat. The other parents insisted on their Children eating cooked meat and using human implements like plates, knives, and forks.

The Children squatted around the carcass and stripped the meat off the bone with their bare teeth. None of them showed the slightest concern that so many other people were putting their mouths all over the same carcass.

Link didn't comment on it, either. He sat next to Dina, took the skewers she handed him, and ate them while he and the Children talked.

"Where have you been staying?" he asked. "I haven't seen you and none of the other hunters have mentioned seeing you, either. You must have gone far out of our range."

"We went down the southern gorge," Adrian replied. "Then the Black went on a side mission to scout the eastern fork of the river as far as the Great Divide."

"The what?" Dina interrupted.

"The Great Divide," Adrian repeated. "It's a ridge of steep cliffs that separates this part of Prideland from the west country. We haven't explored that yet."

"No, I mean before that. You said the Black went on a side mission to scout the eastern fork of the river."

He blinked at her. "What are you asking me?"

"What's the Black?" she asked.

"These three." He waved at Karim, Kaiser, and Kenji. "They're the Black."

"You can't call them that!" she exclaimed. "They have names."

"It's easier to call them the Black."

"It's insulting," she told him. "They're people. Use their names."

"They call themselves that," Naia interjected. "Karim was the one who told us to start calling them that."

"It's quicker than calling them by their names," Riggs chimed in.

Dina turned to the three brothers. "Are you okay with this?"

"Of course," Karim replied. "It makes sense because.....we're black."

"I know that," Dina countered. "It's just....."

"It's the same as calling those four the Pygmies." Iona pointed at Naia, her sister Nova, and their brothers, Duke and Darius.

Dina realized in that moment that these names weren't intended as any kind of slur against the parties in question. The names were simply descriptive.

Karim, Kaiser, and Kenji were.....well, black. Naia, Nova, Duke, and Darius really were pygmy compared to the rest of these Children. Why not just come right out and call them what they were? It was quicker than listing all their names.

Adrian dismissed the subject by turning to Link. "You should come with us the next time we go down the southern fork. There's so much territory down there that we haven't explored yet."

"Did you run into many cats out there?" Link asked. "That's the other parents' main objection. They're worried you'll be in danger from the cats."

"That isn't their main objection," Karim growled.

"You should come, Link," Adrian insisted again.

"I'd like to," Link mused and took another bite off his skewer.

"What's stopping you?" Iona asked.

Link glanced at Dina. "Nothing, I guess."

Link's nephew Riyadh spoke up from the other side of the circle. "You could come, too, Dina."

"We should split into gangs," Naia's brother Darius suggested. "We could cover more ground that way."

"We should find out if there are any cantons past the Great Divide," one of the Auroras named Aries suggested.

"We have a lot of ground to cover before we start exploring beyond the Great Divide," Adrian replied. "Let's find out what's on this side of Prideland first."

"We don't even know which cantons are in this part of Prideland," another Aurora named Indigo pointed out. "We should find out who's in them and who they belong to."

This sparked another flurry of conversation. Dina listened in fascination. She didn't realize until now how far the Children's private social hierarchy had already developed.

She'd been telling the other parents for months that the Children needed to establish their own way of relating to each other and everyone around them.

She didn't realize until right now that it had already happened while everyone's backs were turned. Adrian had become their undisputed leader. They all followed his word to the letter. They obeyed him much better than they obeyed their own parents.

"What are we going to do about the other parents?" Dexter finally asked.

"What is there to do about them?" Link asked. "They have their own way of doing things."

"We should keep their Children away from them," Dexter's brother Brock suggested. "We should build a canton of our own in the jungle where the Children can stay so their parents don't get any silly ideas about locking people up."

"That's nonsense," Link fired back. "No one is locking anybody up."

"They'd like to," Kaiser pointed out. "The parents would lock up their Children if they could get away with it."

Link opened his mouth to protest when Darius interrupted. "We don't want to build another canton anyway. We're already in a canton. We don't need another one."

"Then we could just build a camp in the jungle—our own camp," Kenji suggested. "It doesn't have to be permanent. Those who want to stay in the jungle could stay in the jungle. Those who want to come into the village to see their parents can do that without putting everyone else at risk."

"What do you say, Adrian?" Rome asked.

Adrian shrugged. "It won't matter. Soon we'll be old enough to come and go as we like. No one will be able to make us go anywhere we don't want to. Then the people who don't want to see their parents won't have to come back to the village at all."

Dina cringed. "If you're all finished eating, it's time to get ready for bed. Throw those bones outside, Rex. You Auroras clean the blood off the floor and then all of you bed down for the night. It's getting late."

They did as she told them. She carried the pot of embers to the kitchen counter and put the skewers on top of the coals to burn off the last drips of juice and fat.

The Auroras got a bucket of water, scrubbed the floor clean, and dried it with the mop.

The other Children stretched out on the floor, wrapped themselves in the blankets Dina left out for them, and started to curl up according to sibling groups.

Dina finished cleaning up the house, shut the front door, and blew out some of the lamps to darken the room.

Then she started the bedtime routine she'd been using with the Children since they'd all been born. She sat down on the floor next to the first sibling group she came to, which were the four Manx boys.

She rubbed Rey through the blanket and ran her fingertips over his fur. She did the same thing to all four boys and they pushed their heads into her hands. Bedtime was one of the few times they accepted any affection from her.

"You all had fun out in the jungle, didn't you?" she began.

"Why can't we live in the jungle all the time?" Riggs asked.

Dina sighed. "I guess it's like Adrian says. You will when you get older. None of you is fully grown yet, but you will be soon. You're between being Children and adults, so give yourselves time to grow."

"Brock is right," Rome growled. "We should stop the parents from interfering with their Children."

"How about you leave that for the Children to handle?" Dina suggested. "I think they can deal with their own parents in their own way."

"I don't like seeing them make the Children leave the group when the Children don't want to," Rome muttered. "That's wrong."

"No one is making those Children do anything," Dina pointed out. "If I tried to make you stay in the village, would you do it?"

Rey looked up at her with huge eyes. "You wouldn't do that, would you?"

"Of course not. I'm proud of how independent you are. I want you to test your strengths in the jungle. I know you'll be all right."

"You should have been all the Children's mother," Rome snarled.

She had to laugh. "I think I have enough Children already, sweetheart. Now go to sleep. I'm sure you all have another big day of climbing, hunting, and exploring tomorrow."

She kissed each of them, tucked them the rest of the way in, and moved on to the next group, which was the Pygmies.

The four smallest Children curled around each other, rubbed their bodies against each other, and twisted together in a knot. Duke already had his eyes closed.

Naia's deep blue eyes peered up at Dina from out of a nest of blankets. "Dina....can I ask you a question?"

"Sure, sweetie," Dina replied. "Anything you want."

"We're Children of the Pride, aren't we?"

"Of course you are. You know you are."

"But you told us once that the definition of a species is that a species can't reproduce with another species."

"That's right. The Children are unique in the history of life. I can't think of any other time when you Children would have been biologically possible."

"If that's true....." Naia hesitated and then blurted out, "Will we be able to mate? If we only came into existence because of some mutation like you said, we might not be able to reproduce....with each other, I mean."

Dina cringed again. She wouldn't have felt comfortable talking to any normal human ten-year-old about this.

These weren't normal human ten-year-olds. If they continued to develop at the same rate, they would become mature in less than two years.

"I can't answer that, sweetheart," Dina replied. "You're a completely new species. It might be that you can't produce offspring. I really don't know. I wish I could give you the answers you want, but we'll just have to wait and see what happens when you get older."

Naia clamped her eyes shut tight. "I hope we can."

"I hope you can, too, sweetie." Dina kissed her and then turned to the other Pygmies. Duke was already asleep.

Darius and Nova listened in silence. Dina couldn't tell if Nova had any reaction to the subject, but Darius did. He scowled at Naia and his features hardened.

Dina kissed Nova and then ran her hand down the fur of Darius's face. "Don't worry too much about this now," she told them. "If it happens or if it doesn't, we won't be able to do anything to change it. We'll just have to keep going and deal with whatever comes."

She kissed each of them and moved on to the next group, which was the Auroras. They all bundled together in a huge heap. The older Auroras curled up with the younger ones in no particular order.

"Tell us the story of how you fought the cats to escape from Prideland, Dina," Briar urged.

Dina laughed. "What do you want to hear that for? I've told you a hundred times."

"Tell us again," Aries exclaimed.

"Tell about your fight against Fallon and Khalid," Amir chimed in.

Dina glanced over at the four Manx brothers, but they all lay on the floor watching her. They didn't object to her story about how she killed their father.

They never objected to that any more than the Black objected to her telling the story of maiming Khalid so she could get to the Pod and escape from this planet.

She kicked herself for calling Karim, Kaiser, and Kenji, 'The Black', but if they wanted it, who was she to argue?

She took a deep breath. "Well, when I decided I needed to escape from Prideland, I snuck out of Renfroe's house while he was out hunting. I took the iron poker from the fireplace. I knew I needed a weapon, but I couldn't go to the kitchen or the cook helper would have found out I was trying to escape."

"I would have killed the cook helper," Karim growled. "I wouldn't have let any stupid helper get in my way."

Dina burst out laughing. "Well, when it happens to you, you can pull the escape your own way. Anyhow, I ran as far as the market before the sentinel cats caught up with me. I knew they would be after me as soon as they realized I was making a run for it, so I tried to get as far as I could before I turned to fight them."

"Skip to the part where you fought Khalid," Israel called.

"No, tell the part about where you hooked the dead cat on the poker and waved it in their faces," Aries countered. "That part is funny."

"How about I sit here and say nothing and all of you can tell me the story?" Dina teased.

"No, you tell it," Kaiser replied.

"Skip to the good parts, though," Darius told her.

"Well, when the sentinel cats attacked me, I swiped at them with my poker and one of them got stuck on the hook. I kept waving the cat in their faces and yelling, 'Who's next?'"

Rome chuckled under his breath. "That's great! Who's next? I wish I could have seen their reactions."

"They backed off," she went on. "They didn't want to fight me and wind up on the end of my poker, too, but when they disappeared into the darkness, I knew I had to get out of there. I knew they would go get their bigger friends and it would be all over. I kept on running until I got to the power station. I climbed into one of the Elite Battalion's barrels, pushed it into the river, and floated the rest of the way out to the jungle."

Naia made a face. "That's really gross. I couldn't have done that."

"It was a clean barrel," Dina told her. "There was nothing in it."

"And then you went out to the Pod....." Aries prompted.

"But when you got there, the power packs were already dead," Dexter added.

"No, she fought Fallon and Khalid before that," Kaiser corrected.

"No, she fell down the hole under the tree first," Kenji interjected.

"Skip that part," Adrian cut in. "That part is boring."

"You guys know the whole story anyway," Dina replied. "When I crawled out from under the tree, I approached the Pod and Fallon and Khalid came out of the undergrowth to stop me from leaving."

"They planned to kill you, you mean," Brock interrupted.

"It's the same thing," Dina replied. "Anyway, Fallon attacked first while Khalid hung back and watched. I gutted Fallon with my poker and then Khalid attacked me and I injured his leg."

"Yeah!" Karim murmured. "That would teach him not to mess with you."

"Anyway, then I went on board the Pod and found that the power packs were dead."

"So you wired a bunch of other scavenged ones to the ship and got the engines going," Naia chimed in. "You're so smart, Dina."

"Anyway, that's the end of the interesting part," Dina replied. "Now it's time for you all to go to sleep."

She kissed and cuddled the rest of the Children more quickly than she should have, but none of them seemed to mind too much. They were all growing out of that kind of motherly affection.

When she finished, she blew out the last lamp, but not before she spotted Link standing in their bedroom doorway. He leaned his shoulder against the door frame smiling at her.

She knew that look, so she blew out the light and tiptoed across the room making sure not to step on any of the Children on her way there.

She slipped her arms around Link's waist and rested her head on his chest in the darkness. Now, when she was alone with him, she could finally shut her eyes and put aside all the cares of the day.

He hugged her back, kissed her on the forehead, drew her into the bedroom, and shut the door.

They both took off their clothes, slipped into bed, and came together with their arms around each other. Dina sank into the warmth of his body and every nerve dissolved in pure relaxation.

"Did you miss me?" he whispered.

"Of course," she whispered back. "Did you think I didn't."

"I just wanted to hear you say it."

"You shouldn't even have to ask," she told him. "I wish you wouldn't stay away for so long. Did it really take you all that time to find a deer?"

"Sometimes I have to travel a long way."

"You shouldn't stay out so long. The farther you go, the more likely you are to run into cats."

He didn't answer for a minute. She might have deceived herself into thinking he was falling asleep, but she knew better.

She propped herself on her elbow and looked down at his shadowy face in the darkness. A faint glimmer of moonlight shone on his cheeks, hair, and beard. "What's wrong?" she whispered. "Did something happen? *Did* you have a problem with cats?"

"No," he replied. "That's the thing. There aren't any cats around here and even fewer to the west. They don't come out this far and they definitely don't go any farther."

"I don't believe it," she countered. "Just because you didn't see them doesn't mean they aren't there."

"Adrian would have told us if the Children had seen any cats out there. The Children went west and they covered a lot more territory than I did. There are no cats in that direction...and do you want to know why? They don't come out this far because they're afraid of the Children."

Dina snorted and put her head back on his chest. "You're dreaming."

"Think about it," he whispered into her hair. "We could go west and start over somewhere where we wouldn't have to constantly defend ourselves against cats. We could live there—free—with the Children. We wouldn't have to guard ourselves every single second and waste all this manpower on keeping watch for cats to come along and attack us."

Dina almost lifted her head to argue back....and then she realized that he was right.

"Do you think that's what Adrian is doing?" she finally asked. "Do you think that's why he and the Children are doing all this exploring—to find somewhere they can be free?"

"I don't know about that. It sounds like they're just curious—kind of like how they want to meet their own kind in the other cantons. Maybe they haven't thought that far in advance.....or maybe they *have* thought of it. I don't know, but it's worth thinking about, don't you think?"

"I guess so," she murmured. "It would be a lot better than staying here and having the other parents constantly harping on us for letting our Children run around in the jungle."

Now it was his turn to stay silent for a minute. "Would you go with me?" he whispered. "Would you leave here and rebuild with me out there if I asked you to come with me?"

Her head shot up again and her breath caught. They'd been living together for a year and raising all these Children together, but this sounded like something a lot more serious.

He ran his fingers through her hair and then pulled her down to kiss her. "I love you," he whispered. "Whatever future we're going to have, I want to have it with you. We stayed in this canton because we had to, but we don't have to stay anymore. The Children are growing up. They won't need us at all in a few months. Then we'll be free to go anywhere we want, but I bet you they would come with us. What do you say? Will you go with me?'

"Yes," she whispered back. "Whatever future we're going to have, I want to have it with you. It would be a dream come true to rebuild somewhere away from cats—somewhere our Children could live free and grow up in safety. That's the whole reason we left Prideland in the first place, isn't it?"

He pulled her deeper into his mouth and that kiss answered all the questions crowding her mind. Her spirits soared thinking about the life of potential and promise waiting for her in a land without cats—a land of unlimited opportunity where a person could get anything they wanted if they just worked hard enough to make it.

Chapter 4

Dina must have dozed off. She woke up in darkness with her arms around Link's chest. His ribs rose and fell with his breathing. He was still asleep.

Dina couldn't tell what woke her up, but after a few breathless minutes of listening, she heard voices whispering outside.

She slipped out of bed, pulled on her clothes, and tiptoed out into the main room. All the Children were asleep, too.

She opened the house door and spotted four people standing a few dozen yards from her house. They whispered with their heads together.

The sight of them made her scalp prickle. Now she knew something was wrong.

She strode over to them and discovered Meredith Fellows, Nicholas Lockerby, Cook, and Paul Frasier standing on the grass in the moonlight. They were all members of the Council that made decisions for the village.

"Is something wrong?" she snapped.

"We were just discussing how to get in touch with you without waking up your Children," Nicholas Lockerby replied.

"You could have just come and knocked on the door," she countered and didn't even try to keep her voice down. "They can hear well enough. If you woke me up with your whispering, you probably woke them up, too. They've probably been listening to every word you say. You all have Children. You should know."

Meredith tried to wave that away, but it came out more as a squirm. "We'd like you to come and address the Council, Dina."

Dina groaned. "You can't be serious."

"We need to decide what to do about them," Nicholas went on.

"What do you mean by, 'do about them'?" Dina asked. "What is there to do about them? They're people with minds of their own. What could you possibly do to them?"

"That's what we need to discuss," Meredith replied and waved toward the house nearest to the gate. "If you aren't doing anything else, would you mind coming over and addressing us now?"

"I was sound asleep if you really want to know," Dina spat.

"Come over....please," Nicholas replied. "Now is the only time we can talk without the Children around."

"You're crazy," Dina countered. "We could have had this conversation yesterday or during any of the other three days when the Children weren't even in the village. Now they're right over there in my house."

"This afternoon's events have forced our hand," Meredith replied. "We didn't realize things had progressed this far."

"Things?" Dina demanded. "What things?"

"Just come," Paul urged. "Please. We can discuss all of this at the Council meeting."

She groaned again and dragged herself across the canton to the house where the Council met. This was the stupidest idea in a long list of stupid ideas—as if the Council or anyone else could do anything about the Children.

She walked in to find the place flooded with light and full of people—including people whose Children she knew for a fact were in the village right now. These people were really sinking to a new low by sneaking around behind their Children's backs.

The crowd parted to let the four Councilors cross to their table on the other side of the room. Murmurs greeted Dina when she walked in and the crowd parted for her, too.

Everyone backed away and gave her a clear path to approach and present herself to the Council. She took a deep breath, squared her shoulders, and determined to get this over with as quickly as possible.

She did her best not to lose her composure even before the meeting started, but it wasn't easy to keep it. She didn't come all this way and go through all these trials to let someone take out their insecurities on her Children—any of them.

She'd committed herself to raising all these Children as her own and that's what she did. She didn't treat Adrian and Iona any differently than she treated any of her other Children.

She felt the same protective fire toward all of them—including the Children of her deadliest enemies. Fallon's, Khalid's, Tom's, and the Hellions' Children were just as precious and important to her as Adrian and Iona would ever be.

"Thank you for coming, Dina," Nicholas began. "We've asked you to come here and discuss with us what steps we can take to mitigate the threat posed to this village by the Children's activities....."

"Threat!" she blurted out. "The Children don't pose any threat to the village! Are you insane? We came out here and spent a year defending this village because of the Children. We all came here to give them a safe home where they could grow up in peace."

"We all understand that, but things are different now," Meredith replied. "The Children roam freely through the jungle without any regard for the danger they're courting for the rest of us...."

"We haven't had an attack in more than eight months and we haven't seen a cat in more than six," Dina countered. "Did it ever occur to you that the Children going out into the jungle is what's keeping the cats away?"

"That's ridiculous," Paul returned. "The Pride is dedicated to wiping out all the Children. We all lost Children in the attack on the other canton...."

"That was when the Children were helpless babies," Dina pointed out. "If the cats still want to wipe out the Children, why haven't the cats come out this far? They haven't mounted even an exploratory trip to find out where we are. The Children have been out there for three days and Adrian says...."

"We aren't interested in what Adrian says," Meredith snapped back much too harshly considering she was supposed to be an impartial councilor here and not a concerned parent. "Adrian is the problem we're all here to solve."

Dina felt her hackles rise and fought to push them down, but she failed in the end. "Adrian is not a problem to be solved," she snarled. "He's a boy who has as much right to live freely and explore his environment as anyone else does."

"I think what Meredith is trying to say...." Nicholas interjected.

"I know exactly what Meredith is trying to say because she just said it," Dina snapped. "If you think Adrian is some kind of problem to be solved—or that the Children are posing some threat to this village that's greater than the threat against them—then *you're* the problem to be solved, not the Children."

Dina forced herself to stop talking before she made this any worse than it already was. She had a harder time controlling her rage against these people.

She shut her eyes and drew in a steadying breath and concentrated hard to face the Council and stay calm.

"The bottom line is that the Children do pose a threat to the village," Meredith went on. "The farther they go on these exploration trips, the more likely they are to lead the cats back to us."

"They aren't a threat—not to us," Dina growled in a shaky voice. "They're our own Children. What the hell are any of us doing here if we're going to turn on them and start treating them as our enemies?"

"They're cats," Paul countered. "They're more cat than human."

"That's not true," Dina fired back. "You don't know them. You don't let yourselves know them."

"They definitely aren't human," Nicholas pointed out. "How are we supposed to know they won't turn against us with no warning?"

"They definitely will turn against us if we push them away," Dina argued. "They'll grow up one way or the other. You can't stop that. You can't keep the Children confined to the village if that's what you're suggesting. They're going to go out into the jungle with our permission or without it. Our best strategy would be to harness the Children's abilities in our own defense."

"What do you mean?" Meredith asked.

"They can see, hear, and travel better than any of us," Dina replied. "They cover more ground and they can move silently if they need to. They could be our earliest warning that cats were moving into the area. You might not want to take Adrian's word for what goes on out in the jungle, but he knows more about what goes on out there than we do. He can see and hear more of it than our guards and sentries can see from their watchtowers. You'd be foolish not to listen to him. If you were smart, you would make the Children your allies instead of your enemies. I can't believe I have to tell you this about your own Children. I can't believe you're actually sitting here talking about your own Children in the same terms as, 'threat' and 'cats' and talking about them turning against you. It sounds an awful lot to me like *you've* already turned against *them*. You've left them no choice but to turn away from you."

The Councilors exchanged glances and Meredith cleared her throat. "Thank you for coming to address us, Dina. We'll take your remarks into consideration. We will discuss this matter further before we render our decision."

Dina fumed at them for dismissing her like a schoolgirl when she didn't even want to come here in the first place.

She would never stop her Children from going out into the jungle. She didn't give a damn what the Council decided. They could try to restrain their own Children and destroy their relationships, but she sure wouldn't.

All the other Children in the village would go along with hers. That was the thing these parents didn't seem to realize. More than half the Children in the village belonged to her and Link. What her and Link's Children did, the others would go along with.

If she'd learned anything from this afternoon's events, it was that Adrian was in charge of them all now. Something changed in the jungle over the past three days while none of the parents were watching.

The Children had organized themselves into a hierarchical social structure with one definite leader.

The other parents couldn't have failed to notice this. That must be why they found the Children so threatening all of a sudden. The parents finally woke up to the fact that their Children owed their allegiance to someone else now.

The crowd parted again to let her through. She stopped in her tracks halfway across the room when she spotted Link standing in the very back of the crowd. He flattened himself against the wall where no one could see him, but he must have heard every word.

Not that she would have hidden it from him. His Children were as involved in this as the others. He'd invested everything in raising all their Children over this past year. He'd treated all the Children as his own even though none of them was biologically his.

He considered them his. Dina knew that without him even saying it. Every action of his proved it beyond doubt. He put Dina herself to shame with his dedication, attention, and affection for all the Children, even other parents' Children.

He pushed himself off the wall and followed her out into the darkness. They crossed the damp grass to their own house.

She didn't want to talk to him about any of this until they shut themselves up in their own bedroom again, but she had to change her plans when she walked into the house and discovered all the Children sitting up.

They hadn't lit any of the lamps. They didn't need to. They could see in the dark. "What is the Council going to do, Dina?" Amir asked.

Link lit one of the lamps to light the room. "The Council isn't going to do anything. The Council doesn't have the power to do anything to you or to anyone else. You don't have to worry about them. They're toothless."

"The Council doesn't have a clue what to do anyway," Dina added. "They could discuss this for another year before they come to any decision—if they ever come to a decision."

"They won't keep us locked in the village," Adrian chimed in. "They'd have to kill us first."

"No one is killing anyone and no one is keeping anyone locked in the village," Dina fired back. "That's just silly."

"What about the other Children—Leroy and Salvatore and Dion and all the others?" Karim asked. "We can't let these people do anything to them, either."

"No one will do anything to them, either," Link told him. "These people are the Children's parents. These people only want what's best for the Children and for everyone else."

"They're scared," Rome sneered. "They're so scared they don't even know what to be scared of. They're running around with their heads between their legs trying to figure out what they should be scared of."

Dina found herself laughing. "That about sums it up, sweetheart. I couldn't have said it better myself."

"What should we do about them?" Naia asked.

A bunch of the Children turned to look at Adrian, but he didn't acknowledge that they were once again turning to him for leadership. He kept gazing up at Link and Dina.

"I'll tell you what you should do," Dina told them. "You should all go back to sleep now. The party is over. Lie down, curl up, and put this out of your minds until tomorrow morning. Then you can go back out into the jungle and you won't have to worry about these people anymore."

"We'll take Dion and Salvatory and the others with us," Riggs declared. "We won't leave them behind. I don't care what anybody says. None of these cowards better get in our way, either."

"All right," Dina countered. "Lie down, go to sleep, and let tomorrow take care of itself. Good night."

She gave out a few more kisses and blew out the lamp before she and Link went back to their room.

Dina sank into the mattress, but she couldn't relax. She heard more whispering—from the main room this time. The Children weren't going to sleep. They were out there deciding things, forming plans, and establishing their social relationships that not even those people closest to them understood.

Link put his arms around Dina and pulled the covers over both of them, but he didn't go to sleep, either. He held himself stiff and tense in bed while he listened to the Children whispering.

"Are you ready to run away to the west country with me now?" he whispered.

She stifled laughter. "It sounds pretty good right about now, doesn't it?"

He kissed her hair. "I should ask Adrian about it. He can let us know if the Children are interested."

"Not yet," she murmured back. "Wait just a little longer."

"Wait for what?" he asked. "Do you mean wait for this situation to blow up in our faces? We should leave now before that happens."

"If we left now, we might have to leave some of the other Children behind. At least wait until we know for sure that it's best for everyone and not just us. Wait until we know for sure we're doing it for the right reasons and not because it's the easy way out of an uncomfortable situation."

Chapter 5

The Children sat in the sunshine on the grass in front of Dina's house. Adrian sat in the center of the group.

"Israel, Cairo, and Riyadh, you go with Abdullah and Amir to Hardship canton and see if they're having the same problems with their parents there."

"You said we could go to the Hardship canton," Riggs pointed out. "You always skip out on us."

"This isn't about that," Adrian told him. "I need our older Children to deal with their older Children. Pregnant mothers were going out to Hardship long before they came here. All the Children at Hardship will be older than we are. We need someone older so the Children there don't think I'm sending out a bunch of shrimps to negotiate with them."

Snickers went through the group.

"You Manx can go to Northfall instead, and before you Aurora start giving me a hard time, I have another job for you."

"Name it," Indigo told him. "Any job is good enough for us."

"Abdullah and Amir are Auroras anyway," Naia pointed out. "So technically, the Auroras are already on a job."

Adrian's head shot up and he grinned at her. "Thank you. I have a job for the Pygmies, too."

"Yay!" Nova squeaked. "Are we going to another canton?"

"No, midget," Adrian told her. "The other cantons would eat you for lunch." Her face fell. "Don't worry. It will be something good."

Dina watched and listened from the steps of her house while she scraped the flesh off the deer hide from last night. She had to marvel at the way Adrian's mind worked. He didn't act like a ten-year-old boy at all. He acted more like he was seventeen.

He divided the Children into gangs according to sibling groups. Nearly everything they did seemed to center on keeping the sibling groups together.

"Manx can go," he finally ordered. "Anyone going to Hardship can go, too. Get over there and come back here tonight. We'll wait for you."

The four Manx boys stood up at the same time and bounded away across the grass without saying goodbye to anyone.

They ran on all fours like cats, covered the distance in no time, and rocketed away into the trees. They vanished in seconds.

The group going to Hardship canton took longer. Link's three nephews that were going took a long time to take their leave from their two sisters.

The same thing happened with the Auroras. The siblings seemed to have a lot to say to each other before they parted ways even for one day.

Adrian didn't protest this or hurry anyone along. He just waited until they all left and sprinted away into the trees, too.

He turned to the four Pygmies. Naia and Nova grinned at him in anticipation of finding out what job he would assign them.

He broke into a matching grin when he saw their faces. Dina had rarely seen him so delighted.

He opened his mouth to speak, but right then, Troy Engel came over to them. He barely glanced at the Children and strode over to Dina. "You aren't going to let them go out into the jungle again, are you?'

She bent over her work. She would have liked to pretend he didn't exist, so she just mumbled for the thousandth time, "I'm not letting them do anything. No one can stop these Children if they want to do something."

"You don't even try to stop them," Troy countered. "Now Leroy, Devon, and Franco are back at my house saying they'll never come back to the canton at all if I don't let them go out with Adrian and the rest of your group."

Dina shrugged. "Maybe if you gave them a little more leeway to exercise their independence, they wouldn't feel the need to exercise it for you. Just something you might want to think about."

Dina became aware of the rest of her Children listening in rapt attention—and not the good kind.

"Where *are* Leroy, Devon, and Franco?" Adrian asked. "Are they at your house?"

Troy whipped around like he just noticed the Children sitting there. "Of course they are," he snapped. "Where else would they be?"

"Do Sasha and Shelby want to come out, too?" Naia asked. "We agreed yesterday that we would all go down the river to the....."

"Whatever you agreed to yesterday doesn't mean anything," Troy countered. "I'm their father. I decide if they're going to go. If I think going out with you wouldn't be the best thing for them, then they won't go."

"Be reasonable, Troy," Dina murmured. "You're letting yourself get all mixed up in this hysteria. I know you care about your Children, but this isn't the way to do it."

"You won't keep them here against their will," Karim cut in. "If they want to go, we'll make sure they go. It's you whose words don't mean anything."

Just when Dina thought the confrontation couldn't get any worse, Meredith, Nicholas, and Paul walked over at that moment and joined the happy bunch.

"The Council has come to its decision, Dina," Meredith informed her. "We've decided to bar the Children from leaving the village unless they have their parents' permission."

"Why are you telling her when we're sitting right here?" Adrian interrupted. "Do you think we're deaf or something?"

Meredith didn't turn around. She answered over her shoulder without looking at him. "I'm not talking to you, Adrian. I'm speaking with Dina here."

"If you're coming to a decision like that, you better be talking to me," he fired back. "If you make any decision that concerns us, you better have the backbone to look us in the eye and tell us to our faces."

She finally turned around and confronted him. "Fortunately for us all, Adrian, this decision doesn't concern you because you do have your parents' permission to leave the village. This decision concerns those Children who don't have their parents' permission to leave the village. I'm sure you'd agree that what happens to those Children is their parents' decision, not yours."

She started to turn back to Dina, but he just kept right on going. "No, I don't agree that what happens to those Children is their parents' decision. If their parents decide to confine them to the village against their will, then you can bet your ass I'm gonna do something about it."

"You don't need to curse to get your point across," Dina cut in.

Adrian got to his feet. The Children had two different ways of getting to their feet when they'd been sitting down. They could get to their feet in the normal human way or they sometimes just sprang to their feet in a catlike way. They would lift off the ground or floor and land on their feet without seeming to exert any effort at all.

Adrian used his normal human way of getting to his feet this time. It was slower and produced more of an authoritative impression on anyone watching him get up.

Meredith understood his intentions loud and clear and then all the other Children stood up, too. The Black moved in to surround him and all the other Children assembled behind Adrian in what could only be the prelude to a royal showdown.

"We're leaving the village now," he informed Meredith and the other councilors, "and we're taking Leroy, Franco, Devon, Sasha, Shelby, Salvatore, Dion, Elio, Kabir, Zen, and Santos with us."

Meredith opened her mouth to argue back, but right then, Troy's five Children all rushed over. Leroy, the oldest boy, grabbed Adrian by the arm. "Don't leave without us, Adrian! We're going with you."

"I told you to stay in the house," Troy snapped. "You aren't going anywhere unless I say so."

Just then, another two boys and two girls came out of nowhere. They stormed across the canton glaring at everyone. "We're leaving," Dion announced. "We're with you, Adrian."

"Get in the back," Adrian ordered.

The nine Children obeyed him instantly, hustled behind the other Children, and took their places in the very back of the crowd. Now all the other Children blocked Meredith, Troy, and the other councilors from getting anywhere near their own Children.

"We're going out into the jungle now," Adrian clipped. "Any other Children who want to come with us are welcome to come. They don't need their parents' permission and we'll keep using this canton as a base whenever we need to. You can go have another Council meeting and decide to lock us out, but we'll just keep coming back."

He turned around and walked off. The Children parted to let him through exactly the way the crowd at the Council meeting parted to let Dina through.

The Black glared at the councilors in pure, undisguised hatred before they stalked off to follow Adrian.

All the other Children gave the adults pointed looks before they left, too. Even the Children who didn't have their parents' permission made sure to give their parents challenging glares before the whole party strode through the gate.

More Children came out of their houses to join Adrian's group. Children flocked to him from every direction. Some had to fight off their parents who tried to hold their Children back and stop them from leaving.

In the end, all the Children broke away and joined up with the group.

They walked upright in slow, dignified procession until they got outside the fence. Then the whole party bounded away on their hands and feet, rocketed into the treetops, and took off at dizzying speed.

Dina heaved an almighty sigh. "What in the world are you thinking, Meredith? Are you really trying to destroy your relationship with your own Children? Is that what you're trying to do?"

"You might try backing us up once in a while," Troy countered. "You could have stopped them. They listen to you. You could have explained to them why they have to stay here."

"I couldn't do that because I don't agree with you," Dina returned. "Why in the name of God should they stay here—and don't give me that nonsense about the jungle being too dangerous for them. If the Children were going to get hurt or attacked in the jungle, it would have happened before now. They get stronger, faster, and more ferocious as they get older. They'll only become better able to handle whatever is out there—not less so."

"You should support us because you're a parent," Meredith told her. "If they turn against us, they could turn against you."

"That won't happen because I'll make sure it doesn't," Dina replied. "You aren't doing this out of concern for the Children's safety or even the canton's safety. This is all just a power play so you can exercise your control over your Children. That's all it is and that's exactly why we left Prideland. If you wanted that, you should have stayed there."

Chapter 6

D ina came out of her house toward sunset and raised her hand to shield her eyes from the setting sun. The evening rays touched the treetops to the west.

"Is something wrong?" Link asked from his seat on the steps.

"No...." Dina murmured. "Adrian told his two scout groups that he would meet them here when they got back from the other cantons, but the Children still aren't back yet. What if something went wrong?"

"Nothing went wrong." Link bent over the stick he was whittling. "They're already back. They just don't want to come into the canton because they don't want to confront their parents. The Children are hiding from us. That's you letting the other parents get in your head again. You've never worried about the Children before and you don't need to do it now. Nothing has ever gone wrong with them in the past and it isn't going wrong now."

She sighed and sat down next to him. "Maybe you're right and it's time to leave here."

He put his knife and stick away. "Come with me. We'll go out there, find them, and bring them in. Then you'll see that everything is okay."

He took her hand and they headed for the trees. "I envy how certain you are about everything," she told him.

"I have to be to make up for your doubts. You defended the Children so well at the Council meeting. You really put the fear of God in everyone. I see it as my job to give you that confidence. You share your doubts with me and no one else, so I have to counter them by being certain for both of us."

"You always know the right thing to say," she murmured.

"You said all the right things at the Council meeting."

"Then why can't I convince them to change? I agree with Adrian. Those Children don't belong in the village if their own parents are going to hold them down."

"Just don't let anyone else hear you say that."

"I won't. They would hang me. They might hang me either way since I'm such a terrible mother."

He put his arm around her shoulders and kissed the side of her head. "You're an outstanding mother—the best I've ever seen."

She couldn't answer with this lump forming in her throat. She put her arms around him as they kept walking into the trees, but in a little while, they heard branches rustling in the canopy.

They found the Children sitting in the treetops. They weren't leaping around or playing. They just sat there talking, including Troy's, Meredith's, Nicholas's, and all the other Children whose parents had been causing so much trouble.

"Are you coming back to the house?" Link asked. "I didn't go hunting today. You kids ate all the food last night."

"We just ate," Adrian informed him. "We went hunting, so we aren't hungry."

"I guess you and I are out of luck," Dina murmured under her breath to Link.

He bit back a grin and called up, "Come back to the house. We can deal with your parents."

"We are dealing with them," Karim growled. "We're dealing with them by staying out here."

"Maybe they'll learn something if we don't come back for a few more days," Salvatore added.

"Don't be like that," Link countered. "They care about you. I'll make you a deal. You can all come back to our house. You can stay there while Dina and I explain things to your parents. What do you think of that idea?"

"Not much," Dion muttered.

"So you're just going to stay out in the jungle for the rest of your lives?" Link asked. "You're never going to come back—ever again—any of you?"

The Children exchanged glances and then everyone turned to see what Adrian would say.

"All right," he finally agreed, "but none of us will talk to the other parents and we're all going to our house. If any parents try to interfere with us, you deal with them. We're sick of it."

"I understand and I don't blame you at all," Link replied. "You leave the other parents to me and Dina. You don't even have to talk to them."

The Children hesitated and then Adrian muttered to those nearest to him, "Come on."

He dropped out of the branches and landed lightly on the ground forty feet below where he'd been sitting.

The other Children copied him, leapt off their branches, and landed all over the jungle floor beneath where they'd been sitting.

Link and Dina turned away, rejoined hands, and headed back toward the village. "You always know what to say," she murmured under her breath.

He squeezed her hand, but he didn't answer.

They left the trees with the Children trailing behind them. Relief flooded Dina's heart when she didn't see any parents by the gate. The path to her house lay clear and unobstructed before her. Maybe just maybe she and the Children could get inside before the parents showed up to ruin everything.

She and Link made it as far as the steps to their house before it all went south. Adrian, Iona, the Black, and some of the Pygmies led the Children. The others followed in a loose convoy with the Manx and Osiris's Children in the very back.

Troy's Children were just passing through the gate with Dion and Santos when Troy, Meredith, and three other parents came out of their houses to converge on the line.

"Where have you been?" Troy snapped. "You've been gone for hours."

Leroy turned away from his father. "Leave us alone. We aren't talking to you."

Link and Dina turned around to intervene and so did Adrian. "We invited them to come stay with us," Dina replied. "We thought....."

"No one is talking to you, Dina," Meredith snapped. "No one gave you any license to invite our Children to your house or anywhere else." She turned back to her sons. "Get in the house. We need to have a serious talk."

"We aren't going anywhere with you," Santos fired back. "We only agreed to come back to the canton at all because Adrian said we could go to his......"

"Adrian is not your mother or your father," Meredith countered. "Adrian doesn't make the rules. Now come on. Don't make me have to....."

She grabbed his arm to pull him out of line. A bunch of other Children had also either turned around and gathered nearby to intervene, but none of them got there fast enough.

Santos spun around impossibly fast, gave a feral snarl, and slashed his mother's arm with his teeth. She yelled out in pain and surprise, let go of him, and Santos sprang out of range. He stopped a few yards away and crouched there glaring at her with blood dripping from his teeth.

"Don't you ever touch me again!" he hissed. "Don't any of you ever touch any of us again! You keep away from me!"

Link and Dina both tried to move between Santos and the rest of the parents, but neither Link nor Dina got there soon enough.

The other Children gathered around Santos, narrowed their eyes at the assembled parents, and then they all moved off toward Dina's house.

The parents gaped at their Children in horror, but none of them dared to step out of line again.

Adrian and those nearest him went inside. The rest of the Children filed across the threshold one at a time and eventually they all disappeared into the house.

Meredith stood there clutching the gash in her arm while blood soaked through her sleeve. She came to her senses when the Children vanished inside Link's and Dina's house.

"This is your fault, Dina," Meredith snarled. "You had no right to intervene."

"I tried a million times to warn you about this," Dina countered. "We invited the Children to our house to try to make peace between all of you, but you just don't get it. You can't keep flexing your authority with these Children. That won't work anymore. If they don't stay with us, they won't come back to the village at all and none of you will ever see your Children again. Is that what you want?"

No one answered and Link and Dina finally turned away. The parents were all still standing there when Link and Dina entered their house.

They walked into the usual scene of dozens of Children sprawled all over the floor. The only difference was that, this time, they brought all the other parents' Children with them.

Troy's, Meredith's, Nicholas's, and a dozen others lounged on the floor with the rest. Iona went to the cupboard and took out all the blankets to pass around.

Handing out blankets and bedding everyone down had always been Dina's job. Now she saw her daughter doing it. This whole situation was evolving so fast. The day was coming so fast when the Children didn't need anyone anymore.

Dina passed her hand across her eyes and groaned. "This is not good."

"It could have been a lot worse," Link murmured in her ear. "Only one person got hurt. I was expecting more."

She looked up at him. "There has to be a way to stop this."

"The only way to stop it is for the Children to move out to the jungle permanently."

"We won't do that," Adrian interrupted from his place on the floor. "Not now. Now we have to show them that we can come and go as we please. If this didn't happen today, we probably would have stayed out in the jungle. Now we have to keep coming back here to teach them that they can't tell us what to do."

Dina groaned again. She would have protested, but Link only said, "That makes sense. The sooner they learn, the better."

"Why do they have to be so stupid about it?" Santos growled. "Why can't they just understand that we need to move around?"

"I wish everyone in the village was like you and Dina," Leroy interjected. "We could be happy here if they didn't keep trying to stop us from going outside."

"I wish I could say they were trying to protect you, but I think it's gone beyond that now." Link entered the room and sat down on the floor. He had a hard time finding an empty patch of floor, but the Manx boys moved aside to make a place for him. "I think Dina is right and the parents just want to control you. I don't see any other rational explanation for why they would act like this."

"But why?" Karim asked. "Why do they need to control us when you don't?"

Link shrugged. "Maybe they're scared because they *can't* control you. Maybe that's the problem. Maybe they thought they'd have more time before you grew up—time when they could influence you and get you to do things their way. I don't know."

Adrian turned around, cocked his head, and looked up at Dina. "What's wrong, Dina? Why don't you sit down with us?"

"Don't you start telling us what to do," Devon growled across the room. "Don't tell us Santos did wrong by defending himself."

"I wasn't going to." She finally came out of her trance enough to enter the room. She sat down next to Link.

So many Children crowded the house that they had to sit body to body and shoulder to shoulder. She sat close to Link, but she still wound up bumping into Dexter, Brock, and a few other Children. None of them could avoid nudging and elbowing each other.

The party didn't have anything to eat tonight, but none of the Children seemed to mind. There wouldn't have been room on the floor to cook anything anyway.

Some of the Children started curling up to go to sleep right away. Others just talked.

"I don't want to leave the village," Indigo told Adrian. "I don't want to leave Link and Dina."

"You don't have to because we aren't leaving," he told her. "We're here now, aren't we?"

"What about us?" Salvatore asked. "If we keep coming back here, it could lead to more clashes with the parents. Are we really going to go that far—to attack our own parents."

"No one is attacking anybody," Adrian countered. "No one will mess with us after this. They'll leave us alone."

"They won't stop trying to make their point," Link cut in. "They might not try to physically restrain you, but I doubt they'll change their minds and suddenly decide that it's okay for you to come and go as you please. They'll keep making the same arguments that you should stay put and do what they say."

"Then they'll keep getting the same answer," Adrian replied. "We'll just keep doing what we want until they get the message."

Chapter 7

A rustle in the trees outside the canton made Dina look up from the wooden spoon she was sanding with a rough stone.

Every rustle in the trees made her look up. The Children were out there somewhere, but they rarely came into the village anymore. When they did, they didn't stay long.

She bent over her work and told herself to stop looking. Keeping a constant watch on the jungle wouldn't make the Children come back. It wouldn't soften relations between the Children and their parents, either.

Almost as if her thoughts made it happen, Troy and Nicholas walked over to her house. Meredith didn't show herself. She was finally learning.

Troy sat down on the step next to Dina. "The Children are out there in the trees," he began.

"I know," she replied without looking up.

"Aren't you going to go out there and talk to them?" Nicholas asked.

"I wasn't planning to," Dina replied. "I planned to sit here and go on with my own business until they decide to come back."

"Aren't you even a little bit curious about what they're doing out there?" Troy asked.

"Not really. I already know what they're doing. They're hunting, climbing, running, jumping, traveling, exploring—all the things Children their age are supposed to do."

She stopped sanding to run her fingers over the wooden surface. It was getting smoother, but it wasn't smooth enough to use yet.

Nicholas cleared his throat. "We came over here to ask you to go out there and talk to them. They've been gone for a month."

Dina looked up for the first time. "Why don't you go talk to them yourselves?"

"Because....." He broke off.

"Are you afraid of your own Children?" Dina demanded.

"Not them," Troy replied. "More like what's out there in the jungle."

"Nothing would bother you with the Children around," she told him. "If it's safe for me to go out there and talk to them, then it's safe for you to go out there and talk to them."

"They understand you better," Nicholas pointed out. "You have more rapport with them."

She bit her tongue to stop herself from telling them for the millionth time that there was a very good reason for that. These parents could have had more rapport with their Children if the parents only treated the Children differently.

"What exactly would you like me to talk to them about?" she asked. "What would you like me to tell them that we haven't already talked about?"

"You could invite them back to the village," Troy suggested.

"So they can get into another fight with you? I think I'll skip it."

"Don't you want to see Adrian and Iona?" Nicholas asked. "Don't you even want them to come back to the village?"

She put her spoon down with an exasperated sigh. "Why is it so hard for you to believe that the rest of the Children are as much my Children as Adrian and Iona? Do you really think I care more about seeing them than the rest of my Children?" She shook her head and went back to work. "I really don't understand you people at all. I really don't."

"Okay, fine," he countered. "Don't you at least care about seeing all your Children?"

"I would see them a lot more often if the rest of you didn't treat them as your enemies," she muttered under her breath. "You're the reason they won't come back to the canton."

"Go see them for us, Dina," Troy urged. "Please."

"What could you possibly stand to gain if I did?" she asked.

"Tell us where they are. Tell us that they're okay. Tell them we miss them and we love them and we want to see them."

"But not that you're sorry for treating them so badly and that you promise to make it right?" She snorted. "You have it all backward."

"Just go see them," he repeated. "Please—for us."

She groaned and set her spoon aside. "All right. I'll go. Just don't expect it to do any good."

"Thank you," Troy replied. "We really appreciate it."

She put her spoon and sanding stone away, brushed the dust off her clothes, and headed for the gate. She really ought to have her head examined for doing this.

She didn't go to put the other parents' minds at rest. She wasn't didn't even go because she held out any hope of convincing the Children to come back to the village—because there was no hope of that.

She only went to satisfy her own curiosity about what the Children were doing. They didn't leave the area—not completely.

If Adrian was still sending out scouting parties to contact other cantons and explore the surrounding countryside, he always kept some Children close to Riverbend canton. He must be using it as a base.

She headed for the spot where she'd heard rustling earlier, but she didn't find any Children there. She didn't see any sign that they'd been here before, either.

She ventured farther into the jungle and tensed as the safety of the canton slipped into the distance behind her. What if the parents were right and the jungle was too dangerous for human beings?

She pushed that thought out of her mind. She'd gone out into the jungle farther than this before. Link and the other hunters went much farther and they did it on a regular basis. They always came back unhurt.

She heard more rustling and branches snapping ahead and to her left. She turned in that direction, but when she got there, she didn't see any Children there, either. So she had been wrong. Adrian wasn't using the canton as a base.

Her heart sank. The Children must be staying farther away from the canton than she realized.

All these weeks, she'd comforted herself by thinking they were right outside the fence. She could tolerate them staying away for so long because she thought they were so close.

Now she found out they weren't—if they were using anywhere as a base at all. Maybe they just kept wandering around, hanging out in the treetops, and never staying anywhere for long.

She followed the rustling sounds, but she couldn't be sure the Children were the ones causing those sounds. She never saw them.

The sounds disappeared as soon as she got near them, only to start up again a hundred yards deeper into the jungle. Were the Children testing her? Were they trying to lead her away from the canton for some reason?

Maybe they wanted to see just how brave she really was. If the jungle was so dangerous, how far was she willing to go? How much danger was she willing to put herself in to find her Children?

She shouldn't have come out here unarmed, but she couldn't turn back now. The thought that the Children might be testing her made her push on. Whatever dangers she might find out here, she'd faced them before with less. She could do it again.

She walked for over an hour before she found the Children. When she did, she didn't find any camp, base, or headquarters. They were just hanging out in the treetops.

The noise got louder as she drew nearer. Dark shapes hurtled back and forth in the high canopy. Shouts and laughter echoed through the jungle and led her to the Children.

She expected to find them playing—and they were—just not in the way she thought.

They started fifty yards to her left and raced across her path heading west. Some voices came from farther away while others sounded like they were right on top of her.

Their voices became more distinct and recognizable as Dina approached.

"Get him, Karim!" Naia shrieked.

"Get behind him, Riggs!" Brock yelled. "He's trying to break away!"

"Riyadh—Israel—cut him off through those vines!" Adrian ordered. "Come on Franco! Close that hole on the right!"

"Here comes another one!" Aries called. "They're moving in trying to free him!"

"Watch out behind you, Dexter!" Iona shouted.

Dina pushed forward trying to see what they were doing. It sounded like they were hunting something. She froze when she actually spotted Children in the high branches.

They *were* hunting something. They'd surrounded three cats with another three skirting the Children's position.

Karim, Riggs, Riyadh, Israel, Franco, Devon, and Link's nieces Egypt and India surrounded a panther, a puma, and a large tabby cat perched in the branches of a single tree.

The Children had cornered the puma on a branch that was way too small for it. The puma had backed as far out onto the branch as he could and crouched there yowling and screeching at the Children.

The puma flattened his ears against his head and bared his teeth, but he didn't dare to move anywhere. He couldn't retreat any farther without breaking the branch.

Children surrounded him on all sides. Riggs was the smallest of the advancing Children. He inched out onto the branch getting closer to the puma.

The puma slashed its claws at Riggs, but Riggs stayed out of range and kept pressuring the cat into backing farther away—which he couldn't.

Karim perched on a branch just above the puma, right where Karim's black fur and eyes would intimidate the cat the most. The others surrounded the cat on every other side so he couldn't get away.

More Children swarmed around the tree on the ground in case the cat tried to drop out of the branches.

Kaiser, Adrian, Rey, Rome, Osiris's daughters Calliope and Emerald, and the Auroras Abdullah, Amir, and Aurelio had separated the panther from his friends. Kenji, Cairo, Sasha, Shelby, and the Pygmies had backed the tabby into the crook of a branch twenty feet from the others.

Three more cats moved in on the Children's location, but these cats couldn't get near their friends with so many Children around. The rest of the Auroras and twenty other Children formed a barricade to stop these cats from saving the three captives.

Dina stared at the scene in slack-jawed horror when she realized the truth. The Children weren't just defending themselves against these cats. The Children must have gone out of their way to hunt these cats down.

At first, she thought the Children might just be fooling around or testing their strength and abilities.

The instant she showed up, Karim dropped off his branch and collided with the puma. The cat gave a spine-chilling shriek and whipped his body around to counter Karim's attack.

Guttural growls and hisses came from both of them as they plummeted out of the treetops. All the Children started yelling and then Karim and the puma smashed into the ground from fifty feet up.

Dina caught one glimpse of the two of them locked in a death struggle. Karim bared his fangs trying to dive for the cat's throat and then all the other Children rushed in to envelop the pair.

Karim and the puma vanished under a wave of bodies. Their brutal roars and howls set off everyone else. Amir charged the panther. Amir sprang from another branch, landed within striking range of the panther, and slashed the cat across the foreleg.

The panther whipped around trying to grab Amir with its teeth. Adrian and Kaiser both closed from either side and all the other Children attacked at the same time. The Pygmies descended on the tabby with teeth and claws.

The Children who'd been guarding the hunters sprinted to close with the three cats moving in from behind.

The three prey cats went down in a swarm of Children and the other three cats turned tail and ran for it. Adrian, Kaiser, and Amir brought the panther crashing to the ground and more Children pounced to tear the cat apart.

The Pygmies and their friends finished off the tabby in the branches. Too many Children up there crowded around their prey for Dina to see what they did to it.

As soon as they finished, Naia and Darius pulled away and looked down from the treetops. Blood covered the two Children's silky white fur.

Naia raised the tabby by the tail and bellowed in triumph. "Ha ha! We got him! Do you see this, you bastards?! Any of you that comes back into our jungle will get some of this!"

"Who's next?!" Darius roared into the treetops. "Do you hear that, you stinking, mangy bastards?! Who's next?!!"

They both burst out laughing, grabbed each other, and bounced up and down on their branch. The cat's body flapped in Naia's hand.

The Children on the ground took longer to subdue their much bigger victims. The noise of howls and snarls still drifted from the spot where Karim brought the puma down.

Eventually, one Child after another peeled themselves out of the stack. They stood up still staring down at the ground underneath them.

They finally separated enough for Dina to see Karim pinned under the puma's body. The puma still had his mouth locked around Karim's throat, but Karim had shredded the puma's stomach and pelvis so badly that the puma must have bled to death before he could suffocate Karim.

Blood and gore saturated Karim's fur. Blood pooled underneath him and more slashes and bite marks covered the puma's back and sides where the other Children had attacked him.

Rex, Riggs, Franco, and Devon pried the puma's body off of Karim. "He's dead, Karim," Franco told him. "You can get up now."

Even then, they had to work hard to crack the puma's jaws apart and heave the body off. It thumped on the ground and Karim dragged himself to his feet. "He was heavy!"

"You're a mess," Rex told him and then they all started laughing.

They clasped each other's hands and Devon clapped Karim on the back. "That was an awesome drop! That bastard never saw you coming!"

Karim's eyes sparkled with delight. "I figured I better bring him down before he made a desperation move. He might have gotten away from us otherwise."

They left the puma lying there and went over to where Kaiser, Rome, and Aurelio were still putting an end to the panther. Adrian, Rey, Abdullah, and Emerald held the cat down against its best efforts to break free.

Rome seized the cat by both sides of its face and dove for its throat to slash its neck. Kaiser clamped his jaws around the cat's neck from behind and gave it one brutal twist to snap the cat's spine.

The cat gave one last frantic convulsion and then flopped bleeding on the ground. Blood drenched all the Children holding the cat down and Emerald and Rome both got trapped underneath the cat's body when it fell.

The Children had to wriggle out from under the panther before they got to their feet. Adrian looked around and saw Karim, Rex, Devon, and the others watching from a distance.

"Who's hurt?" Adrian asked. He craned back his head and yelled up into the branches. "Is anyone hurt up there?"

Naia glanced behind her. "Duke got cut on the face....and it looks like Cairo and Shelby have some scratches." She bent over the branch and examined everyone on the ground. "Is everybody all right?"

"We're okay," he called back and searched the surrounding Children. "Rome has some bad cuts.....and it looks like Karim got a bad gash on his leg."

Dina's eyes snapped over to Karim. He was already covered in so much blood that she didn't notice any cut on his leg until Adrian mentioned it.

"Come down from here!" Adrian yelled up in the branches. "We'll regroup and head over to the....."

He pushed his way through the assembled Children to approach the dead puma. That's when he noticed Dina standing there watching.

He stopped in his tracks and all the other Children turned around to see what he was looking at.

"Dina!" Riggs panted. "We didn't notice you there."

"We were a little busy," Brock added and some of the Children laughed.

"Is this.....is *this* what you've been doing out here?" she gasped. "You've been out here.....hunting cats?"

Adrian shrugged. "Pretty much. We have to establish our territory. We can't have them coming in here hunting *us,* can we?"

Dina shut her mouth with difficulty and gulped. Her maternal instinct told her to step in and start taking care of the Children's injuries, but she couldn't bring herself to move.

"How long have you been doing this?" she choked.

"A few months," Iona replied. Dina didn't see where Iona had been during the hunt. She came out of nowhere now, but she had blood all over her light golden fur, too.

Just then, Naia, Darius, and the other Pygmies leapt down from the high branches. Naia still swung her tabby by the tail.

She held it up for the others to see. "We brought back a trophy." She laughed and then noticed Dina. "Dina! Where did you come from?"

"She came from the canton, of course," Riggs replied. "Did the other parents send you again?"

"I was curious to find out what you were doing out here....." Dina trailed off. "Now I know."

"What's the big deal?" Adrian asked. "So we're hunting cats. They hunt us—or they used to. They know better now."

"Do you always get hurt like this?" Dina asked. "This is exactly what the other parents are worried about—you getting hurt."

A hush fell over the group. "Do you have to tell them?" Leroy asked. "Can't you just keep it to yourself?"

"Why should I do that if you're so proud of yourselves and it's no big deal? You should want them to know what you're doing. Are you ashamed of it?"

"Of course not," Adrian snapped. "It's just that things have already been so strained between us and the canton. We didn't want to make it worse. That's why we stayed out here—so they wouldn't find out."

Dina compressed her lips. "I think you should come back to the village and tell them—or at least show them that you're hurt. We can look after your injuries there and you can deal with your parents at the same time. You don't have to stop what you're doing, but keeping secrets from them sure won't help."

"You won't try to convince us to stop what we're doing?" Iona asked.

Dina squirmed. "I won't say I like it."

"Why not?" Karim asked. "You were the one who taught us to fight back against the cats."

"Fighting back to defend yourselves is one thing," she replied. "Hunting them down and killing them is something else."

"Why is it something else?" Adrian demanded. "This is our territory. They would come around hunting us and killing us if we didn't establish ourselves. We have to kill any cat that encroaches. That's the only way they're going to get the message that they can't come here hunting us."

Dina spun around to stare at her son. He barely came up to her chest, but she got the impression again that she wasn't dealing with a ten-year-old boy. He'd grown into something so much more than that.

She shook those thoughts out of her head. "Just come back to the village and let me clean up your wounds. We can't do it here."

All the other Children glanced at Adrian to hear his decision. He kept staring at Dina. He didn't look sideways at the other Children's injuries. This kind of thing really must happen all the time.

Dina cringed at the thought. How many cats had the Children killed? All this time, she thought they'd just been living in the jungle playing around.

Now she found out the truth and she didn't know what to think.

Chapter 8

Everyone in the canton stopped what they were doing when Dina led the Children out of the trees. People stood and stared as she led Karim, Adrian, Kaiser, Abdullah, Rey, and Emerald to the river.

Dina brought a bucket from her house and tipped water over their heads one Child after another. Karim rubbed down his fur and blood soaked the grass around his feet.

The other Children came forward one after the other so Dina could drench them, too. They cleaned themselves off and then left to make room for the others.

Rey and Abdullah splashed water on each other and laughed. "Do you mind?" Dina snapped. "You're getting me wet now."

"Aw, have some fun!" Abdullah told her. "When was the last time you went swimming?"

"I really don't remember. I was on the *Savannah* for years before I came here."

"You should go down the river with us to the canyons," Rey told her. "That's where we usually go."

Dina looked up. "You do?"

"It's a lot more fun than *this* place." He grimaced at the canton with all the people standing around gaping at the Children. "We can play all we like there and no one bothers us."

When she finally finished washing the blood off the Pygmies, the whole party returned to Dina's house where the Children sprawled on the grass drying off in the sunshine.

"Come over here and let me look at your leg, Karim," Dina told him.

He didn't move from his place. He lay on his stomach while Iona ran her fingers through the fur on the back of his neck.

"It isn't that bad," he muttered. "Just leave it alone."

"Let me take a look at it either way." Dina sat down on the steps leading into her house. "It isn't my fault you have a mother. Let me do a mother's job and take a look at it."

He groaned in annoyance and rolled over, but he didn't take his head away from Iona. He pivoted his body sideways so his legs pointed toward Dina.

Iona kept running her fingers through the fur on his forehead and cheeks. Dina did her best not to notice the way they were acting toward each other.

She took her mind off them to bend over the cut on Karim's leg. She had to push his fur apart just to see it. It turned out to be a lot deeper than she imagined.

The cut tore out the cuff of his already frayed pants where they covered his thigh. His black skin separated to reveal a deep gash almost to the muscle, but at least it wasn't bleeding anymore.

He didn't even flinch when she touched it. "We should bandage this up to stop it from getting infected."

"I am NOT going around with a bandage on my leg," he countered. "Forget it. You aren't dressing me up like an old man to go running around in the jungle."

"You can't go out there with it hanging open like this." She looked up at him. "Doesn't it hurt? It looks painful."

He shut his eyes and turned his head away so Iona could stroke the side of his head and rub behind his ears. "It isn't that bad. I've been hurt worse than this a bunch of times."

Dina glanced up at Iona, but Iona didn't see Dina looking at her. Iona gazed down at Karim with a magnificent smile of admiration and affection. Iona didn't pay any attention to Dina at all.

Like something out of a distant dream, Dina's gaze skimmed the rest of the Children's group. They'd always curled up together, rubbed and stroked each other, and slept and lounged in piles of bodies.

Dina had always seen that behavior as part of their feline nature. Now it took on a whole new meaning.

Adrian, Abdullah, Keith, and Rome lay in a heap with the Pygmies. Adrian closed his eyes and let his head fall against Naia's side.

None of the others who said they were injured showed any sign of pain or distress over their injuries. Dina couldn't even really see where they were injured.

She took one look at Karim's leg and stood up. "Stay here. I'm going to get the bandages."

"No!" he barked. "Just leave it alone."

"You have to put something on it," she insisted. "A cut that bad could kill you if it got infected."

"I'll take care of it, Dina." Iona got up and Karim had to move his head out of her lap. "We can put some Vaga sap on it."

"What?" Dina asked. "What's Vaga sap?"

"That's just what we call it. That's what we use on wounds that are too big. I'll get it."

She took off toward the gate and vanished into the jungle. Karim lounged where he was and didn't move.

Iona came sprinting back a second later holding what looked like a black marble between her fingers. She ran straight past all the staring villagers and squatted down next to Karim's leg.

"I'm going to put it on now," she told him.

He shut his eyes. "Go ahead."

She pinched the two sides of the cut together and smeared the sap over the incision. The sap stuck to his skin and fur and glued the cut closed.

She smoothed the top and plastered the goo over the entire cut to completely close it off from the outside air. Karim didn't move through the whole procedure.

Iona finally spread the sap into a solid plate from one side of the cut to the other. She let go of his leg, wiped the remaining sap on the grass, and tapped her finger on the black surface. Dina couldn't see the cut anymore at all.

Iona's finger made a quiet tapping sound. The sap had solidified.

"That's amazing!" Dina exclaimed. "Where did you get that?"

"It's the sap of a vine that grows out in the jungle," Iona replied. "It's what we always use on wounds that are too big to just leave open."

Dina glanced around at the other Children. "Maybe we should do the same thing with the others."

"They'll be fine." Iona sat back down and went back to running her fingers through Karim's fur.

He didn't purr, but he did roll onto his stomach so she could continue stroking the back of his neck the way she had been before.

Dina looked away. She never would have felt uncomfortable about seeing her Children acting affectionate with each other. Now she couldn't unsee the obvious implications.

They were all growing up. If they didn't act like Children in any other way, why should they express their affection for each other in a childish way? They all spent so much time together. It was bound to lead to more.

That was the moment when Dina spotted Troy and Nicholas talking to Meredith and some of the other parents. They all watched the Children, but none of the parents had worked up the courage to come near them—yet.

Dina ought to do something to head the parents off at the pass, but she couldn't bring herself to do that. She was the one who convinced the Children not to keep their hunts a secret from their parents. She couldn't forestall the inevitable moment when they found out.

Troy finally worked up the nerve to split away from the others and came over to Dina's house. She read his expression as he approached.

The other parents hung back and watched from a distance—as if them staying on the other side of the village could stop anyone from seeing that they were a part of this confrontation.

Troy started out by plastering a casual smile on his face. His expression changed when he got nearer and saw some of the Children bleeding.

"What happened?!" he snapped. "How did they get hurt? How did you all get hurt? Did something happen? Did the Pride send out another party to attack you?"

Adrian answered without opening his eyes or lifting his head off Naia's fur. "They're always sending out parties to attack us. That isn't new—but if you really want to know, this wasn't one of those parties. It was just a random bunch of cats wandering around in the jungle."

Troy's jaw dropped. He stared at Adrian, but Adrian still didn't open his eyes.

Troy spun around to gape at Dina and then Troy's wide eyes skimmed the rest of the Children. "You....fought cats?! You....got hurt....fighting cats?!"

"They didn't get hurt *fighting* cats," Dina interrupted. "They got hurt *hunting* cats. The Children have been out there hunting down any cats that encroach on their territory."

Troy opened and closed his mouth more than once before he managed to choke out the word. *"Territory....."* he rasped. "You're....you're staking your claim on *territory?*"

"Calm down, Dad," Leroy drawled from across the circle. "We've been doing it for months. You just didn't know about it. Nothing changed just because you found out about it."

"You......" Troy blurted out, but he couldn't finish.

He blinked at the Children and then turned around to stare at Dina.

She actually felt sorry for him. He'd been the least problematic of the parents. She didn't really blame him for getting alarmed that his Children were out there in the jungle hunting down any cats they could find.

She didn't tell him what the hunt had actually been like. He and the other parents would have gone into hysterics if they found out.

He cleared his throat with an effort and turned back to the Children. "Leroy—Devon—Franco—could you come over here for a minute? I need to talk to you."

Franco groaned and rolled his eyes. "You go," he growled to Leroy. "You're the oldest. You deal with him."

Leroy snorted and got to his feet. Troy pretended not to notice that Franco and Devon didn't obey him. Sasha and Shelby watched their brother walk away with their father. Neither of the two girls made any move to get up or involve themselves in the interaction.

Dina pulled her wooden spoon and sanding stone from inside the doorway. She made a show of sanding her spoon, but everyone present could hear exactly what Troy and Leroy were saying to each other.

"How long has this been going on?" Troy demanded.

"I already told you," Leroy countered. "We've been doing it for months. I don't know why you're making such a big deal about it now. It isn't like we were supposed to just go limp and let the cats hunt us down. We do it all the time."

"You weren't supposed to let the cats hunt you down. You were supposed to stay in the village—or at least near the village," Troy returned. "We've been telling you this all along. It was bound to end with someone getting hurt."

"No one got hurt—or at least not that badly," Leroy told him. "We've gotten hurt way worse than this. You just never found out about it."

Troy gasped. "You got hurt?! When?! Why didn't you tell me?"

"This is why. If you keep kicking up a stink about everything we do, we just won't tell you. You won't stop us from doing it. I don't know when you're gonna get that through your heads. We won't stop hunting the cats. You sure act like you don't want us to come back to the village at all."

"If this is what you do in the jungle by yourselves, maybe you shouldn't go out with Adrian anymore," Troy went on. "He's a bad influence on you—on all of you."

Leroy changed his tone in a heartbeat and dropped his voice to a deadly snarl. "Don't you dare say a word against Adrian. We wouldn't be alive right now without him. He's done a hell of a lot more for us than you ever have."

"How dare you talk to me like that?!" Troy fought his own voice under control. "We raised you! We risked our lives to take you out of Prideland so you could grow up somewhere safe and free. You have the option to run around in the jungle right now because of us! Adrian didn't do that."

Leroy hesitated for a moment and then his voice changed again. "Maybe not, but he's in charge of us now. We need someone who understands our ways—someone who can lead us to deal with the situation we're in right now. That isn't you. It isn't anyone in this village. It has to be one of our own and he's the one. If you don't like it, then you can stay here and we won't see you again."

He turned his back on Troy and walked back to the group of Children sitting on the grass.

Troy stared after him, which brought him around to staring at the Children. The others pretended he wasn't there. They also pretended they hadn't heard that conversation.

Dina couldn't keep her head down anymore. She looked up at Troy and another pang of sympathy stung her when she saw his tortured expression.

He stared at his Children lying on the grass. Leroy went back to the cluster where he, Brock, and Riyadh had been lounging with Egypt, Nova, and India.

Riyadh lay with one arm draped over Nova's fluffy white fur. Brock and Shelby lay curled around each other.

Leroy sat down and Egypt scooted over to his side, put her arm around his shoulders, and rested her head on his shoulder. How did this happen? How did all the Children pair off into couples so fast?

Troy shuddered, shook himself out of his dazed trance, shot Dina one glance, and walked away to go rejoin the other parents. Dina expected them to come back and make another scene about the Children getting hurt, but the parents didn't do that.

Some of those parents' Children had gotten injured today, but they didn't approach to find out how their Children were or even to find out how they got hurt.

No doubt Troy would spread the news sooner or later. He might even be over there telling everyone right now. That might lead to another explosive confrontation.

Adrian must have been thinking the same thing. He dozed with Naia for a while, but in a few minutes, he raised his head and cast a critical glance around the canton.

He got to his feet. "Let's get out of here. It's time we were going."

Dina sprang up, too. "You don't have to leave so soon. Stick around. Link will be back soon. We can have dinner together."

"I don't think so," Adrian told her. "Maybe another time."

She winced when she heard that biting tone in his voice. They were leaving—as in leaving. They weren't just going out into the jungle to play.

Her voice trembled when she asked, "When will I see you again? When will we see you again?"

He heard that tremble and turned around to face her for the first time. How long had it been since he gave her this much direct attention? She couldn't remember.

"You will see us again," Adrian replied. "I don't know when, but we'll come back soon. We aren't leaving—not like that. We'll come find you. Don't worry."

She found herself consuming him with her eyes. She didn't want to stop looking at him—at all of them. These were her Children and now they were leaving.

They might not be leaving permanently, but an irrevocable break had torn them apart somewhere along the way. Whatever they had been to her in the past, they would never be that again. They would never be the babies she carried everywhere and took care of every single day.

She fought the urge to kiss him in front of everyone. She couldn't do that. He was growing into a leader more powerful and authoritative than anything she could have imagined.

Having his mother kiss him in front of everyone would have been the worst thing she could do to him.

She couldn't even get her voice to function well enough to say goodbye as they all got to their feet, filed through the gate, and out into the jungle.

Everyone else in the village stood back and watched them go. None of the parents stepped out of line to stop the Children or even to say goodbye.

In a minute, the undergrowth swallowed the Children and they vanished without a sound. They didn't disturb a single leaf and then they were gone.

Chapter 9

Dina submerged a shirt in the freezing cold water of the pool at the base of the waterfall. Her mind wandered while her hands went through the usual routine of scrubbing the shirt, beating it against the rocks, and then rinsing it.

She started on the second shirt when she noticed movement in the trees nearby. She glanced up and froze when a group of Children appeared out of the jungle.

Neither Dina nor any other parent in this canton had seen their Children in nine months and these weren't Children who'd grown up in Riverbend canton.

Dina had never seen these Children before. They were strangers and they didn't approach. They hovered near the line of foliage and cast wary glances at her, the gate, and the sentries in the watchtowers.

The Children stayed there on the fringe of jungle for at least five minutes before one of them whispered to the others. They all turned around to face the jungle and then their group parted to let a different party of Children move into the open.

Dina's stomach twisted when she saw Adrian, the Black, Iona, the Manx boys, the Pygmies, and all the other Children she'd raised with her own hands.

She stood up, but she didn't go near them. They'd been gone for almost a year and she never could have imagined they would change so much.

Adrian had grown six inches and nearly doubled in size. His shoulders, back, chest, and legs bulged with muscle and the fur around his face and head had darkened.

The stripes radiating outward from his cheeks had turned brighter white. They gave him an even more distinctly tiger-like appearance.

The three black boys had grown even taller and bigger than Adrian. Tania had been tall, but Adrian's commanding presence cast everyone else in shadow. The three brothers surrounded him in a guarding posture and everyone cut those four boys a wide berth.

Everyone in their party had grown. They looked like they might be sixteen or seventeen in equivalent human years, but their expressions had matured far more than that.

The four Manx brothers hadn't grown as tall as the others, but they'd also put on massive amounts of muscle that gave them a blocky, powerful, deadly look.

They'd also inherited the hard, cruel, piercing glare that Dina remembered so well from their father, Fallon.

The Pygmies were all still petite and delicate, even the boys, but all four walked with a graceful, springy step. Their crystal blue eyes darted from one object in the landscape to the next. They were as ready to fight and defend themselves as everyone else.

Adrian scanned the canton, murmured something to the strange Children who'd come with him, and advanced into the open.

Dina jolted out of her trance and hurried over to meet them. She couldn't stop her heart from turning a somersault when she came face to face with Adrian.

He was taller than she was now and much bigger, but he smiled with the same warmth. "Dina! It's so good to see you!"

She hugged him. "I'm so glad you're back! Tell me all about where you've been and what you've been doing." She went from one Child to another hugging them all. "You're all so big! You look like you're almost fully grown."

"It's good to see you, Dina," Karim told her. "We've missed you."

"You should have come with us, Dina," Riggs chimed in from the back. "You would have liked it out in the jungle."

She found herself beaming at them. "I'm so proud of you all! Look at the way you've grown up!" She stopped in front of Iona and folded the girl in her arms.

Dina became aware that she wasn't hugging a girl anymore. Iona was becoming a young woman.

The girls no longer went around shirtless the way they used to. They'd fashioned tops for themselves and all of them had developed breasts.

"Is Link in the canton?" Adrian asked. "We want to see him, too."

"He went out hunting. He'll be back soon. Why don't you all come to my house—I mean our house. You're very welcome." She glanced behind the group toward the trees. "Who are your friends? They're welcome, too."

"They won't enter the canton," Kaiser replied. "Their parents drove them out of their home canton. Now they don't trust humans anymore."

"That's a shame," Dina replied. "Did you explain to them that it isn't like that here?"

"It is like that here," Riggs countered. "We can go to your house because we're your Children, but we're the only ones. The rest will stay out in the trees."

Dina's spirits sank. "I guess I can't argue with that. Do you want to come inside now?"

"Just a minute," Adrian replied and turned back to the jungle.

He retreated to rejoin the stranger Children he'd brought with him. He conversed with them for five minutes before they nodded and shrank away into the undergrowth.

All the rest of Adrian's party went with them. Only he, Iona, the Black, the Pygmies, the Manx, and the Auroras came with him.

He walked straight through the gate without a sidelong glance at the guards and sentries. They aimed their weapons at him and the other Children advancing through the gate, but the sentries didn't attack nor did they try to shut the gate to stop the Children from entering.

Dina led the way to her own house. The Children sat down on the floor, but they didn't sprawl and lounge the way they used to. They stayed sitting up like the guests they were.

Dina hustled behind the house to where Link had left the remnants of an ox carcass hanging from the eaves.

She untied it, lugged it back inside, and laid it on the floor in the center of the group. Then she sat down to join them.

"Where have you been all these months?" she asked. "We wondered if you would ever come back."

"I told you we would," Adrian replied. "We've been organizing with the other cantons—or the Children from the other cantons."

"Are they all as hostile as ours?" Dina asked. "Which canton did your friends come from?"

"They call it Moonlight canton," Naia replied. "It's the canton closest to the city from here."

Dina perked up. "Oh! That's Frank's old canton."

"Some people call the city Zuno, but we don't know if that's the real name," Naia went on. "It's just a name people call it when they need to distinguish it from all the other cities in Prideland."

Dina glanced around the room at all the Children. They weren't Children anymore. They were adults. "Wow, you all know so much more about Prideland than I do. I've never been to any of those places."

Rome laughed at her. "We didn't go to Zuno, of course."

"No, of course not," she murmured.

"Has anything changed here?" Adrian asked. "Are the parents still as entrenched as they were when we left?"

"I wouldn't know. We never talk about you—or anything related to any Children. I guess people are happier to let it drop, but we don't have a problem as long as you aren't around."

"Then us coming around will cause another problem." He compressed his lips. "Nothing ever changes."

"You should come out into the jungle with us, Dina," Riggs repeated. "You don't belong here any more than we do."

She tried to laugh it off. "I couldn't travel the way you do. You would leave me in the dust in a few minutes."

No one answered for a minute, and in that silence, Dina heard Link talking outside. The voices drifting through the open door didn't sound as tranquil and at ease as they usually did.

She got to her feet, crossed the room, and saw Link talking to the guards at the gate. Link carried another deer on his shoulder and one of the guards pointed to the tree line where the Children from Moonlight canton had first appeared.

They held a long conversation pointing at different parts of the jungle before Link nodded and headed for the house.

Dina stepped aside to let him enter. She bumped into Adrian, the three black brothers, and Riggs and Rome. They all stood behind her watching Link, too.

He split in a grin when he saw them all waiting for him. He sweated under his load and Adrian and the boys surrounded Link when he walked through the door. "Let us help you, Link," Rome told him and they lifted the deer off his shoulder.

He laughed at them. "Clean it before you swallow it whole." He laughed loudly and grabbed Karim to hug him. "Look at you all! It's so great that you're here! I missed you so much!"

He went through the room hugging everyone and kissing the girls on their cheeks.

Riggs, Rome, Kaiser, and Kenji laid out the deer and started cleaning it. Link clasped both his hands around Iona's cheeks, kissed her, and then moved on to Naia and Nova.

"It's going to be wonderful having you all around again. Life is so boring without you here." He came to the end of the room and glanced around. "Where are my kids?" His expression changed. "Don't tell me something happened to them."

"They're fine, Link," Iona told him. "They stayed out in the jungle."

"Oh. Then I'll go see them there." He turned back toward the door.

Adrian stepped into his path. "Don't go anywhere, Link. Stay here."

"What are you talking about? I want to see my kids." Link tried to push past Adrian to get to the door.

Adrian straight-armed him back and lowered his voice to a deadly murmur. "I said stay here, Link. You can't go out there."

"I was just out there." Link rounded on Adrian. "What are you doing? Get out of my way. You aren't going to keep me as a prisoner in my own house."

Adrian didn't budge. "Your kids are fine. They're right outside the village."

"Where?" Link demanded. "You can't stand there and tell me they don't want to see me. If there was a problem between me and them, they never mentioned it. I want to see them. I need to see them. I need to see that they're okay."

"You can see them soon," Adrian replied and sidestepped in front of Link when Link tried one more time to bypass him and get out of the house. "I'm warning you, Link. I won't let you go out there."

"*You*....won't let....*me*........" Link snapped. "You don't *let* me do anything. This is my house and my village. I come and go as I please."

"Not this time," Riggs cut in. "Just leave it alone, Link."

"Leave my own kids alone! Are you insane?" Link glanced around the room, but in that moment, he saw something that made him stop pushing to get past Adrian.

Adrian planted his bulk between Link and the door. Riggs, Rome, Kaiser, and Kenji remained squatted over the deer carcass they were cleaning, but they were the only boys in the room who didn't surround Adrian in a wall of solid muscle.

Karim, Rey, Rex, and the Auroras formed a circle around Link and Adrian. The boys didn't have to move between Link and the door. Their presence communicated loud and clear that they wouldn't let Link go out there.

Then Link glanced over his shoulder at Dina. She didn't move nor did she offer a word of protest. Whatever the Children had been doing out in the jungle, it had grown much bigger than Link, Dina, or anyone else they knew.

Adrian softened his stance first, stepped around Link, and returned to his place on the floor. "Come sit down with us, Link. We came all this way to see you. Let's not turn it into a conflict."

Link followed Adrian with his eyes and stared down at Adrian in stunned confusion. "At least tell me where my kids are."

"Naia just told you. They're out in the jungle right now—right outside the village."
Adrian turned back to the ox they'd all been eating a few minutes before. "You can see
them soon. I promise."

Chapter 10

Adrian didn't look at Link again. Adrian kept his back turned. Link stared at him and then at everyone else.

The other Children gazed back at him and most of them smiled at him in warm affection, but none of them contradicted Adrian's decision.

Link must have seen the writing on the wall because he gave in and sat down on the floor between Dina and Adrian.

"There are a bunch of Children out there from another canton," Adrian finally explained, but he waited until Link capitulated first. "They've had bad experiences with humans and they don't want humans around. I assigned some of our group to stay with these other Children on a rotating basis so our visitors don't get lost or think we abandoned them. Your Children will finish their rotation in a few hours and then they can come to see you. Just don't go out into the jungle. We worked hard to forge this alliance and I don't want to ruin it by having some humans come around and scare our friends away."

Link blinked at nothing. This visit was heading in a direction neither he nor Dina ever anticipated.

Fortunately, Riggs and Kenji came over just then with the freshly skinned and gutted deer carcass. They put it between all the Children who divided between it and what little remained of the ox.

"Why don't you light a fire, Dina?" Kenji told her. "You and Link should share this with us."

She got to work and brought over a pot of coals to cook the meat for herself and Link. The Children ate it raw the way they always did.

Dina did her best to change the subject. "Have you visited many other cantons?"

"About ten," Adrian replied. "Some are better than others. Some are so friendly the Children don't want to leave. Others are far enough away from Prideland that the Children don't recognize the danger—at least not yet."

"Are mothers and Children still coming out from Prideland? Are the cats still killing any helper that gets pregnant?"

"Definitely," Iona replied. "When we visited Hardship canton, a group of four mothers showed up while we were there. They were all in fear for their lives. They said they would have been killed if they'd stayed."

"What about cats bringing their Children out the way Amaryllis, Osiris, and Elyse did?"

"I haven't heard of that anywhere else," Adrian replied. "So far, those three are the only ones we know about who have done that. All the others are actively involved in hunting the Children down and killing them as soon as they're born."

Dina shook her head over her work. "That's terrible. It's such a waste."

Adrian turned back to Link, but before he could speak, Dexter climbed the steps and stopped on the threshold. "Cain and Jackal are asking to see you, Adrian. They want to leave and they want to see you first. They insist."

"What's wrong?" Adrian asked. "I told you boys to give them anything they needed."

"We have been. I don't know what the problem is. They won't explain themselves to anyone but you."

"I better go see what they want." Adrian stood up. "The rest of you stay here."

This order apparently didn't apply to the Black. Adrian headed outside and the Black went with him.

Link and Dina followed them as far as the threshold. Dexter stayed behind, too.

Link and Dina stopped at the doorway and watched Adrian, Karim, Kaiser, and Kenji cross the grass.

The Children from Moonlight canton met them there at the tree line where they'd appeared the first time. More Children came out of the undergrowth and formed a big loose mob that spilled into the open.

"Should be we worried about this?" Link murmured in Dina's ear.

"Something's coming," she whispered back. "Something big."

Those words brought back a distant, long-forgotten memory. It had fallen so far beneath her conscious mind that she didn't even remember it until right this minute.

She'd had a vision the night she realized she was pregnant with Adrian and Iona. She'd fallen unconscious and seen a vision of a tree that grew out of her—a tree that exploded and destroyed all of Prideland with it.

This was it. This was the tree. Adrian.....he was doing something—something she couldn't even fathom right now because whatever he was planning was still in its infancy.

Whatever he was planning would be the explosion that laid all of Prideland to waste. She didn't know what would happen in the future, but this was it. It all started right here—with these Children.

The Children entered the jungle, and a few minutes later, Adrian and the Black came back with Link's nieces and nephews and Osiris's Children.

Those nine made up the rest of Link's and Dina's Children All the others stayed in the jungle where they wouldn't see anyone.

Troy's, Meredith's, Nicholas's, and all the other Children who'd grown up in Riverbend canton never even showed their faces where their parents might see them.

Adrian and the Black brought everyone back to Link's and Dina's house. Link hugged his Children and welcomed them home as warmly as all the others. Then everyone sat down in their usual places.

The tension dissolved and their conversation resumed as though it had never been interrupted.

The sun started to go down, so Dina lit the lamps to brighten the room. "Why did the Children from Moonlight leave?" Iona asked.

"They don't like being this close to people," Adrian replied. "Even being this close makes them uncomfortable. They're going back into the jungle, but we'll meet up when the time comes."

"What time is that?" Dina asked.

Adrian pretended not to hear and turned to Link. "I want to ask you a favor, Link."

"What is it?" Link asked with his mouth full.

"We'd like you to train us—to fight. We want to fight back against the cats and we need training."

Link's head shot up and so did Dina's. "What do you mean—you want to fight back? Isn't that what you've been doing? Haven't you been hunting cats in the jungle? Isn't that your favorite pastime?"

None of the Children treated this as a joke. "We've only hunted small groups of cats when all of us worked together could overwhelm them with numbers. The Pride is sending out more search parties now. We need to organize and we need training. A confrontation is coming where all of us will have to defend ourselves against a large number of cats. We won't have numbers on our side, so we'll need to be able to fight better than they can now."

Link took another bite before he answered. "I'm not sure I'll be able to help you with that. You have such different abilities than mine."

"Please, Link," his nephew Riyadh urged. "You're the only man in the village who knows anything about fighting."

"I don't know about that," Link countered.

"You're the only man in the village who knows anything about fighting who will be willing to help us," Adrian replied. "We also need training in weapons. We don't have that."

"What do you need weapons for?" Link argued. "You have teeth and claws. What more weapons do you need?"

"We need to exploit every advantage we have over the cats," Adrian replied. "We have their speed, strength, and agility, but we also have all the advantages of humans. We need to use those advantages against them. We need to use all the cats' vulnerabilities against them. It's the only way we're going to win."

Link stared at him and then down at the food in his hands. No one made a sound and the silence hung heavy over the room.

The oppressive feeling of something massive coming toward Dina became unbearable. So this was the huge thing. It had been building for a long time—years, maybe.

"What do you say?" Adrian finally asked. "Will you help us?"

"I was just thinking," Link muttered.

"What were you thinking?" Adrian asked. "Tell me what's on your mind. Anything you can tell us will help us."

"And we need all the help we can get," Riggs added.

Link looked up. "Has this happened before? Have you had these confrontations with the cats—large groups of them against you when you couldn't use your numbers?"

"Not yet," Karim replied. "We've had no choice but to avoid them before now. We don't dare to engage with them when we don't have the strength to win."

Link looked away again. "I see."

"What's wrong?" Riyadh asked. "Don't tell us you want us to stop fighting and run away from them. We can't do that."

"I wasn't thinking that," Link replied. "I was thinking about the advantages you have over the cats."

"What advantages are those?" Adrian asked. "Besides what I just mentioned."

Link looked up again and his expression cleared. "It's like you said. You have all the advantages of humans and none of their weaknesses. It's the same with the cats. You have all their advantages and none of their weaknesses. You can't lose. You just need to learn how to use your skills and abilities in the right way."

Now it was Adrian's turn to pick his jaw up off the floor. "You're serious! You think we can't lose?!"

"Why should you? Think about it. The human way of warfare is to hit your enemy from afar—somewhere they can't hit you back. Humans use bows and arrows, spears, projectiles, artillery—anything to attack your enemy with some distance between you. The human way of warfare is to avoid hand-to-hand combat at all costs and to weaken your enemy as much as possible before you engage them directly. That's what you need to do. You need to learn to use weapons like you said, but you also need to perfect your close combat skills so you can beat the cats when you do engage with them."

"How do we do that?" Naia asked. "How would *I* do that? We're too small."

"Then you have to rely on speed, agility, and pure batshit craziness—like Dina did when she fought the sentinel cats—and when she fought Fallon and Khalid. You might not have strength and weight on your side, so you compensate by being more vicious, more determined, and willing to go farther than your opponent. You go where they won't go and do things they aren't willing to do."

"How does that help us defeat the Pride if they send a big group of cats after us?" Kaiser asked.

"You have the jungle on your side," Link replied. "If that fails and you have to fight them in the open, you need to bring in your friends from other cantons. There are plenty of people out there who want to fight back against the cats—people like me and Dina. You just don't know who they are or where they are. You need to call in every ally you can find, so you need to prepare the Children from other cantons to be ready to fight side by side with humans. Whatever experiences those Children had in their home cantons, the Children need to put those experiences aside and fight with those humans who are ready to support the Children's cause. Those people are out there waiting to hear from you. The Children aren't in any position to turn those allies away just because some of you had bad experiences."

Now it was Adrian who looked down at the food in his hands. "You're right. I didn't think of that."

"In the meantime, you need to work on your weapons training—and you need to start thinking big-picture. You won't be able to keep avoiding conflict with the cats, so you need to start preparing. You need to start thinking about choosing your battleground and drawing the cats into positions and situations that are the most favorable to you and the least advantageous to them."

"How do I do that?" Adrian asked. "Do you mean luring them into the jungle?"

"I mean start thinking strategically. You might fight them in the open, but you planted your own people on either side of the battlefield in hidden locations. Then, when you get the cats where you want them and engage them in battle, you spring your flanks on them and bring them down."

"Yeah!" Riggs cheered. "That would be perfect!"

"That's just one example," Link countered. "There could be plenty of other examples of using the terrain to your advantage. The cats of the Pride are just cats. They might be sentient, but they're just animals. They don't have the ability to strategize and think in tactical terms—and I'm quite certain none of them has any military experience. None of them has ever planned any battle or war before. They'll be totally unprepared for you to do it."

Adrian cocked his head. "How do you know so much about it? Where did you learn all this if you grew up in Prideland?"

"I was just about to ask the same thing," Dina chimed in.

Link laughed and his cheeks colored. He lowered his gaze back to his food. "Never mind about that. If we do this training thing, you need to bring in all your people from the jungle. It won't work to just train some of you......" He hesitated. "Then again, maybe it would work. I could train all of you and then you could go train the rest of your people."

"We have forty more out in the jungle right now....." Adrian began.

"Forty!" Link gasped. "Are you serious?"

Adrian nodded. "I didn't think it would be a good idea to bring them all into the village at once. It's bad enough just the thirty of us coming to see you."

"Oh, right," Link muttered. "I didn't think of that. No, that definitely wouldn't work, then."

"So when can we start?" Naia asked. "We needed this training last year."

"We can start tomorrow," Link replied.

"What about the other parents—and everyone else in the village?" Brock asked. "They won't like it."

"I'll deal with them," Link replied.

"How will you do that?" Dina asked. "They won't be happy about all these Children hanging around, especially not if you're training the Children to fight the cats."

"That's exactly how we'll convince them to let me train the Children to fight cats. I'll explain that training the Children to fight cats is the best way to defend the canton. You said before that you hunted any cats that trespassed on your territory."

Adrian nodded. "We had to. It was us or them."

"Exactly. You hunting cats is the reason we're still here and no cats have come after us yet. Training you to fight will give the canton much better protection than all those guards and sentries out there."

"You can say that again," Kaiser growled.

Link stood up. "Right. We have a big day tomorrow, so you kids will need to get to sleep. Are you sleeping here or going back out into the jungle?"

"Here if it's all right with you," Adrian replied.

"Of course it's all right with us," Dina told him. "This is your home. You're always welcome here."

Link carried what was left of the deer and ox carcasses to the eaves behind the house. Dina distributed blankets to all the Children and finished cleaning the room. They curled up together and she blew out all but one of the lamps.

She made a circuit of the room tucking everyone in and kissing them good night the way she used to. It gave her a strange feeling to be doing this with people who were already essentially adults, but they would always be her Children.

She moved over to where the Manx, the Black, and the Pygmies all lay together in one big pile. Dina stroked Kenji's cheek and then raked her fingers through Kaiser's fur. He always liked that when he was little.

"Was it nice at Northfall Canton?" Dina asked. "What was it like there?"

"We didn't go to Northfall canton," Kenji replied. "We aren't allowed to go there."

Dina's eyes widened. "Why not? Adrian made it sound like you all went there."

"Tania lives there," Karim growled. "Adrian sent us to Hardship canton instead."

Dina's eyes popped even wider. "You don't go there....because Tania's there?! She's your mother. Don't you want to visit her?"

"No way!" Karim countered. "She's a traitor and she hates us even more than the cats do. She's our enemy. I would kill her if I ever laid eyes on her again. If anyone else stabbed us in the back the way she did, we wouldn't hesitate."

Dina opened her mouth to argue back, but words failed her. Karim glared at Dina, but he didn't see her. His anger shot past her to some other, unseen dimension.

Dina glanced at the other two brothers. "Do you two feel the same way?"

Kenji's features spasmed, but he gulped and said, "Adrian says seeing her would be bad for me. He says it's best if we all stay away from her."

"Do you think that's true?" Dina asked.

"Of course," Kenji replied. "Adrian's always right."

She glanced at Kaiser, but he wouldn't even look at her. He kept his head turned away and pretended not to hear.

Their reactions shocked her into silence. She couldn't bring up Tania again. Talking about Tania obviously upset all three of them and Dina didn't blame them.

She'd only told them once that their mother left them with Dina to raise. None of the Black ever brought up the subject again until now.

How ironic that they all instinctively understood how much Tania hated them. Dina never told them that Tania hated them, but they all sensed it without being told.

The Black had grown up around dozens of Children whose parents had sacrificed everything to save them from the Pride. Link, Dina, Troy, Meredith, Nicholas—all these people had given everything just to be able to raise their Children.

Some, like Link's sister Lyric, had given their lives protecting their Children from the cats. Even some cat parents had taken their lives in their hands to bring their Children to safety.

There could have been any of a thousand reasons why Tania moved away and left her Children in Dina's care. Tania wouldn't have been the only one to do that.

She *was* the only one who outright hated her own Children and couldn't stand to look at them or even stay in the same canton with them.

Dina didn't like to think about how the Black found out about her. Maybe Adrian was right and the three boys were better off without Tania in their lives. In fact, Dina was certain that they were.

She finished saying good night to all the other Children, crossed the room to blow out the last lamp, and tiptoed to the bedroom. Link's dark outline blocked any light coming from inside.

He stepped out of the way to let her in and shut the door behind her. They both took off their clothes in the dark and got into bed.

She slid over next to him and put her arms around him. His body radiated heat into her and his smell flooded her nostrils.

She relaxed into the blissful feeling of having him here with her. This house didn't feel the same when he went out hunting.

He let out a deep sigh as his weight sank into the mattress. She expected him to go straight to sleep, but after just a few seconds, he twined his fingers into her hair and pried her head up to kiss her.

His lips consumed her and his earthy scent intoxicated her. His mouth became more insistent and ravenous. He pushed her mouth open and his tongue devoured her mind.

She let her head fall back as he leaned forward to push her down on the bed, but just as fast, he hooked one muscular arm around her waist and pulled her on top of him.

He didn't let go of her hair or her mouth. He used her head to steer her into position and he pulled her legs onto each side of his waist.

Her body ignited when she straddled him. His other hand guided her hips in a steady rhythm that drove her out of her mind.

She moaned and his breath quickened in her nostrils. He stiffened between her legs. It would be so easy to lower herself on top of him and let him take her—for the first time.

They'd been living together for almost two years and they'd never gone all the way. Was tonight the night they both gave in and let the inevitable finally take over?

He kept one hand laced in her hair while the other explored her body. He eventually slipped his hand between her legs and penetrated her with his fingers.

She swooned in an agony of delight and copied him to stroke him with her hand. They matched their rhythm rising to the stars.

He broke off her mouth and his eyes glistened up at her in the darkness. "I want you," he whispered. "I want all of you."

"You have me," she whispered back. "You have all of me."

"I mean like that. I want you like that."

She caught her breath. "Are you saying you're ready for.....*that?*"

He hesitated, but the wild look of rising passion didn't leave his face. "I guess not."

She winced. She wanted him, too. She wanted him more than anything, but they'd agreed not to have any more children. They already had enough.

She drilled herself down on his hand harder and faster. Her hips pumped his fingers deeper inside her and she stroked him at the same rate.

His breathing became more strained in his nostrils until they both gasped in release and she buckled on top of him.

He clasped her head in both hands and demolished her mouth in a thousand kisses before they both collapsed together in each other's arms.

She let herself sink into the darkness of his embrace. She wanted him more than anything, but this one line—this was the line neither of them could cross.

"We could go west," he whispered into her hair. "We could go west and start over. We could have our own children there."

She clamped her eyes shut against the vision that flooded her mind. Starting over somewhere with Link—having his children and having a real family—she would give anything for that—anything except the Children she already had.

This was just a fantasy. That's all it was. Link would never be able to leave his Children. He was just as committed to them as Dina was to her own Children.

Link had just committed himself to training them and helping them in their campaign against the cats. He wouldn't be ready to leave for a long time—if ever.

She was just about to fade out into unconsciousness when he ran his fingers into her hair and used it to push her head back. He lifted her face and her eyes floated open to meet his.

"Tell me you would do it with me if we could," he whispered. "Tell me you would go west with me if I asked you to."

"You know I would," she whispered back. "I love you. I love you more than anything. I've never loved anyone as much as I love you."

He ran his other hand down her body to her belly. "Would you have my children.....if we could? Would you really do that for me?"

"Of course!" she breathed. "You know I would love to do that. I would be doing it now if we didn't have all these other Children to take care of."

He eased in and kissed her again. Their bodies came together in a torrent of heat, but neither of them escalated.

Just being with him was enough....and yet it wasn't enough. It was the best of a bad situation.

They both eventually stretched out, exhausted and frustrated, but Dina never doubted that Link felt the same way about her that she did about him.

She didn't allow herself to think about what going west and starting over with him meant. She didn't allow herself to think about what it would mean if they ever got to a time when the Children didn't need them anymore—a time when their obligation to the Children didn't trump everything else.

Chapter 11

L ink strode up and down the line of Children standing in front of him. "Step forward and stab!" he yelled. "Keep your feet in line! Don't cross them! Flex your knees and spread your weight as wide as you can! Step forward and stab! And....shuffle back! Now step forward and stab!"

The Children advanced with their knees bent and their legs angled wide to give them a broad base of support. They kept their feet separated, advanced, and each of them stabbed the air with a knife.

Link walked between them checking their stance and technique. "Keep your non-dominant hand up! Your opponent could have killed you by now, Dexter. Don't stab until you get to the end of your step, Adrian! Use your weight and momentum to drive the blade forward. Don't stab until you get into your new position. Now shuffle back."

The Children scooted back to where they started.

"That was really good," Link told them. "That was better than I expected. Now we're going to add a block. You're going to bring your arm down in a sweeping, half-circle motion in front of you like this....."

He started with his arm raised and his hand positioned in front of his face. He brought it down in a chopping motion.

"You're going to imagine your opponent stabbing at you with a knife or another weapon. You're going to block that strike and then stab with your own weapon. Understand? Like this."

He took the knife that Riyadh had been using and went through the sequence at an angle to the group so they could all see him.

"How does this help us against the cats?" Rey asked. "They don't use knives."

"That's why you aren't in charge of this army," Link told him. "You need to start thinking bigger. If you fight the cats and win, they'll bring out every tool in their arsenal to finish you off. The cats have millions of helpers in the cities who will all be using weapons to come after you. Now go through that sequence using the block and stab. Go!"

He moved out of the way and the Children advanced across the open ground outside the canton fence. It was the only place big enough for all of them to move around without bumping into each other.

They followed his instructions to the letter. Then he set them apart in pairs, armed each of them with a short, blunt stick to act in place of the knife, and instructed them on how to spar with each other.

"We're using the honor system here," he told them. "If your opponent lands a hit on you, you have to admit that you lost and concede the point."

He had them spar with their fake knives for a while.

"Now you're going to take turns and each of you will put down your knife. You'll spar with each other using any fighting style you want to. You can fight the person as a cat or as an unarmed person or a combination of the two. It doesn't matter what you do as long as you don't get stabbed first—and no teeth or claws. Just pretend."

Laughter answered him and then the Children got down to wrestling and scrapping with each other. They went through multiple matches each with everyone scoring victories on everyone else.

Sometimes those Children fighting bare-handed prevailed, but plenty of times, the person with the fake knife stabbed or slashed their opponent first and "killed" the other Child.

"Excellent!" Link declared after fifteen minutes of this. "That was excellent! Move back into position over there."

They returned to their starting line. All the Children grinned at each other and flushed with pleasure that they were actually learning to fight.

Link paced up and down in front of them again. "Now we're going to test your strategic thinking and battle planning. We're going to divide into two groups. One group will go out into the jungle, disappear into the undergrowth, and start planning to assault the canton. The other group will stay here and defend the walls."

A bunch of Children gasped. "You want us to assault the canton—on purpose?!" Calliope exclaimed. "You're joking!"

"No, I'm not joking and you better do a damn good job because those of us inside the walls will be using every means at our disposal to stop you—including using weapons.

Imagine you're assaulting a village of subsidiaries who are out to kill you on the Pride's behalf."

"But what about.....what about *them?*" Aries pointed up at the watchtowers.

"I'll deal with them." Link went through the group pointing out each person one after the other. "Adrian, you can start out there since you're so hot to become our new military commander. Take Kenji, Israel, Iona, Rey, Emerald, Brock, Abdullah, Briar, India, Riyadh, Kaiser, Duke and Nova. The rest of you stay here with me. Go on. Get out of here."

Adrian grinned at his comrades and they took off running into the jungle. "Now what do we do?" Karim asked.

"Come over here and man the walls." Link strode over to the guards at the gate and waved at them. "Give these kids your weapons. They're gonna take over the defense for a while."

The first man they came to gaped at Link with his eyes hanging out of their sockets. "We can't do that!"

"Why not? We're doing a training exercise." Link threw back his head and called up to the sentries in the watchtowers. "Come down here and give these kids your weapons."

"Um.....we can't do that," one of them replied. "We're under orders not to leave the fence unguarded."

"You aren't leaving it unguarded. Come down."

The guards and sentries exchanged glances. Someone must have told the Council members what was going on because Meredith, Nicholas, Cook, and Richard Shriver raced over just then.

"What are you doing, Link?" Meredith demanded. "You can't leave the fence unguarded."

"I'm not leaving it unguarded," he repeated. "We're training a whole new army of guards." He snatched a bow from the nearest man. "Hand over your arrows. These kids are taking over until the other group assaults the fence."

"Assaults the.....!" Richard choked on the words. "The Children are assaulting the fence?!"

"We're doing a training exercise," Link spun the other way. "Aren't any of you going to hand over your weapons? Do you want these kids to defend the canton or not?"

A few men stepped forward and held out their weapons, but Nicholas lunged forward and waved them back. "No! Don't give them anything! You can't do this, Link! You can't protect the canton this way."

"I can't protect the canton?!" he countered. "Are you stupid? Why do we have these guards and sentries if we aren't going to defend the place?"

"That's different," Richard replied. "We have to defend the canton from the....."

"Here they come!" Karim called from the gate. No one had even thought to close it.

Everyone rushed to the fence. Three men grabbed the gate and started to haul it shut.

Dina stood up on the steps of her house where she'd been watching the whole scene. Link stepped onto the lowest fence rail so he could see over the top. Naia, Karim, Cairo, and Aries jumped onto the fence and perched on top of the posts.

Adrian, Israel, Riyadh, and Kaiser emerged from the trees beyond the river. The four boys didn't approach the canton. They just showed themselves and then receded out of sight.

Link jumped down and spun around to confront the Council members. "Are you going to arm these Children now?"

"No!" Richard snapped. "This is a disaster waiting to happen, and when it does, you'll be the one responsible, Link."

He groaned in exasperation and climbed back up on the fence. "We'll just have to defend the canton without weapons."

"What do we do that?" Cairo asked.

"You know what to do," Link fired back. "Fight them any way you can."

The words barely left his mouth before the same four boys broke cover and sprinted across the open ground. Rey, Abdullah, and Brock followed right on their heels and charged the fence.

The rest of the defenders rushed forward to mount the fence to meet the invaders, but they didn't get there in time. Adrian and Israel hurtled off the ground, soared through the air at dizzying speed, and collided with Aries and Karim.

The four boys crashed down on the ground inside the fence and rolled over and over each other battling for dominance. Riyadh and Kaiser sailed straight over Cairo and Naia to land inside the fence right amongst the shocked Council members.

Keith, Riggs, Rome, and Aurelio converged on the spot, attacked without mercy, and pinned down the invaders. The other defenders swarmed in to subdue them just as Rey, Brock, and Abdullah breached the walls.

Aries and Karim jumped down into the mayhem and a battle broke out right there in the dirt behind the fence. The defenders enveloped the attackers in an instant.

The battle might have ended there, but at that moment—in the moment when the defenders had the attackers pinned down on the ground, Kenji, Iona, Emerald, Briar, India, Duke, and Nova came swarming over the fence from either side.

They must have been lying in wait because Dina didn't see them even from her elevated position.

Iona, Emerald, Briar, and Nova came from the lefthand side of the gate. Kenji, India, and Duke came from the righthand side.

The seven of them avoided the wrestling match happening on the ground. The second wave of attackers raced along the top of the fence to the watchtowers. India, Duke, and Briar scrambled up their support posts, attacked the sentries, took their weapons, and threw the men out.

The men would have fallen to their deaths, but the three Children made sure the men caught hold of the ladders before they fell.

India turned the sentry's bow on him and aimed the arrow in his face. "Get down! Get down now!"

Duke and Briar conquered their watchtowers in seconds. Iona charged Richard and snatched the bow out of his hands. He was too stunned and horrified to fight back.

She, Emerald, Kenji, and Nova rushed through the canton disarming all the guards and turning their weapons on everyone. "Get over there in the center! Get over there! Nobody try anything!"

The seven Children of the second wave herded the guards and sentries together. The Children even included Link and the Council members in their sweep.

Iona rushed over to the Children scrapping on the ground. She jabbed the tip of her arrow into each of them one after the other. "You're dead, Karim! You're dead, Cairo! Back off! You're dead! You have to concede the point and surrender. You're dead, Darius! We won the game!"

"You can all put your weapons down now," Link told them and pushed Kenji's arrow out of the way. "It's over. Adrian's group won."

Adrian's people exploded in cheers, hugged each other, and jumped up and down. The defenders picked themselves up, dusted themselves off, and moved off to regroup across the yard.

"We would have had you if these dopes had given us some weapons," Cairo grumbled.

"Just admit that the best team won," Brock countered. "We had you with that flanking maneuver. You all would have had your backs turned and we would have taken you either way."

"That was outstanding," Link exclaimed. "I'm proud of you all."

"Rematch!" Dexter called. "Let's switch sides! Defenders into the jungle and attackers defending the village. Come on, Link! Give us a chance to even the score."

Link glanced around and shrugged. "All right. Switch it up. Karim—you take your crew out into the jungle."

Adrian turned to the Council members standing there staring in slack-jawed horror. "Are you going to arm us now?"

"No weapons," Link interrupted. "The other team wasn't armed and you can't be, either. Just man the fence and stop them from getting in."

Adrian turned to the Children nearest him. "We need to pull another strategic maneuver like Link says."

"How do we do that?" Brock asked. "The fence is too narrow and they would see us trying to hide people on either side."

"No, we already pulled that last time," Adrian decided. "We have to do something new—something they won't suspect."

His team gathered around him listening.

He cast a flinty glance around the village and nodded once. "I know. Split up between the houses and hide. As soon as they get over the fence, we'll come out and put them down. Iona, Brock, and Israel—you go into that house there. Abdullah, you take India and Riyadh to that house there."

He went through his group splitting them up into twos and threes and assigning each cluster to a different house.

Last of all, he, Kenji and Kaiser returned to Dina's house. "Stay here, Dina," Adrian told her. "Keep doing what you're doing. Don't move and don't do anything out of the ordinary. Act like we aren't here."

"How am I supposed to do that when you *are* here?" she asked.

He only grinned at her and pulled his two comrades inside. The other Children retreated inside different houses and shut the doors. In a few seconds, the canton returned to its usual quiet state with no one moving around.

Only the stunned, shocked Council members standing by the gate and the absence of any sentries gave any clue that something wasn't quite right.

Dina held her breath. Adrian's idea would be risky, but it was brilliant in its simplicity. He used the only resource available to hide his people where the opposing team would never find them—until it was too late.

Link stepped up onto the rail, looked over, and murmured, "Here they come."

Dina didn't hear or see anything until Riggs, Aries, and Cairo vaulted onto the top of the fence. They leapt down into the yard and the rest of the Children followed.

They landed on top of the fenceposts. Dexter, Rome, Calliope, and Amir stayed crouched there. The others sprang down into the yard, but there was nothing there. They didn't find anyone to attack or anyone defending the canton at all.

The others spread out searching for anyone who might offer any resistance. The intruders checked behind every house and even under the houses where the stilts held them off the ground.

The invaders regrouped in the middle of the yard. "Where are they?" Keith asked.

"This is another one of Adrian's tricks," Karim growled.

"He couldn't just make himself and his team vanish," Darius pointed out.

"They didn't vanish," Naia countered. "They're hiding. They're waiting to jump us as soon as we go looking for them."

"We need to stick together," Rome decided. "We can't let them split us up."

"So....what do we do?" Darius asked. "We can't just stand here doing nothing."

"Why not?" Amir asked. "We took the canton. We should be declared the winners. What do you say, Link?"

The whole group turned around to hear Link's response, and at that moment, Adrian, Kaiser, and Kenji charged out of the house.

Dina couldn't figure out how they did it, but the rest of Adrian's team burst out at exactly the same instant. They closed on the other team in a blink, attacked everyone, slammed them down on the ground, and piled everyone on top of each other.

Somehow or other, the defenders maneuvered the smallest intruders to the bottom of the pile where their larger teammates' weight held them down.

Kenji, Brock, Kaiser, Israel, and Abdullah sat on top of the stack and raised their arms in triumph. "The winners! We're the winners!"

"Get.....off......me....!" Karim roared.

"Admit defeat and we'll let you go," Adrian countered.

"NEVER!!" Karim thundered.

Link stepped in. "Adrian's team is the winner again. You can get off now."

Adrian and his friends jumped off the pile and grabbed each other in celebration. "Ha ha! Undefeated!"

Karim climbed off the stack with as much dignity as he could muster and glared at the winners. "We'll beat you next time."

"There won't be a next time because you'll be fighting on the same side from now on," Link interjected. "That was just for fun. Now we need to go back to weapons training. Each of you get yourselves a bow and arrows and set up some targets out on the grass that you can shoot at."

The Children turned around. All the guards and sentries stared at them. The Council members hadn't moved.

"Okay, scratch the weapons training for today," Link decided. "Everybody come back over to my house and get something to eat. We'll continue with this after lunch."

Chapter 12

Dina looked up when Link walked into the house. "Is everything all right?"

"Where were you, Link?" Iona asked.

"Never mind about that." He shut the door behind him and Dina saw the sky outside before he secured the latch. The stars had come out while he'd been gone. It was long past sundown.

He sat down on the floor next to Dina and she handed him a wooden plate loaded with meat she'd roasted for him. "I expected you over an hour ago."

"Thank you." He bent over his plate and started eating without explaining anything.

She bit her tongue and didn't ask where he'd been. It must have been somewhere serious if he didn't tell her or the Children where he was.

The Children had been talking nonstop about their training game. "We should do it again out in the jungle," Adrian was saying. "We'll get the other Children to help us. We might even find some cats to practice on."

"What about getting hold of some weapons?" Karim made a disgusted face toward the door. "And I don't mean from this place."

"I know where we can get some," Dexter called out. "The Children at Northfall have been amassing weapons for a long time."

"Good thinking," Adrian told him. "What other human battle techniques could we use, Link? Tell us more."

He kept his head down and muttered into his plate. "Well, there are all kinds of booby traps you could set up—falling weights, nooses set up on the ground that snatch a person by the foot and lift them into the air or throw them into hidden spikes that kill the person, pits dug in the ground and covered with nets and leaves to hide them so the person falls into the pit—there are a thousand different booby traps you can set up in the jungle. There are hidden barricades and fortifications you could set up so you make your enemy think you're retreating, but instead, you lead your enemy to a fortification where they either fall to a hidden trap or you spring some other weapon on them there."

"Ho ho ho!" Kaiser chortled. "We are gonna have so much fun setting this up!"

Adrian stared at Link in dumbfounded amazement. Dina could just see the wheels turning in Adrian's head. He was born for this.

"There are also bottlenecks you can use to herd your enemy into a narrow place they can't get out of," Link went on. "That's one of the oldest tricks in human warfare. If you get your enemy running through a narrow gap, it takes fewer defenders to destroy the enemy because the enemy can only send a few people through at a time."

Dina spun around to stare at him. Now she knew for certain that there was more to Link's story than he ever let on.

He couldn't have been born in Prideland if he knew about that. He must have come from somewhere else. He must have learned all about human warfare before he came here.

She didn't have time to ask before Kaiser stretched, gave an almighty yawn, and sprawled out on the floor. "This war business is tiring work."

The others laughed and everyone started bedding down for the night. Dina went around the room cleaning up and blowing out the lamps. She almost didn't notice Link heading for the front door.

She caught him before he slipped out into the darkness. "Where are you going?" she whispered.

He glanced toward the Children. None of them noticed him about to leave. "I'm going out. Stay here."

"Hey!" She shot her arm in front of him to stop him. "It's the middle of the night and you've been gone for hours! Where are you going? Just tell me."

He cast one last glance around the house and lowered his voice to a hushed murmur. "I got called to the Council, okay? They want me to answer questions about why I'm training the Children. People are raising objections and I have to go state my case."

"I'm going with you," Dina told him.

"No," he countered. "Stay here. You being there will just complicate things. If you go, everyone will address their questions to you and I need to speak for myself. This is my thing."

"I won't say anything. I'll stand in the back and listen like you did for me. I won't approach the Council." She raised her hand. "I swear it."

He gave her a hard look. "I shouldn't let you come."

"Let me support you. You wouldn't let me do anything else when it comes to training the Children. Let me do this."

He compressed his lips again. "All right, but don't say a word."

"I won't. I promise."

He slipped out of the house and she hurried after him to the house the Council used for meetings. A crack of light shone through the gap under the door to show that people were already inside.

Dina heard plenty of voices even from her own steps and those voices didn't sound happy at all. Of course not.

Link opened the door and a tide of noise hit her in the face. People packed the house all talking at once.

They fell instantly silent when Link walked in. The crowd parted and the tension spiked off the charts when he approached the Council table.

Troy, Salman Kramer, and Harmony Leach all already stood in front of the table. Salman and Harmony both fired off remarks at the Council.

"Is this what we left Prideland for—to have our village assaulted by our own Children?" Salman was saying.

"This is exactly what we've been warning about since the beginning," Harmony interjected. "The Children could have been subject to all kinds of influences while they were out in the jungle and we would never know about it until....."

None of the three realized Link was here until the silence descended over the crowd. Harmony glanced over her shoulder and then all three froze when they saw Link standing behind them.

"Link—thank you for joining us," Fitch began. "We were just hearing general remarks from the community."

Link cast wary glances at the three parents and drew himself up in front of the table, but he didn't speak first.

"Some members of the community take issue with your decision to train the Children to fight," Lucy Callaghan told him. "Could you explain to us what led you to this decision and your reasons for it?"

"What led me to the decision?" Link repeated. "What led me to the decision was Adrian asking me to train the Children so they'd be prepared to defend themselves against the cats."

"And you actually thought something Adrian said was a good idea?" Salman countered. "When are you gonna learn? That boy is the reason we're in this mess."

"That boy, as you call him, is the reason we're in a position to defend ourselves in case the cats ever come after this canton again," Link fired back. "That boy, as you call him, is the reason we're all still alive and the reason the cats haven't attacked us since we came here. The Children have been out there in the jungle defending our lives for the last year and a half. It's thanks to Adrian that the Children have established a buffer zone around our canton where the cats don't dare to come—and if cats do come, the Children hunt them down and destroy them. That's the boy we're talking about—and from what I've seen in the last three days, he isn't a boy anymore. He's a man. He's as much a man or more than any man in this room, including me. I would take him any day of the week over anyone here."

"The Children doing what they have to do to defend themselves in the jungle is different from training them into some kind of army to go out to war against the cats," Harmony pointed out.

"How is it different?" Link asked. "Adrian's point is that the Children have always prevailed because they had numbers on their side. They attacked isolated cats in overwhelming numbers and brought the cats down, but that won't work if the Pride sends out hunting parties where the Children *don't* have numbers on their side. The Children need to be able to defend themselves in all situations, not just the ones that are the most advantageous to them. I can't believe that you as their parents would argue against the Children being able to defend themselves in all situations. I can't believe you would actually suggest leaving them vulnerable to any attack of any kind."

"Actually, Troy was just saying the same thing." Meredith waved at Troy.

Link jolted and spun around to stare at Troy. "He was?"

"He thinks training the Children is a good idea," Meredith replied. "He's the only person here who agrees with you."

"Oh." Link frowned at Troy. "I thought you didn't want your Children to get hurt."

"I didn't—and I don't," Troy replied and then shrugged. "I guess they're gonna get hurt one way or the other. I would rather they get hurt defending themselves than for them to get hurt *not* being able to defend themselves."

"Defending themselves against isolated cats and establishing a perimeter around the canton isn't the same as deliberately hunting the cats down," Salman countered. "We know the Children are hunting cats down. We still have pregnant mothers coming out from Prideland with their Children. What kind of example are you setting for them and the younger Children? If our older Children organize into an offensive fighting force, what is there to stop them from hunting down the search parties the Pride sends out to find them? Even one cat surviving an attack like that could get back to the Pride and then they'll send out even bigger parties to come after us."

Link pointed at him. "See, this is the problem. You think of the Children as us versus them. You think the Pride sending out parties to hunt us is different from the Pride sending out parties to hunt the Children. They're our own Children, for God's sake. Don't you realize that? There is no us and them. They're ours. We're all in this mess together. We should be doing everything possible to help the Children's mission instead of undermining it. The problem is we aren't doing enough. We can't because we're human, but that doesn't mean we shouldn't be doing everything we can do."

"Here, here," Troy chimed in. "I agree."

"Does anyone else here have anything to say in favor of training the Children to fight?" Meredith called to the room at large.

No one made a move. Dina would have liked to speak up, but she promised Link she would let him do this on his own.

A few people shuffled their feet and cleared their throats. No one spoke in Link's favor.

"The decision of the community is clear," Fitch went on. "We ask you to stop training the Children for the good of all concerned."

"No, I won't stop training them," Link replied. "There is nothing in this world that you or anyone else can say to me that will convince me to stop helping my Children survive whatever comes. Asking me to do that would be the same as asking me to throw my Children into harm's way and stand aside without trying to help them. I won't do that. I really don't care if you like it or not. I'm doing it and I'm going to keep on doing it."

"Then we have no choice but to ask you to leave the canton," Meredith announced. "You brought your Children here on the condition that you would help us defend ourselves against the cats....."

"That's what I'm doing!" Link's voice started rising. "I'm the one who is doing that! I'm the only one who's doing it—me and the Children! We had a policy that we would expel anyone who didn't support the Children's interests and help us keep the Children safe from the cats' attacks. You're the ones who are doing that! You're the ones who are acting against the Children's interests and failing to give them every resource they need to cope with the dangers they face. If someone leaves the canton, it should be you."

"That's ridiculous, Link," Nicholas countered. "We couldn't *all* leave. Then you and Dina and the Children would be left here alone."

"That would be better than you undermining us at every turn......but you don't have to worry about that," Link replied. "The Children are organizing all the other cantons to do the same thing so you would have nowhere to go. You might as well stay here—and I'll stay here and train the Children to protect you so you don't have to protect yourselves. You might not like it, but that's the way it is. You don't have the power to throw anyone out of the canton, especially not the Children or any of their allies. I suggest you suck it up and get used to living in a world where you don't always get your way."

He turned on his heel and stormed out of the house. People fell over themselves to get out of his path before he trampled them on his way to the door.

He walked right past Dina without looking at her, blasted through the door, and out into the night. She had to race to catch up with him, but she didn't try to talk to him. She'd never seen him this mad—ever.

He didn't go back to the house. He barged out to the gate, which was closed at this time of night.

He inevitably ran into all the guards and sentries standing around on watch, so he spun away from them and kept storming through the canton. He paced down the fence line and eventually stopped between a few other houses.

He stood there fuming with his back to the houses. Dina tiptoed up to him from behind.

She didn't know what to say to him, so she just stood there in the silence and waited for him to cool down.

That meeting didn't go the way she expected. She didn't expect even one parent to speak in Link's favor.

One was better than none, but the meeting ending with the Council asking Link to leave the canton didn't bode well. What if they decided to grow a spine and actually force Link, Dina, and the Children to leave?

She didn't expect them to muster the courage to actually do that. They were all talk, but they did have the authority to tell the guards and sentries what to do.

That could lead to open conflict between the Children and all the humans living in this canton. Dina could just picture the disastrous results of that.

She shivered in the cold, but it didn't seem to bother Link. She advanced a little closer to him from behind and rested her hand on his back. "Do you still want to go west?"

"We can't go now," he muttered. "We have to make a stand here. Adrian's right about that. We have to make a stand against these people as much as the cats. We can't run away or let them think they can intimidate us. They have to learn that they can't push the Children around and they can't push *us* around."

"At least Troy came around," she remarked.

Link snorted. "One man! What good does that do?"

"It's better than none. You're one man and so is Adrian. You're doing what has to be done to make change. Maybe Troy can do the same thing."

He humphed under his breath. He didn't turn around.

After a minute, he growled, "I'm sorry. I shouldn't take this out on you."

"You aren't taking it out on me. You stood up for yourself and the Children. I'm proud of you." She slipped her arms around his waist from behind and rested her head against his broad, muscular back. "I'm glad we agree on this. It would be terrible if we didn't."

"Yeah," he muttered and finally tilted his head back to rest his skull against hers. "Thank you."

"I didn't do anything. I just stood there."

"That's what I mean. It helps a lot to know we're together on this. I don't have to worry about you changing your mind."

"No way. I would train the Children if I could, but I can't. Only you can do that. I'm proud of you for doing whatever it takes to prepare them."

He pried himself out of her arms and turned around. "We're going to continue to have problems with the other parents—and the Council."

"I know."

"Maybe we should leave. Maybe we should go out into the jungle and leave these people to their own devices."

"We can't do that," she pointed out. "We would leave them defenseless. These are the Children's parents even if they're clueless idiots. We have to stay at least until the danger has passed."

"The danger will never pass. That's the problem. The Children will always be in danger from the cats—and any people who stay out here will always be in danger from the cats."

She heaved a deep sigh. "Then we can't leave at all."

He breathed a matching sigh and turned his eyes to scowl at the village houses. "Yeah. I know."

She slipped her hand into his. "Come on. Let's go back to the house. The Children are probably wondering where we are."

"I'm sure they already know," he grumbled, but he followed her back to their house.

They made it as far as the steps before Troy came out of the shadows. "There you are. I was looking for you."

"What do you want?" Link snapped. "I said all I have to say in there. I'm not going to go through it all again here."

"That isn't what I want to talk to you about," Troy murmured. "I was wondering if you would do me a favor."

"What is it?" Link countered. "I'm not going to do anything right now. I'm going to bed."

"I don't mean now. I mean later......whenever....."

"What's the favor?" Link demanded. "I won't do anything to weaken the Children if that's what you're asking."

"I'm not asking that. I'm asking.....if you would......tell my kids.....when you see them.....tell them I'm proud of them. I don't expect they'll ever come back to this canton and I don't expect they'll ever want to see me again. I don't blame them for that. They're better off in the jungle without me. Just tell them. Tell them I'm happy about what they're doing....and I'm proud of the people they're growing up to become. I wish I could do more. I wish I could do what you're doing, but I'm no good at stuff like that. Just tell them that, if they ever need anything from me, they only have to ask. They know where to find me. Tell them I'm staying here so they know where to find me if they need me. Tell them I'll do whatever they need me to do—even if it means helping them fight the cats. Tell them I made a mistake and I realize that now. I might not be able to make it up to them, but tell them I want to if they ever find a way."

Link stared at him in the dark for a long time. When Link finally spoke, he murmured in a soft undertone that trembled with buried emotion. "All right, man. I'll tell them when I see them."

"Thanks." Troy glanced back and forth between Link and Dina. "You're doing the right thing. You always have been. I was stupid not to see it before. If either of you need anything, you should tell me, too."

"Thanks, man," Link replied. "We will."

Troy walked off into the dark. The door to his house let lamplight stream into the darkness and then shut it off when he went inside.

Link and Dina stared after him and Dina's stomach twisted at those words. It must have cost Troy a lot to say all that to Link of all people.

Troy really must have woken up to the gravity of his mistake if he could tell Link that. Troy didn't go so far as to ask Link to bring Troy and his Children together so he could tell them to their faces that he'd changed his opinion.

He really understood what he did and said to drive them away. He accepted that they didn't want to see him. He understood well enough not to ask them to come back from that so he could feel better about himself.

He just made himself available to them. He offered whatever help they needed when they needed it and how they needed it. He was prepared to leave it at that and walk away.

Link finally sighed again, climbed the steps, and he and Dina slipped into the dark house. No one moved or sat up. The Children lay on the floor sleeping—or pretending to sleep.

They gave no sign that they heard what happened at the Council meeting or what Troy said outside, but Dina felt certain that the Children did hear. Word would get back to Troy's Children one way or the other. They would get the message. What they did with it after that would be up to them.

Chapter 13

Link paced up and down the field outside the canton fence. "Block—and stab—and block! Advance—and block!"

The Children parried each other's strikes and some advanced while the others retreated. They worked in pairs going through the techniques he'd taught them.

They stabbed their training knives upward toward their opponents' heads, straight toward their opponents' chests, and then downward toward their opponents' stomachs.

The opponent—whoever that happened to be at the time—blocked or deflected the attack and then went through a matching sequence of attacks for the first person to block.

Dina leaned against the fence to watch and she wasn't the only one. Everyone in the canton who didn't have anything more urgent to do gathered around the gate watching the Children train.

They'd been at it for hours and none of the other residents left to go back to work. Even the guards and sentries who should have been keeping watch assembled there to see what the Children were doing.

The group of Children on the field had grown to more than seventy. Dina had been right about word spreading to the Children in the jungle.

Troy's Children and the Children of every other parent in the canton had come back to join Link's training camp. All the Children who'd grown up at Riverbend canton were here now taking part.

No one from the canton went out there to greet or interact with their Children. The canton's residents kept their distance and the Children were too busy training to stop and socialize.

Link finally clapped his hands once. "That's really good! You're looking great. Now put your weapons aside and come over here. We're gonna do another war game."

"Yes!" Riggs and Kaiser high-fived each other. "We're gonna slaughter you slouches."

"Be careful I don't put you on opposite teams," Link interrupted. "Gather around and listen up. We aren't going inside the canton this time since that obviously hurt some people's feelings. Team One will stand out here and defend the walls. Team Two will attack from the jungle."

He strode through the group separating the Children into teams.

"Since you all thought the first time had an unfair advantage with Adrian on their side, I'm going to level the playing field this time," Link announced.

"How are you going to do that?" Iona asked. "There's only one Adrian."

"I'm going to take command of the second team," Link told her. "Adrian's team will defend first and my team will attack first."

"I want to be on Link's team." Brock shoved between the other Children to get closer to Link.

Link pushed a few people away and pulled others closer to him. "Karim, Darius, Amir, India, Shelby, Dexter, Israel, and Amber—you go with Adrian. Riyadh, Franco, Sasha, Salvatore, Blaire, Legacy, Elio—you come with me."

The Children exchanged jokes and excited looks as they divided into teams. It took a long time for Link to work his way through the whole crowd.

"Now here's what we're going to do. Listen up!" he yelled. "I'm not going to repeat this. If you miss what I'm about to say, you lose. Each team will divide into two. Half your team will be armed and the other half unarmed. Those of you who are unarmed will have to do your best against your armed opponents."

The excitement started to fade and the whispering stopped as all the Children started to realize exactly what he was suggesting.

"The defending team won't have any warning of what the attacking team is going to do," Link went on. "You'll just have to cope with the situation as it unfolds. Understand? Do your best not to hurt your friends, but don't hold back when it comes to either defending the canton or taking it."

"What do you mean by 'taking it'?" Adrian asked. "How will we know if the attacking team succeeded in taking the canton if you can't go inside or breach the walls?"

"You'll have to defend the walls well enough to stop them from getting inside," Link replied. "We'll all know if the attacking team overruns you well enough to breach the walls if they want to." He turned away and yelled over the Children's heads. "Team Two—grab your weapons and head out to the jungle."

Link strode past the gate and pointed at the sentries. "Shut the gate and resume your posts to defend the fence from attack!" Link shot Adrian a wild grin. "Good luck, kid."

Adrian burst into a matching grin and turned to his friends. They gathered into a huddle to discuss their strategy, but they had to wait for Link and Team Two to get out of earshot.

The guards and sentries got busy dragging the gate closed, so all the onlookers had to retreat back inside.

The guards and sentries scrambled to resume their posts and all the human residents hustled to find places where they could watch the battle.

Dina returned to the top step of her house. Other spectators whose houses were farther away from the fence actually climbed onto their roofs to watch.

Dina couldn't hear what Adrian was saying to his team. She couldn't see Link or any of his team out in the jungle, either.

Adrian gave instructions to his group and they spread out in front of the fence. He positioned those with weapons at the front to meet the invaders. Those without weapons hovered right outside the fence and they all tensed for the incoming assault.

Nothing happened. The silence dragged one minute after another and still the second team didn't show themselves.

Some of Adrian's defenders exchanged glances. "Maybe something went wrong," Karim suggested.

"He's messing with us," Adrian countered. "This is Link's way of unnerving us. Stay alert and keep watch."

A few more tense minutes passed. "How long should we wait?" Shelby asked.

"This is what he's trying to teach us," Adrian countered. "We have an advantage because we know they're about to attack. We wouldn't have that in a real fight. It would come out of nowhere. Now pay attention. He's going to try to pull a fast one on......"

A whoosh of rushing wind jolted everyone into spinning around to face the jungle. Dina didn't see anything at first and then a cloud of arrows exploded out of the trees. It came from deep enough inside the jungle that no one could see the attackers.

The arrows came from the jungle far to the left of where Link took his team. The assault came from close to the waterfall and the arrows whistled skyward before they arced downward and plunging for the first group.

India and Amber both screamed and tried to back away, but the fence blocked them. "Stand firm!" Adrian roared, but it was too late and the defenders had no way to protect themselves.

Dina's stomach turned watching all those arrows fall. They would kill any Child they struck.

Even Adrian ducked under his arms as the arrows plunged from high in the sky. They stabbed down at the defending Children.....and bounced off.

Adrian looked out from under his arms and examined one of the arrows that had fallen on the ground. Someone had wrapped a strip of cloth around the arrowhead so it wouldn't hurt anybody.

"Holy crap!" Dexter breathed.

"Anyone who got hit is down," Amir pointed out. "A hit like that means we're out."

"You're right," Adrian replied. "Who got hit?"

He was still looking around at his companions when another flock of arrows erupted out of the jungle. These came from far to the left, too, soared high overhead, and then dove for the canton itself.

Dozens of arrows landed on the house roofs and even on the watchtowers. Without a moment's hesitation, a second assault whizzed past Adrian's group and arrows thumped into the fence.

Adrian and his comrades looked all around them. Everyone inside the village stared at the second batch of arrows. The attackers had fixed the red flowers of jungle vines to the arrow tips.

"What does it mean?" Darius asked.

"It's fire," Adrian muttered. "He set fire to the fence and the houses." Adrian's shoulders slumped. "He won. This is what he was trying to tell me. He won without ever setting foot on the field."

"LOOK OUT!!" Karim thundered.

The Children spun around just in time for Link's team to break cover and charge across the field. The Children bellowed in feral war cries, covered the open ground in seconds, and brought the first team down easily.

Link didn't rush in with the rest of the team. He sauntered out of the undergrowth and watched from a safe distance as his team closed with Adrian's group.

The Children attacked, wrestled, and slammed each other onto the ground outside the fence, but the whole assault ended in a matter of minutes.

They were still going at it when Link strolled across the river and advanced on the piles of bodies. "You can stop now."

"We can still win!" Israel panted from under Kaiser, Kenji, and Abdullah. "We aren't finished yet."

"How many of you got hit by the first wave of arrows?" Link asked.

Adrian pried himself out from under Riggs, Rome, Salvatore, and Devon. "He's right. We all got hit. There would have been no one left to defend the canton." He nudged Karim, who had his elbow locked around Elio's neck. "You can stop now. It's over."

Link clapped Adrian on the shoulder. "You did well. I'm proud of you."

"We didn't do anything," Adrian muttered. "We just stood here while you took us down."

Link beamed at him. "You're learning. That's what's important. You need to think laterally."

"How could we have defended against that?" Adrian asked. "That was the whole point, wasn't it? We couldn't have defended ourselves against that. We were sitting ducks."

"That's where advanced intelligence comes in," Link told him. "You defend yourself by knowing your enemy is there before he attacks. You defend yourself by stopping him from getting into that position in the first place. Come on. Let's go inside and talk it over. Hey! Stop moping about it. I did this so you could learn—not so you could feel bad about yourself." He turned to the fence. "Open the gate!"

The guards and sentries dragged the gate aside. The word must not have come down from the Council yet that Link wasn't welcome in this canton anymore.

He, Adrian, and the rest of the Children entered and headed for Dina's house. The Children settled down on the grass. Link sat down crosslegged next to Adrian in the middle of their group.

All the Children started talking about their latest war game. Dina couldn't hear Link's and Adrian's conversation over all the other voices.

She stood up and went into her house to see about finding the Children something to eat, but they'd already finished off all the food.

She was just going back outside when Troy came over carrying a freshly skinned ox carcass over his shoulder.

He set it down in the middle of the Children's group and they gathered around to eat it. He would have walked off without a word, but before he could leave, Leroy looked up and smiled at Troy. "Thanks, Dad."

Troy smiled back at him and returned to his own house without saying anything.

"So what's our next campaign?" Adrian asked Link.

"I was thinking we should do a jungle campaign," Link replied. "You know the terrain around here better than I do. Maybe you could set up another game with some of your friends from the other cantons."

Adrian's eyes brightened. "Yeah! Good idea! We need to start doing joint maneuvers with them so we establish our communications and all work together."

"Exactly." Link hesitated and then asked, "Are there any cats around this area right now?"

Adrian shrugged. "Who knows? We would have to send out a scouting party to find out. Why do you ask? Do you want to do a maneuver on the cats?"

"I guess you've already done maneuvers on individual cats and small groups. We already know an overwhelming number of Children can take down one cat or a small group. It would be interesting to test your abilities one on one."

Adrian's jaw dropped. "You mean....one of us against one cat?"

"What better way to prove to yourselves that you can take them? It's like you said. You can't always count on having the advantage of numbers. It would be even better if one of you could take a group of cats, but let's start with baby steps. If you found a cat in the jungle, you could send one of you against it and see what happens."

"What if the cat wins?" Darius asked from Link's other side. "One of us could get killed—especially one of us Pygmies. We couldn't take a panther or a tiger."

"That's the point," Link replied. "You could have your people standing by to bail the person out if the cat starts gaining the upper hand. It will be even more important for you Pygmies to learn to fight cats who are bigger and stronger and heavier than you are. You need to prove to yourselves that you have the skills to compensate and overcome whatever advantage your opponent has, even when they have the advantage of numbers and size."

Adrian frowned and rubbed his chin. "You're right. It's a lot more complicated than I thought."

"Don't make it more complicated than it has to be," Link went on. "Just think about it. Think about plugging the holes in your defense. Analyze your weaknesses and work on overcoming them. The best part is that the cats aren't doing any of this. They aren't thinking about overcoming their weaknesses. Their whole defense centers around eliminating the Children. The cats aren't planning for you to fight back or for you to use strategy to do it. That's your greatest asset."

Adrian fell into a thoughtful silence. No one said anything else for a while.

All at once, another shout went up from one of the watchtowers. "We got company! It's the Children from the other canton! They're coming back!"

Chapter 14

A drian, Link, and all the Children scrambled to their feet, hustled to the canton gate, and stared across the river toward the jungle. The strange Children who'd visited last time clustered in the same place under the trees.

"It's the Children from Moonlight canton. I better go talk to them," Adrian decided. "Come on, Black."

Karim, Kaiser, and Kenji flanked him as Adrian strode out onto the field. The Riverbend Children stayed packed around the gate watching.

The sentries in the watchtowers aimed their bows at the visitors, but after only a few minutes, the sentries lowered their weapons.

Adrian and the Black advanced and mingled with the Children from Moonlight canton. They talked for five minutes and Adrian waved toward the fence.

"It looks like they're having a council of war," Dina remarked to Link.

"That's exactly what they are having." Link glanced behind him toward their house. "I wish I'd gone hunting and gotten some more food. These Children sure eat a lot."

"Maybe Troy can help us out again," she suggested, but she didn't have time to go ask him before Adrian turned around and headed back toward the gate.

The Children from Moonlight canton followed him and Dina's scalp prickled as more and more and more Children streamed out of the jungle.

They all wore the same ragged scraps of clothing that did absolutely nothing to conceal their fur. Their clothes made the Children look wild and more beast-like than Dina remembered—or maybe it was just because she didn't know these Children.

She'd gotten used to seeing her own Children—all of her own Children including the adopted ones. Their fur looked normal to her.

Seeing these strangers cemented in her mind how alien and animalistic they were. They would never and could never be tamed. They were wild and always would be.

At least a hundred of them followed Adrian across the field. He walked through the gate followed by the Black and all the Children from Moonlight canton poured into the village after him.

The guards and sentries stood back to let them through. Only fifteen men guarded the fence, gate, and watchtowers. They would have been insane to try to fight this many Children, especially since the guards and sentries had seen these last few days how warlike the Children were.

Adrian halted halfway across the canton yard and turned around to call to his new friends. "See that house over there?" He pointed to Link's and Dina's house. "You can gather around that house, but don't go near any of the others. Some of the humans in this village don't feel comfortable around Children."

He turned to continue his march back to Link's and Dina's house. He stopped in front of Link and Dina. "These are my parents," he told the Moonlight Children. "This is their house. We can talk here." He turned to Link and Dina. "This is Cain. He's the leader of the Moonlight Children and this is his brother and lieutenant, Jackal."

Dina nodded at them and mumbled, "It's a pleasure to meet you all. You're welcome to our home."

She would have liked to extend her hand to them, but Adrian's story about these Children's hostility toward humans stopped her.

Link waved toward the house. "Come inside—please. Make yourselves at home. Anything we have is yours."

He led the way into the house. Dina was just looking around at all these Children and wondering how in the world she could ever show them any kind of hospitality.

Out of nowhere, Troy appeared again with a second ox carcass. She would have liked to ask him where he kept getting all this food, but he didn't give her a chance.

He carried it inside and a dull thump resounded from the floorboards when he dropped it in the middle of the room. Then he walked out and went back to his own house.

He made eye contact with Dina as he passed her and he started to smile, but he was already walking away.

Adrian, Iona, the Black, the Pygmies, the Manx, the Auroras, and Osiris's Children led the Moonlight Children into Link's and Dina's house—or as many of the Moonlight Children as would fit inside the walls.

The rest settled down on the grass with the rest of the Riverbend Children. They gnawed on the first carcass Troy had brought over for their lunch.

The Children talked about places in the jungle they all knew about, other groups of Children they knew in different parts of Prideland, and different encounters they'd had with each other and with cats patrolling the area in search of Children.

Dina tore herself away and went into the house. All her own Children sat on the floor with the Moonlight Children while they ate and talked. So many different side conversations fired back and forth across the room that she couldn't follow them all.

Adrian, Iona, and Karim sat in a group with Cain, Jackal, and three of their comrades.

Dina slipped past them and stopped next to Link. They watched from the side of the room and Dina experienced another clenching sensation in her guts.

If the Council could see these Children, the Council members would think twice about ever holding another meeting about the Children's activities.

The Children had gone so far beyond anyone's control. They'd formed their own society with their own rules, their own hierarchy, and their own orientation to the world around them.

The Council couldn't possibly make any decision that impacted the Children. That would be impossible for anyone outside their own circle.

Dina could just imagine the conversations Adrian was having with these leaders from another canton. They were deciding the fate of all Prideland right here on the floor of her house.

The world tilted on its axis. It would never be the same after today. That shift might have happened weeks or months or even years ago, but she sensed it right now.

The Pride's Senate didn't decide anything about Prideland, either. Whatever happened to Prideland, it all started and ended right here.

She couldn't even feel proud of the way Adrian was stepping up to be the leader all these Children needed him to be. She didn't have anything to do with raising him to be that leader. He did it all by himself.

The Children kept talking and negotiating for hours as the day wore on. None of the Children seemed to be aware of the passage of time nor did anyone mention leaving.

Link stayed in the house for the first half hour, but when nothing changed, he took his bow and quiver and left.

Dina brought in water from the river and carried it to all the Children out on the grass. Apart from Adrian, Cain, and Jackal, she didn't see anyone acting like a leader. The

Children all seemed just as intent on negotiating and deciding with each other as if every single one of them was as much a leader as Adrian was.

They finished off both of Troy's carcasses by the time Link came back with another fell deer. He skinned it and the Children went at that one with as much energy and enthusiasm as they'd used to demolish the other two carcasses.

"Are all these Children staying here?" Link muttered to Dina after he finally washed the blood off his hands. "How will we feed them all?"

"You and Troy are going to be busy," Dina replied and got a grin out of him.

The meeting went on until almost sunset when Adrian, Karim, Cain, and Jackal stood up and shook hands. "Thank you," Cain told Adrian. "I look forward to seeing you next week."

"You're welcome," Adrian replied. "We'll meet at the usual place and travel together from there."

Cain nodded and all of his people followed him out of the house. He didn't explain anything to anyone.

When he got outside, all the rest of his entourage got up, shook hands and nodded to those they'd been talking to, and followed him through the gate into the jungle.

Half the Riverbend Children went with them. They emptied out of the canton in a few minutes and left all the stripped bones lying on the grass.

Link sighed. "It looks like the party is over."

Adrian sat back down in the same place and went back to eating. "We're meeting them next week for a joint maneuver to find some cats to fight."

"Are you going to test yourselves one-on-one?" Link asked.

"We can do that anytime," Adrian replied with his mouth full. "We'll meet up with the other canton to organize a wider campaign outside our own territory—outside anyone's territory."

"How will you do that?" Link asked.

Adrian shrugged. "I'll need to talk to the other cantons first. Moonlight is only one. I'll have to travel to the other cantons and talk to them, too. It wouldn't work to do a joint maneuver with only two of us."

"How many other cantons do you plan to get on board before you mobilize?" Link asked.

"We know of ten, but we'll have to plan on some of them not agreeing to go along with our plans. We'll need to get as many on board as possible, so that means contacting as many as possible and some of them dropping off."

Link nodded. "Good idea."

Adrian rolled onto his side on the floor, stretched, and then curled up. "I'm tired. We can do all that tomorrow."

Link stared down at him. Half of the remaining Children bundled up together on the floor the way they used to, but the others left and headed back out into the jungle. Only a dozen stayed behind.

Dina stared down at her Children, too. They didn't get the blankets out of the cupboard the way they used to.

She couldn't go around the room tucking them in. That window had closed. She sensed it.

The Children had grown beyond her, too. She no longer touched them. Not even Link could influence them to become something more human or more socially acceptable. The Children's wild nature forbade it.

They closed their eyes one after the other. Not one of them asked why she didn't tuck them in or kiss them good night. They didn't notice Link and Dina standing there watching them.

The Children lived in another world now—another dimension where humans didn't exist except as some kind of accessory population apart from the Children's own unique society.

Now it was Link's turn to slip his hand into hers and pull her away. He didn't suggest that she tuck the Children in, either.

They weren't children anymore. They were as grown as they were ever likely to get and they didn't need that from her anymore.

Chapter 15

Adrian, Iona, the Black, and the Pygmies crowded the house steps basking in the sunshine. "I'm hungry," Kenji complained. "When are we going hunting again?"

"You can go hunting anytime you like," Naia told him. "What's stopping you?'

"I can't go by myself," he countered.

"Why not?" Adrian asked. "Go get yourself a nice tree lizard."

Kenji stuck out his tongue. "They're too small and they have too many bones."

"Then go get yourself a deer," Kaiser replied.

"Come with me," Kenji urged. "I can't be the only one who's hungry."

"You won't get any food around here," Dina replied from the doorway. "You've eaten every scrap of meat in the village."

"That's why you're hungry," Darius told Kenji. "Your stomach is so bloated that you think you're hungry when you're actually so overstuffed you can't move."

"I can so move." Kenji cuffed him across the back of the head. "You better watch your mouth or I'll thrash you."

"Link told us to test ourselves on opponents bigger and stronger than ourselves," Darius reminded him. "You might thrash me in the end, but you would get hurt doing it. I can promise you that, so you might want to think about it before you go making threats like that."

Kenji looked away.

"I'm sure someone out in the jungle is hunting as we speak," Adrian chimed in. "They'll have something for you when you get there."

"So how long are we sticking around here for?" Karim asked.

"Until Adrian gets bored," Naia replied.

Adrian snorted. "I'm already bored."

"Then why are we still here?" Duke asked. "We could be halfway to Hardship canton by now."

Adrian shrugged. "I don't know. I like this place. Maybe it's because I grew up here. I like it here."

"Except for the people, right?" Kaiser added. "You'd like it better if the people weren't around."

"I don't like it better than the jungle," Adrian replied and cast one last wistful glance at the nearby houses. "Maybe I'm reluctant to leave because I know that, one of these days, I'll leave and never come back. I don't want today to be that day."

Dina turned away and tried to block that conversation out of her mind, but he wasn't saying anything she didn't already know.

She knew as well as he did that he and the other Children would leave someday and never come back. That day would come eventually. When it did, the break between the Children and the village would be irrevocable.

She did her best not to listen to the rest of their conversation, but she had to turn back toward the doorway when Adrian stood up and said, "I guess we better go."

She returned to the threshold expecting this to be goodbye, but before she could move, a thump drew her attention to the far lefthand corner of the fence where it met the cliff face.

She froze when an enormous tiger sprang onto the top of the fenceposts. He perched there for a split second and she got a clear look at him.

He had a tiger's usual orange-brown coat with stripes radiating outward from his face. It wasn't Renfroe and that fact made his appearance so much worse than if it had been Renfroe.

He sprang down into the canton, took one look around, spotted the Children, and charged for Dina's house.

At the same instant, a dozen other large cats bounded onto the fence from both sides. A few panthers, pumas, and some young male lions surveyed the village inside the fence and then leapt down to the ground in the yard.

Screams echoed out of the canton and Adrian and his comrades all sprang to their feet.

Link dove through the doorway, grabbed an axe, and rushed outside. "Get to the jungle!" he snapped. "Quick! Get into the trees! You'll be able to fight them there!" Adrian headed for the fence, but Link grabbed him to stop him. "Go straight through the gate—now, Adrian!"

"I want to fight them!" Adrian yelled back. "We can't just run away!"

"You aren't ready!" Link spotted the tiger getting closer. "Do you really want to take *him?*"

Adrian glanced at the tiger and changed his mind. He cast around to make sure the other Children went with him and they dropped onto all fours bounding toward the gate.

The tiger swiveled to follow them. Dina couldn't stand that.

She snatched the first weapon she could lay her hands on, which was a shovel standing against the wall.

She jumped off the steps and landed in front of the tiger just as Link moved in to guard the Children's retreat.

The other cats ranged through the canton. People ran from them screaming, grabbing their younger Children, and rushing around in search of some way to escape.

The tiger turned toward the gate to follow the Children, but he ran into Link and Dina blocking his path. Troy showed up a minute later holding another axe.

The other cats must have been looking for the older Children, too, because they ignored the younger ones, their mothers, and any other villagers who came out to defend them.

The cats converged on the gate as Adrian and his party dashed out onto the field. Troy and Dina rotated to face the other cats while Link confronted the tiger alone.

The cats closed around the three friends. Dina instinctively backed away from them and she, Link, and Troy blocked the gate. The cats couldn't get through the track the Children down.

She dared to glance behind her and saw Adrian and the others vanishing into the trees. The guards and sentries who were supposed to be stopping these cats from entering the canton in the first place gathered around Dina and the two men.

A dozen people protected the Children's retreat, but at that moment, another ten cats sprang onto the fence and dropped down inside the canton.

These new cats paced around, and when they didn't see any older Children, the cats advanced to join their friends in surrounding Dina, Link, and Troy.

Dina tightened her grip on her shovel. It didn't feel like much, but it was her only weapon against these cats.

One of the pumas yowled at the people blocking his path. The cats could have gotten out of the canton as easily as they got into it, but these defiant humans posed too much of a challenge.

The cats tightened their formation and so did the people. The guards closed into a knot and the cats circled them. When would the attack come?

At least the Children had gotten away. Dina, Link, Troy, and these other men would make their stand here while the Children disappeared into the jungle. The cats wouldn't be able to take the Children there—or Dina hoped not.

This attack confirmed Dina's worst fears. The cats must be escalating their searches. They wouldn't be content to let the Children establish a territory free from cats.

The Pride had to exert its control even here. The cats couldn't allow anyone to defy them, especially not the Children that the Pride had sworn to destroy.

The big tiger who first threatened Link and Adrian growled and lowered his head between his shoulders in an obvious threat. He stalked a little nearer and one of the panthers crouched closer to the ground for the first spring.

At that moment, another growl made the cats look up. Dina's heart stopped when she saw Adrian, Iona, the Black, the Manx brothers, and a dozen other Children perched on top of the fence.

They paused there for a split second just to make sure the cats saw them all. Then, without a moment's hesitation, Adrian dropped right on top of the big tiger that Link said Adrian wasn't ready to fight.

The tiger whipped around to defend himself, but not fast enough. Adrian hit the tiger with all his weight, bowled the cat over, and they went at each other with teeth and claws.

Gut-wrenching growls, hisses, and bellows came from both of them. Their voices got all mixed up with each other. Dina couldn't tell which of them was bellowing the loudest, but Adrian definitely held his own against this much larger cat.

All their limbs flew at once, but the chaos erupting all over the yard distracted her from Adrian's fight. Iona launched herself off the highest fence posts and landed on top of one of the pumas.

The Black went after the lions. Dexter, Leroy, Riyadh, Riggs, Rome, and Aries pounced on the remaining panthers, another tiger, and another puma.

The cats and Children fell into a knockdown-dragout fight all over the yard. Dina charged forward to strike one of the cats, but she had to dart out of the way when Riggs tumbled almost on top of her.

He grappled with the other puma who screeched and shrieked to wake the dead. Riggs snarled and slashed his teeth in all directions cutting the cat's skin open and diving again and again for the cat's throat.

The cat kicked out with his hind legs and Riggs struck without mercy. The cat used its forepaws to hook Riggs's shoulders and hold him in position so the puma could counter Riggs's attack.

In fact, all the cats used the same strategy and it played against them in the end. Riggs didn't have to hold onto the puma. The puma did it for him and that left Riggs's hands free to use his own claws to slash the puma's belly open.

The puma gave one last blood-curdling shriek and tried to pull away. Riggs took advantage of that move, made a last-ditch plunge, and hooked his teeth around the puma's throat.

Riggs didn't lock on. He tore out with a brutal wrench of his neck and ripped the cat's carotid artery. Blood spurted all over Riggs and he sprang clear.

The cat staggered trying to bite the blood shooting from its neck, but it couldn't hold itself up. Its legs buckled and it collapsed on the ground.

Riggs turned to help his nearest comrades. Karim battled one of the young male lions nearby, but the lion backed off when Karim cut his teeth down the cat's shoulder and laid it open to the bone.

The lion leapt clear and paced back and forth a few times. Karim crouched on the ground snarling and baring his bloody fangs.

Riggs sauntered over to him and planted himself next to Karim to face down the lion. The lion didn't come any closer.

Iona wrestled another puma who used his weight to pin her down on the ground. He dove for her throat, but she dodged at the last second, twisted her head sideways, and clamped her jaws around his foreleg hard enough to snap the bone.

The cat gave a hair-raising yowl and shot away from her, but the damage was done. The other Children injured their opponents enough to make the cats back off.

Only Adrian remained locked in a death struggle against the tiger. They pitched all over the place with one of them gaining the upper hand, only to lose it when the other reared off the ground and fought back.

Adrian tried Riggs's trick of slashing his claws at the tiger's underside, but the tiger's thick fur on his belly protected him. The thick ruff of fur around his cheeks and neck also made it impossible for Adrian to get a good bite on the tiger's neck.

The tiger didn't have the same problem and he outweighed Adrian. The tiger kept pinning Adrian down. Adrian had to fight his hardest just to break that hold and the same thing happened again and again.

The last time he did this, the tiger threw his weight against Adrian to knock him down. Adrian rolled three yards away, spun around, and he and the tiger launched themselves at each other for the death blow.

"ADRIAN!!" Dina screamed, but it was too late.

He dove for the tiger at the same time the tiger dove for him. They both cracked their jaws and bared their fangs to tear each other apart.

The tiger dove for Adrian's throat one more time, but Adrian must have anticipated this. He adjusted his attack a few inches to the right, and instead of going for any vital part of the tiger's neck or body, Adrian raked his fangs across the tiger's face.

Adrian's teeth hooked into the tiger's cheek and laid open a flap of skin that exposed half of the front of the tiger's skull. The tiger roared in pain, but Adrian was still flying past him going way too fast.

Adrian stuck out one hand, extended his claws, and scratched the tiger across the eyes.

Adrian landed behind the tiger and the tiger landed closer to the other Children, but none of them moved to intervene.

The tiger bellowed in pain and frustration, but he couldn't see. Blood and ooze gushed from his ruined eyes and he stumbled in all directions trying to decide where to go.

Adrian watched him from a crouch by the fence, but the tiger didn't go near anyone or threaten anyone anymore. He was completely blind.

Adrian's panted so hard that his lips quivered. Blood dripped from a dozen gashes all over his face, neck, and body, but he didn't notice them.

He watched the tiger blundering around, changing directions, roaring at nothing, and slashing his fangs at empty air.

The other Children, cats, and sentries stared at the tiger, too. A dangerous silence fell over the canton. No one moved for a second until Adrian finally stood up.

He strode over to Dina, but he didn't even look at her when he took the shovel out of her hands. He clenched his grip on it, compressed his lips, and carried it over to the tiger.

The tiger didn't see him. The cat kept his back to Adrian and growled and bit at nothing.

Adrian stood over him and stared down at him in smoldering fury, but Dina also sensed Adrian hesitating to kill this cat, now that he was completely defenseless.

Without warning, Adrian raised the shovel, gave one last furious roar, and brought down the sharp edge of the blade across the back of the cat's neck.

The tiger buckled into the dirt and his head flopped to one side. That one blow chopped the spinal column all the way through and the tiger's head hung by the muscle, windpipe, and blood vessels at the front of his neck.

Adrian turned around very slowly. He still held the shovel and his features trembled with suppressed rage.

Half the other cats had suffered crippling injuries and two others besides the tiger were dead. Blood saturated Riggs's coat and both Dexter and Leroy had suffered serious injuries, too.

The cats stood back and didn't engage with the Children again. The cats didn't leave, either.

"Take this message back to the Pride," Adrian growled through gritted teeth. "Tell them we will never lie down ever again. Any cat that comes after us will suffer the same fate. Tell them their days of pushing us around are over and this jungle belongs to us now."

None of the cats moved. They stared at him like they didn't understand a word he just said.

"GO!!" he roared and rushed them brandishing his shovel.

Those cats that could still run turned tail and shot away into the jungle. The others limped after them and Adrian let them go.

A stunned silence fell over the canton, now that the cats were gone—all except for the three bodies. Adrian's tiger, Riggs's puma, and one of the young lions lay bleeding in the dust.

Link recovered first, rushed over to Adrian, and snatched the shovel out of his hand. "You have to get out into the jungle. They might have other cats hanging around waiting for their friends to come back. Take the Children to the west and get somewhere you can regroup in safety. Disappear for a while...."

"I don't want to get to safety," Adrian countered. "This is our chance. This is the first battle in a bigger war....."

"Not now!" Link fired back. "Wait until you have the other cantons with you! You need to organize and negotiate with them. Consolidate your power first. Fall back, regroup, and come back stronger. Go, Adrian! Go now!"

He shoved Adrian toward the gate and herded the rest of the Children away, too. Adrian resisted, but when Link didn't give him a choice, Adrian walked away.

He walked upright. He didn't run.

Chapter 16

Link slumped as soon as the Children vanished into the undergrowth. He turned around and sighed when he saw the three dead cats. "I guess I was wrong about him not being ready."

"How could you let this happen?" Fitch demanded from Link's right. "This is exactly what we've been worried about."

"You're blaming me for this?!" Link rounded on the guards and sentries. "You're on guard here to stop cats from getting near this place—much less over the walls. You've been standing here watching the fight without raising a finger to help your own people. What's your excuse? What do you have to say for yourselves?"

"We warned you the cats would come after us," Meredith cut in. "We could have all died."

"They didn't come after us!" Link countered. "They only came after the Children. If the cats were after us, we would be dead right now. The cats completely ignored all humans and younger Children. They were after Adrian and his group."

"All the more reason Adrian and his group shouldn't be allowed to come back into this canton ever again," Fitch went on.

"How are you going to stop them?" Troy asked. "They just fought cats. We won't be able to make the Children do anything."

"Make them hate you enough and they'll stay away of their own free will," Dina added.

"Say what you want," Link countered. "Those Children are the only thing keeping us alive right now."

"They're the ones bringing these cats here to invade our canton," Meredith argued back. "You heard what Adrian said. He plans to fight the cats no matter where they are. The Pride will keep sending out bigger and bigger parties to attack anyone who helps the Children. If we let the Children come and go from the village, the Pride will realize that we're aiding the Children."

"It looks to me like the Pride already knows about us," Dina remarked.

"We've put this off too long already," Fitch declared. "We'll have a Council meeting tonight to ban anyone affiliated with Adrian from entering this canton."

"You can't do that!" Dina fired back. "You don't have the authority to ban anyone from doing anything."

"Then we'll have to change the rules. This is a matter of life and death for everyone inside the walls."

"Don't you realize what he's doing?" Link countered. "Don't you realize that organizing all the Children into an army is the best defense we could possibly ask for?'

"Army!" Meredith snapped. "They aren't an army. They're Children. They don't know anything about warfare, especially warfare against cats."

"They know more than we do," Dina pointed out. "They know more than anyone else I can think of on this planet."

"We never should have let you train them," Fitch interjected. "I knew it was a bad idea from the start."

"You didn't let me do anything," Link returned. "You don't make the rules for me or anyone else—especially when the rules you want to make put people in danger."

"Put people in danger!" Fitch exclaimed. "Look around you! We're standing here with three dead cats and a dozen more out there injured beyond repair. What do you think the Pride is going to do about that?"

Link shrugged. "I don't really care what they do."

"They'll send out more cats!" Fitch fired back. "They'll keep sending more and more cats until they put us down. As long as cats keep getting hurt here, the Pride will realize we pose a threat to their rule."

"All the more reason to stand up to them," Link replied. "Adrian is right about that."

"Adrian again!" Fitch snapped. "It's always Adrian. Adrian this and Adrian that. All I ever hear about is Adrian. Adrian is a bigger threat to us than the cats are."

"Adrian wouldn't be a threat to us at all if not for the cats," Troy pointed out.

"So you admit he is a threat!" Fitch countered. "He's bringing the cats here to threaten us. If that isn't bad enough, killing the cats outright is the worst. The Pride will never tolerate that."

"What are we supposed to do—let them kill us first?" Dina asked.

Meredith turned away. "We'll hold a Council meeting tonight and decide what to do about this." She waved at the dead cats. "Someone do something about those."

She walked off followed by Fitch and the other Council members. The rest of the residents stared at Link, Troy, Dina, and each other. Then everyone drifted away one person at a time.

No one made any move to dispose of the dead cats. In the end, no one remained by the gate except Link, Dina, and Troy.

The guards and sentries went back to their posts as if nothing had happened. None of them even tried to explain how the cats got inside the fence with so many men on watch. The sentries never once raised the alarm.

The gate had stood open through the whole attack. The cats could have waltzed right in.

Troy finally puffed out his cheeks and turned to Link and Dina. "Don't worry about these. I'll get rid of them."

"Wait, man!" Link called after him. "Will you give me a hand?"

Troy frowned. "With what?"

"Wait here." Link went inside and came out with a length of rope.

He'd spent hours last winter hand-plaiting that rope. He took very good care of it—until now.

He called on Troy again to help him. Each man grabbed the tiger by a hind paw and they hauled the body out to the tree line.

Dina expected them to pitch the tiger into the undergrowth. Instead, Link lashed his precious rope around the tiger's ankles and he and Troy heaved and sweated and gasped lifting the tiger's body into the branches.

They hung it up in plain view of the canton and left it hanging there while they hung up the puma and the lion the same way.

The three bodies dangled there in such a stark threaten to any other cats that might come around.

Dina watched the men coming back. Troy said something to Link out of the side of his mouth and Link laughed nastily.

"People aren't going to like this," Dina told them when they came back.

"I hope they don't," Link snapped. "Whatever they don't like must be right."

He and Troy shook hands and Link and Dina returned to their own house.

"It sure is quiet around here without the Children," she remarked.

"I can just imagine what the Council will say tonight," Link muttered.

"Are you going to go?"

"I might," he replied. "I need a little entertainment to lighten my mood."

She didn't answer that and they didn't talk again as the sun went down. Every time she looked out her door, she saw the dead cats hanging there in the trees.

The Pride would never let this slide. Maybe Fitch had a point about that. They would never let such a blatant challenge go unanswered. If the cats couldn't impose their authority on the Children, the Pride would turn to the next available target—the canton.

Link went out hunting in the afternoon and brought back a tree lizard for their dinner. Dina sat down in the middle of the floor with her pot of coals and cooked it.

The house was empty. It had been empty before, but it felt different now. Something had broken today—something else—and it wasn't the Council's rules—whatever they were.

Adrian had crossed a line today—a big line. He had fought a full-grown tiger and won.

He wasn't the only Child to kill a cat on his own today, but killing that tiger would cement his leadership over the Children. No one would ever be able to tell him again that he wasn't ready to take that role and steer them wherever they needed to go.

Dina felt her Children slipping farther and farther away from her. She's already lost them. She realized that now. If she hadn't lost them before, today ended their childhood. It definitely ended Adrian's and Iona's.

The sun went down, and with the coming of dark, voices erupted in the house the Council used for meetings.

Link and Dina stayed in their own house listening. Dina couldn't make out any words. She didn't want to know, but after two hours of non-stop arguing, Link got to his feet. "Come on," he told her. "Let's go see what they have to say."

She didn't want to go, but if he was going, she had to.

She followed him to the house and they walked into the usual sea of noise with everyone arguing and talking at once.

Link and Dina stayed near the back while she tried to figure out what everyone was arguing about. She didn't see what they *could* be arguing about.

That nonsense about stopping the Children from entering the canton was just a bunch of hot air. If the cats could get in that easily, the Children could do it, too.

After ten minutes of steady hubbub, Nicholas got to his feet and raised his hands for silence.

"We'll start packing up tomorrow morning and convoy north," he announced. "Anyone who wants to come is welcome. No one has to stay behind that doesn't want to."

"All the guards and sentries who've been defending the wall should come with us," Meredith pointed out. "We'll need them to protect us on the journey."

"That means you'll leave the rest of us defenseless!" someone yelled out of the crowd. "Anyone left behind would be as good as dead!"

"The mothers and younger Children will need those guards more than you will," Nicholas went on. "You'll be able to defend yourselves....."

"With nothing but a skeleton crew?" another man fired back. "That's straight blackmail! You're threatening our lives to make us go with you! You're trying to punish anyone who supports these older Children."

"This has nothing to do with that...." Fitch interjected.

"Of course it does!" Troy called out of the crowd. "You didn't get your way and now you want to abandon anyone who wants to hold this canton."

"This canton is a death zone thanks to the older Children," Fitch snapped. "Anyone who stays behind deserves to die."

An uproar broke out over this. As soon as the noise started to die down, one of the mothers yelled out, "I'm not waiting for the convoy. I'm leaving tomorrow morning."

More shouts answered her. Some people nodded. Others pointed at her or swiped their fingers toward the door.

The yelling and arguing went on for a few more minutes. Dina cringed against the back wall and prayed to High Heaven that no one saw her. She didn't want to get involved in this even though she already was involved. She was as involved as she could possibly be.

Meredith, Fitch, and Nicholas each stood up one after the other and tried to speak to the crowd, but no one would stop yelling long enough for the three Council members to make themselves heard.

Dina was about to call it a night when the door opened behind her and Link. It swung inward and she froze when Adrian entered with the three Black brothers.

Karim, Kaiser, and Kenji glared at everyone around them, but Adrian kept his head up and his eyes trained forward no matter what. He didn't acknowledge Link and Dina at all.

The reaction to his arrival spread forward from the door. One person after another fell silent until only those at the very front kept arguing and shooting insults and remarks at each other and the Council.

Adrian advanced into the room and planted himself in the very center of the house, but he didn't face the Council. He turned in a slow circle to eye the rest of the crowd. Had he grown a few inches in the past couple of hours or was that Dina's mind playing tricks on her?

Meredith rallied first. "You aren't welcome in this canton anymore, Adrian. Take your Children and move to another area of the jungle. You've put all of us in danger for the last time."

He completely ignored her, turned his back to the Council table, and faced the crowd. "I came to ask if anyone here is interested in joining us in fighting the cats. We have scouts out there who report more parties coming out from the Pride to hunt for us. We need everyone who is willing to stand with us. I know Troy, Link, and Dina are with us. Who else can we count on?"

"No one is going with you," Fitch cut in. "It's thanks to you that these mothers and younger Children don't feel safe enough to stay in this canton. They're leaving tomorrow morning to go to Hardship canton instead...."

"Hardship canton is in as much danger as everywhere else," Adrian interrupted. "There's nowhere left to run. It's either fight or die....but it's been like that for the Children from the beginning."

He turned just as slowly to confront the mothers and Children—some of whom said they would leave the very next morning.

"You're deluding yourselves if you think you can run away and be safe somewhere else. This planet will never be safe for any Children unless we make it safe. The only way we can do that is by standing up to the cats and forcing them to stop sending out these search parties. They're really just killing parties. The Pride will keep sending them out until they get the message that any cat who comes around hunting us will end up dead or injured. Anything less is cowardice."

"Not everyone agrees with you, Adrian," Meredith sniffed. "Some of us would rather live our lives in peace than take part in whatever war you're planning."

"Then you're cowards," he returned. "You want to hide behind us and let us do your fighting for you. I heard Fitch just now when he said anyone who stays behind deserves to die, but it's you who will die because you won't fight back."

"We're with you, Adrian," Troy called out. "We're ready to fight when you are."

"Who else?" Adrian cast his sharp eyes over the crowd. "Is this why you left Prideland—so you could run and hide all your lives and let other people take all the risk to save your necks?"

"You'll only make the Pride angry," Nicholas told him. "It's bad enough that they come out here and attack us. You'll only make it worse. One of these days, they'll send a force no one can defeat."

"Then why don't you go back to the cities and be their helpers?" Adrian countered. "That's the only way you'll be totally safe from the cats. Some of you are our parents. Are you going to run away and abandon your own Children to fight this war?"

"There is no war," Fitch returned. "There wouldn't be a war at all if you weren't planning to start one."

"The war started a long time before I was born." Adrian cast one last look over the crowd, but he didn't acknowledge the Council again. "Those of you who want to run can run, but you won't find any safety in the other cantons. You won't find any safety anywhere. Anyone who stays behind better be ready to fight. The days of hiding in a hole are over."

He walked out of the house with the Black behind him. The place erupted in noise all over again.

Link turned to the door and nodded to her, but once they got outside, he didn't go back to their house.

He hurried across the dewy grass to catch up with Adrian. "Wait!" Link called. "Adrian—you aren't alone. People in this canton want to help you. Let us come with you. We can help you organize."

"Not yet, you can't," Adrian replied. "I need to negotiate with the other Children first and consolidate my position like you said. Stay here for now. I'll come back and get you when I need you." He glanced behind Link toward the dark houses. "See if you can get anyone else to see sense. Maybe some of them will wake up and change their minds like Troy did. We're all done with the rest of them. No more Council. If someone isn't ready to fight and support us, they're useless to us."

He turned away and would have walked off into the shadows. The Children could see everything in the darkness. They didn't need lights.

Dina couldn't let him walk away like this. This tearing sensation in her heart wouldn't let her. "Adrian....!"

He paused for a split second, looked back at her long enough to make eye contact with her, and then turned away for the last time before he and his friends slipped away into the trees.

Chapter 17

Dina squatted in front of her house scrubbing out a wooden bucket she'd used for helping Link gut the deer and oxen he brought in for food.

He didn't have to hunt as much since the Children had left the area, but he still went out as much as ever. He was out there right now. He went out every day even when he'd just brought in enough food to keep himself and Dina going for weeks.

He didn't mention if he saw Children out there in the jungle and she didn't ask. Maybe he just wanted to look for them to find out if they had returned to the area.

She figured he'd tell her if the Children did return to the area. They'd been gone for another year and things had settled down at the canton again. Most of the people who left following Adrian's first confrontation with the Council had returned long ago, but the Children didn't return.

She didn't hear about any major war between the cats and the Children, either. People came and went from other cantons—including the cantons Adrian said he planned to form alliances with.

Pregnant mothers and those with younger Children kept leaving Prideland. None of those people mentioned anything about the Children fighting cats.

Everyone who left Prideland said the cats were still wiping out any Child they could sink their teeth into. These people said the cats never let any Child survive. The cats would hunt down Children anywhere in Prideland no matter where they might be hiding.

Then, four months ago, a pregnant woman came out to Riverbend canton with the story of cats bringing helpers out into the countryside to watch the cats hunt and reduce escaping mothers and their Children.

The story spread like wildfire and sparked another panic, but no one talked about leaving. There was nowhere left to run unless someone wanted to forge off into the western wilderness and start over from ground zero.

Link didn't mention this again. He'd committed himself to helping the Children in whatever way they needed him to.

He didn't mention going west and she didn't have to ask the reason why. He wanted to stay at Riverbend so the Children would be able to find him when they needed him.

She dumped the dirty water out of the bucket and turned it over to let it drain and dry. She stood up and was about to go inside when she heard more rustling in the jungle.

This sounded far away and she spotted branches swaying a mile off. She almost dismissed it, but at that moment, she saw three Children break out of the upper canopy.

They scampered up the branches, perched in the foliage, and surveyed the landscape. She couldn't tell from here if they were Riverbend Children or if they came from another canton.

The next second, they dropped down into the canopy and vanished. She sighed and turned away. They were too far out to come near the canton. They knew better, but at least they were out there.

She turned away to go back to her work when Troy rushed up to her. "Did you see that? The Children are back!"

"They're hardly back," she told him. "They're in the jungle, but they didn't come near us. They know to stay away from this canton." She started climbing her steps to go inside. "We're no better than Moonlight canton. They drove their own Children away and we did the same thing."

He lunged for her and grabbed her hand. "Go out there and find them, Dina. Tell them we're still waiting to help them."

"Why don't you go out there? Your Children would be happy to see you. They know you're with them."

"You should go. They trust you more."

"We could go together," she suggested. "Why are you hiding from them?"

He tried to shrug that away. "It will look better if you go alone."

She squinted toward the trees. Curiosity got the better of her. Were those her Children out there? What were they doing?

"All right," she agreed. "I'll go."

He exploded in a huge grin that erased the last of her doubts. The Children might not be happy to see her. They'd parted on the agreement that they would come back when they needed something or someone to help them. They hadn't done that yet.

What did she have to lose? If the Children didn't need her or want her around, they could tell her and she would come back to the canton. No harm done.

If they really didn't want to see her, they could vanish into the branches and leave her in the dust. She would never find them and she would come back emptyhanded anyway.

She put away all the tools she'd been working with that day and headed out into the jungle. She had no idea where to look for them, so she headed for the spot where she'd spotted those three Children in the branches.

She lost track of how far she'd gone. She thought she found the spot, but she couldn't be sure. There were no Children here now.

She kept hiking for another hour before she decided to turn back in defeat. Maybe the Children were hiding from her or maybe they never had been here in the first place. Maybe they'd been traveling somewhere else and just happened to stick their heads up right then.

She did turn around, but before she could go anywhere, she heard crashing sounds coming from her right. She followed the noise and emerged from the trees at the top of a steep gulley cutting through the jungle.

The almost vertical sides formed walls around two open, grassy banks of a small river snaking through the gulley. The sun shone on the undulating banks with only a few trees dotted here and there.

It gave her a perfect vantage point to see everything going on below her. She froze when she saw fifteen Children break out of the undergrowth at the head of the gulley nearest her. They ran on all fours and closed the distance with a mob of large cats coming from the other direction.

Dina couldn't possibly mistake this group for anything other than one of the Pride's hunting parties. They'd sent out their biggest, heaviest, strongest tigers, jaguars, panthers, and lions.

All those cats ran at their top speed on a collision course for the Children, but the Children didn't break off. They charged picking up speed to close the gap.

Dina's guts tightened when she saw Adrian, Iona, the Black, and the rest of her own Children in the mob. They were all here and they didn't falter once.

They crossed the grass in seconds and the two sides closed in a raging battle of claws and teeth.

Whatever the Children had been doing during the past year, their fighting had developed beyond anything Dina ever could have imagined. They attacked with terrifying ferocity that even took the cats aback.

Adrian selected the biggest tiger in the group and slammed into the cat so hard that Adrian bowled the tiger down the bank. The tiger scrambled to use his weight to overwhelm Adrian, but it didn't work.

All the Children had developed a unique fighting style that combined the advantages of more mobile human arms with the kicking, slashing hindleg motion of cats.

Adrian used his arms to grapple the tiger's forelegs against his body. From there, Adrian could yank the cat in any direction.

The tiger tried to bite him, but Adrian threw the tiger sideways, slammed him down on the ground, and in an instant, Adrian wrenched the cat onto his side with his forelegs still pinned.

The cat tried to kick out, but Adrian avoided this by maneuvering his own body to the side of the cat's hind legs. The cat couldn't hit Adrian with his claws.

The cat thrashed and writhed, but Adrian overpowered the cat, twisted him onto his side, and dove for the jugular. The cat tried in every possible way to tear himself out of Adrian's grip, but Adrian's arms were too strong.

He consolidated his bite on the cat's neck and tore. The tiger flailed, but it was too late. Adrian leapt clear and the tiger spasmed again and again as his blood gushed from the bite.

Adrian spun away, left his victim lying there, and charged a jaguar who teamed up with a panther to corner Karim and Kaiser near a stand of trees. Adrian blasted into them, grabbed the jaguar, and overpowered him, too.

The other Children all used the same fighting style. They used their arms to keep out of the way of the cats' hind legs, manhandle the cats into unfavorable positions, and finish them off too fast for the cats to fight back.

The Children slaughtered ten cats and maimed five more. The tide turned in the Children's favor and a dozen surviving cats broke away to make a run for it.

"Get up those hills, Kaiser!" Adrian ordered. "Get in front of them and head them off! Come on!"

His voice sounded lower and more resonant than Dina remembered it. It sent a chill up her spine when she realized who that voice reminded her of. Adrian sounded like Renfroe. Adrian had Renfroe's deep, rumbling voice that would make anyone tremble.

The Children finished off the cats they still held and took off up the gulley to catch the rest. Dina had to change her position to watch the end of the fight.

The Children didn't just drive the cats off. The Children raced up the hills, along the ridges, and overtook the cats in a few seconds. The cats sprinted at their top speed, but they couldn't get away.

Kaiser and Karim dove down into the gulley and veered to come back at the cats from the front. The cats swerved to both sides searching for any way out.

They ran into Iona and the Manx coming from the left and Kenji, Riyadh, and the Auroras coming from the right.

Adrian, Cairo, Israel, and Leroy drove the cats from behind and the four groups of Children closed the net to trap the remaining cats there.

Dina lost sight of them again, and when she clambered up another hill to see what they were doing, the Children were all piling on top of the cats.

Hideous screeches, growling, and tearing noises drifted up the gulley walls....and then all the Children stood back dripping with blood. The cats lay dead on the grassy bank. Not one of them survived.

Adrian ran his wrist across his mouth. "Get up to the ridges and make sure we got them all," he ordered. "Then get back to the camp and send out the scouts to circle our perimeter. This is the second hunting party in a week. They're bound to send out another one soon."

"We should check over....." Kenji turned around and pointed up at the ridges. The words died on his lips when he saw Dina standing there. The rest of the Children looked up and saw her, too.

Adrian nudged Kenji's shoulder. "Go do it. I'll talk to her. Let's go. We don't have time to mess around with this. You come with me, Karim. The rest of you get moving."

Chapter 18

The Children split up. None of them disobeyed Adrian even to come greet Dina. Even Iona left in a different direction to go search a different part of the countryside.

In that brief interlude, Dina saw all she needed to see of the Children. They'd grown again in the last year. They weren't teenagers anymore.

Adrian didn't look any taller or bulkier, but his features had matured. He definitely wasn't a boy anymore.

Karim, Kaiser, and Kenji had grown taller and bulkier and so had the male Auroras. They had all put on muscle.

They all dwarfed Adrian, but his authoritative attitude had only deepened. His influence over them had become undeniable—as if it hadn't been before.

He and Karim sauntered slowly up the hill to meet her. She left the hilltop and dropped into the gulley where she came face to face with them under the trees.

Now, when she stood in front of them, she realized her mistake. Adrian *had* gotten bigger, but not by much.

He exuded power and unstoppable authority that made her cringe.

"You're a long way from the canton, Dina," he began. "Don't tell me you came all the way out here just to see us."

"Does that surprise you?" she asked. "You've been gone for over a year."

"I guess we have."

"You said you would come back and tell us when you needed us to help you," she pointed out. "We thought we would have heard from you months ago."

"We don't need you." He turned to Karim. "You can go catch up with the others. I'll meet you back at the camp."

Karim dipped his chin once and took off running through the jungle without saying a word to Dina.

"Are you....?" Dina glanced down into the gulley. "Are you hunting cats like this all the time?"

"Whenever the Pride sends out a hunting party. Why do you ask?"

She opened her mouth to say something and changed her mind. What could she say? Pointing out how dangerous this was didn't seem to cut it.

He read her mind. "You knew it would come to this. The Pride keeps escalating, so we have to escalate, too."

Her mouth fell open, but she stopped herself from gasping outright. "Do they send out parties regularly? How often do you do this?"

He shrugged. "Every couple of days, I guess."

Now she really did gasp.

He looked up at her and her heart stopped at the look on his face. His stripes had become more distinct. Everything about him looked like the spitting image of Renfroe except that Adrian walked upright.

She could still make out the human face under his fur. He wasn't a cat, but damn! He looked so much like his father that Dina shivered.

"Are you going to tell me how dangerous this is and how we shouldn't be doing this?" he demanded. "We have no choice now....and we wouldn't stop even if we could. Anyone who comes after us better watch out because we won't hold back."

"I wasn't about to say that." She heard how tiny her voice sounded.

"Why did you come out here?" he asked. "You were safe at the canton. We make sure no cats go near there."

"I.....is it so hard to believe that I wanted to see you?"

This was apparently not what he wanted to hear. He turned away and compressed his lips. "What are they doing back at the canton, anyway? Do they have younger Children there? The same thing will happen when the Children grow up."

"Yes, we have younger Children there. They're starting to explore and climb."

"I hope the parents learned their lesson last time," he muttered. "I would hate to have to come back to Riverbend canton and liberate those Children to give them the life they deserve in the jungle."

She gulped down rising alarm. This was her son and yet she didn't know him at all. He'd grown up into someone completely different from what she expected.

"Why don't you come back to the canton and find out what it's like?" she suggested. "Then you can see for yourself how it is for the younger Children."

"I don't think so. I don't belong at Riverbend canton anymore." He stopped suddenly, glanced behind him, and pricked up his ears to listen. "Kaiser found something."

"He did? What did he find?" Dina asked.

"It isn't another hunting party." Adrian faced from and kept walking. "You can come back to our camp. The others will be happy to see you."

She studied the side of his face. "Are you happy to see me?"

"Of course!" He barely glanced at her. "I just didn't expect you. I thought you'd stay at the canton. I suppose it gave me some comfort to think that you and Link were safe there and not out here involved in all of this."

"We want to be involved in all of this. If you and the other Children are involved in it, then we want to be, too."

"Why would you want to be involved in *this?*" he countered. "It's just a lot of hunting, killing, and organizing everyone to stay on top of patrolling our territory."

"We want to be involved because you and the other Children are our family," she told him. "We love you and we want to be wherever you are. We told you that before you left the canton. Did you think we made that up?"

He frowned at her like she was speaking another language, but just then, Aries, Amir, and Kenji came back. "There's another hunting party, but they're heading south toward Bluerock Falls. Duke and Dexter are following them to keep an eye on them. They'll send us word if the cats change course."

"Bring everyone back to the camp," Adrian ordered. "We need to discuss our next campaign."

The three boys ran off into the jungle and left Dina and Adrian alone. She didn't break the silence. The training and planning that Link and Adrian laid back at Riverbend canton was coming to fruition. It just wasn't turning out to be what Dina expected.

She didn't know what she did expect, but she never expected this. Some part of her never fully accepted that Adrian and the other Children would ever grow up.

More than their bodies had grown up. They'd grown up mentally and in every other way. Their original drive to explore, fight, and defend themselves had also grown up—into this.

She should have seen this coming. She should have realized that they would grow into a mature fighting force with big ideas about how to face any threat the Pride sent out against them.

Adrian didn't break the silence, either. Whatever he'd been doing out here with these Children, his plans and ideas had obviously grown beyond anything Dina could imagine. Why shouldn't they? He was the one facing these threats—not her.

She, Link, and all the other parents had been living safely behind the fence at Riverbend canton. Adrian was right about that. No wonder he was surprised that she left it to find him. She had no reason to leave it—not with the Children guarding the countryside.

He hiked back over most of the territory she'd covered to get here. He could have run that distance in a few minutes, but he walked slowly by her side. When the paths became too narrow, he led the way single file.

He turned off westward before they got anywhere near Riverbend canton. He dropped into some steep ravines that got steeper until they became deep gorges. He entered terrain she'd never seen before or even known existed.

He followed a crooked footpath overgrown with vegetation. They had to fight their way through vines and overhanging branches.

Dina and Adrian made it to the bottom of a sheer canyon before the path leveled out. They broke out into a slightly less dense part of the jungle, and in a few minutes, she spotted Children moving through the canopy at high speed.

They called back and forth to each other, leapt from branch to branch, and their laughter rang through the canyon from every direction.

"How many Children do you have down here?" she asked.

"About five hundred." She gasped out loud, but he only glanced at her over his shoulder. "Most of them have escaped from hostile cantons. Others come and go between us and their own camps. We have a network of bands all over the country."

She shut her mouth with an effort. Five hundred Children! She never dreamed the group would grow so large.

The path wound down the canyon and eventually came to an enormous camp hidden in the middle of the wilderness.

It was really more of a town with dozens of rough houses built among the trees. The houses had been constructed of branches lashed together and thatched roofs.

Countless Children clambered through the branches overhead and walked back and forth between these houses.

Dina hardly recognized any of the Children. They were all strangers to her, but they weren't strangers to each other.

They talked, worked together, and she even saw some couples getting intimate with each other either in isolated corners or through the open doors of their houses. None of them made any effort to hide what they were doing from each other.

Adrian made it halfway through the camp before a group of young men came up to him. They appeared to be about seventeen in human equivalent years—the same age Dina's Children had been when they left Riverbend canton.

"We searched the south gorge like you asked," one hulking boy with speckled brown and yellow fur told Adrian. "There was nothing down there."

"No cats?" Adrian asked. "No Children or people?"

"Nothing," another boy with lighter mushroom-grey fur replied. "I don't think anyone has even been down there before."

Adrian frowned. "That's odd. The cats should have used it to flank us by now."

"Maybe they haven't thought of it," the first boy suggested. "They don't think. They aren't creative. They don't try to do very much other than coming straight at us."

Adrian scratched the side of his neck. "You're right. I keep expecting them to pull some genius maneuver out of their ears."

"What do you want us to do about it?" the second boy asked. "This is the third time we've gone down there and found nothing."

"Keep an eye on it," Adrian replied. "I don't want them getting the jump on us. The south gorge is the only way they could come up on our camp without us knowing about it."

"How often do you want us to keep an eye on it?" the first boy asked. "If you want to keep an eye on it, you should post guards down there all the time."

"Every three days should be enough. If you see anything or smell any sign that cats have been going down there, we'll think about increasing our patrols of the area."

"What do you want us to do in the meantime?" a third boy with almost white fur asked. He had one black circle around one eye. "If you put us on any other patrol, we won't have time to go down there every three days."

"Kick back here with your wives for a few days," Adrian told them. "You've all earned a break."

The boys left and Adrian went over to one of the largest houses. An awning had been built against the side wall with a large table underneath it.

Maps of the surrounding countryside lay spread out on the table and he started studying them.

Dina hesitated to intrude on his planning, but her curiosity was getting to the breaking point. "What did you mean when you said those boys had wives?"

"They're married," he replied without looking up. "That's what a wife is, isn't it?"

"You mean....."

His head shot up and he drilled her with a piercing look. He could skewer someone with his eyes exactly the way Renfroe did.

"Why does it surprise you to find out that we want to marry and have families and children just like everyone else?" he demanded. "Being biologically unique doesn't mean we don't want the same things everyone else wants."

"I didn't mean that," she stammered. "I just meant....."

He kept staring at her so intently that she trailed off. What did she mean? Why did it surprise her to find out that the Children's society had developed as far as that?

Before she could make a fool of herself by answering, her own Children showed up. All the Children who'd attacked the cats in the gulley returned along with the Pygmies, the rest of Osiris's Children, and the rest of the Auroras.

They laughed and talked loudly while they relived their favorite moments of hunting down and slaughtering those cats.

"Did you see the way that jaguar tried to run away after I tore out his throat?" Dexter crowed. "He planted right on his face in the dirt and got it all in his mouth." He burst out laughing. "You should have seen it!"

"One of the panthers sat on his own tail when he fell over," Rome added. "He balanced there for at least five seconds before he hit the ground."

The others laughed. They all headed for the awning and crowded around Adrian's table.

Naia walked right up to him, put her arms around him, and tried to kiss him on the cheek, but he turned his head and kissed her on the lips instead.

Dina found herself gawking at them in stupid shock. They'd always acted so affectionate toward each other. How could she be so blind that she didn't see this coming?

Then she spotted Karim in the very back of the group. He carried Iona piggyback on his back and she nuzzled her face into his neck from behind. She didn't look up when the group stopped under the awning.

Dina heard her muttering something into his fur and he burst into laughter at something she said. His face lit up and he lowered his eyelids like he might be blushing under all his dark fur.

Dina barely heard the rest of the other Children's conversation with Adrian. They gave him reports about what they found in different parts of the Children's territory, where groups of Prideland hunting parties were and which directions they were moving, and different groups of Children who'd engaged the cats and the outcomes of those encounters.

He followed all their remarks on the map, but he didn't make notes or anything else to indicate where everyone was or what they were doing. He just traced each location and movement with his fingertip and brought up amazing amounts of information out of his memory.

"Who do we have on duty as runners?" he asked no one in particular.

"Enoch, Dutton, and Creed," Kaiser told him.

"Good. Send Dutton and Creed out to Northfall and tell them to get out a squad to intercept the hunting party moving in on Northfall from the east. Tell them not to let a single one of those bastards get away. Get Enoch to head for Hardship and inform Magnus and Layton about that hunting party traveling down the broken ridgetop. Tell Magnus not to do anything until the hunting party drops into the valley and moves into the gap between the standing stones. Then the Hardship defenders can strike, but not before."

Kaiser left to carry out his orders. Adrian went through a few more orders and received reports from Children Dina didn't know. Everyone seemed to have forgotten all about her until Naia looked up and saw her standing there.

"You should stay with us tonight, Dina," Naia suggested. "You're too far away from Riverbend canton to go home tonight."

"Yeah, you should stay and be our guest," Adrian agreed and he turned to Naia. "Do we have enough food?"

"We can get it if we don't." Naia grabbed Dina's arm and pulled her out from under the awning. "Come with me, Dina. I'll show you where to go."

Chapter 19

A drian went back to talking to the other Children, but Dina could already see that this wasn't a social meeting. They kept discussing their strategy and he kept pointing out features of the landscape on his map.

Naia towed Dina into the house adjoining the awning. "You're the first human visitor we've ever had! This should be fun."

She squatted down near some bundles of belongings in the corner. The house had no furniture or interior rooms of any kind. It was just one room with a dirt floor.

Naia rummaged around in her stuff and brought out a rock and a piece of metal. "It's been so long since I learned how to use this. Let's see if I remember how to do it."

"What are you doing?" Dina asked.

"Lighting a fire to cook your dinner." Naia looked up, met Dina's eye, and burst into musical laughter. "No one ever cooks around here. Some of these Children have never even seen food being cooked before."

"Wow, that's incredible." Dina found her gaze migrating toward the door.

Children walked back and forth outside...and then Dina spotted Karim and Iona again.

He was in the act of putting her down. She turned around, slipped her arms around his neck, and kissed him. It was a full, open-mouthed kiss where their tongues mingled before they pulled away.

She gave him a seductive look before she let her fingers trail out of his hand and she walked away into the camp.

"Naia?" Dina faltered.

Naia didn't look up from what she was doing. She fished a handful of wood shavings out of another bundle, put the shavings on the floor, and struck the rock and the piece of metal against each other to make sparks.

"Hmmmm?" Naia mumbled.

"You and Adrian are......" Dina broke off. She couldn't come up with the right word. "You're together, aren't you?"

"We're married," Naia muttered under her breath. "We got married last year." Her head shot up, her eyes popped, and she gasped. "You didn't know, did you? Oh, my God! I completely forgot that you didn't know!"

"How could I know? I haven't seen you since you left Riverbend canton."

"We got married before that."

Dina froze staring down at the girl—at least, Naia still looked like a girl. She had the same petite, delicate stature and features. She looked as childlike, innocent, and vulnerable as she'd looked as a girl, but Naia wasn't a girl anymore.

She was the same age as Karim and the others. Naia and the other Pygmies were just smaller and slighter, but they were just as developed. They were adults.

All those Children out there—they were all big enough to be fully mature. They were three years old—old enough to be fully grown and sexually developed by feline standards.

Their bodies had certainly matured enough for that. Why shouldn't they mate—or in this case, marry?

Dina gulped down her shock. No wonder the Children separated from human society to establish their own community.

This shock Dina was feeling right now—this was the reason the Children had to go off on their own in the first place.

They didn't belong in human society. Human expectations about what they would do and how they should act—none of those expectations applied to them.

Adrian and the Black looked like they would be about twenty in human equivalent years. That was plenty old enough to get married and.....

Dina's mind went into another tailspin. What if they could reproduce? What if the Children could have young of their own? They would establish a whole new species. Then what?

Adrian....and Naia......

Karim and Iona were obviously a couple, too. They kissed in front of everyone—in front of Adrian and in front of Karim's brothers. None of them even looked sideways at Karim and Iona kissing.

No one acted at all surprised about Adrian kissing Naia. Why should they act surprised? Adrian and Naia were married.

If they had children of their own, that would make those children......Dina's grandchildren.

Her hand flew to her head trying to process all of this. Naia didn't notice a thing. She got her wood shavings burning and added some twigs to make the fire blaze up.

"Yay! I did it!" she cheered. She put the stone and steel away, left the house, and came back a minute later with a claw pot. "We'll take it out into the camp. Everyone will be happy about having a fire tonight. It's been so long since we had one."

She got busy using a piece of bark to scoop the burning sticks into the pot. She used it to carry everything outside.

Dina followed her. Naia squatted in the center of the camp. It was really another village—a village of Children.

One of these days, the galaxy was going to have to stop calling them Children and come up with a different name for them. They weren't children anymore if they ever had been.

Naia dumped her fire onto the ground and started adding to it. She built it into a blaze and the other Children gathered around. The sun was going down anyway.

The Children settled down on the ground exactly the way they used to settle down on the floor of Dina's house in Riverbend canton. They sprawled, lounged, and leaned their bodies all over each other.

Many of them wrapped themselves around each other in lovers' embraces. They kissed, fondled, and curled up together in plain view of everyone.

Naia went back and forth to the house with the awning. That must be hers and Adrian's house.

The thought gave Dina another wave of vertigo. She had to reorient herself to all of this. Her son was married and she never even found out about it until a year after the fact.

Were Karim and Iona married, too? What difference did it make if they put that name on it? They were together.

They sat down together across the circle and he nuzzled his head against her cheek and down her neck. He pushed her over onto the ground, crawled on top of her, and then rolled off to lie on the ground with her in his arms.

Naia returned with the skinned, butchered leg of some animal. She put it down on top of a piece of tanned leather, started cutting off pieces of it, and skewering them to cook over the flames exactly the way Dina used to cook for herself and Link back home.

Adrian didn't show up for another hour. God only knew where he'd been and what he'd been doing.

He sat down next to Dina and sighed. "We'll travel as far as Brookhollow tomorrow. That will get you close enough to Riverbend canton for you to make it home."

"What are you going there for?" she asked.

"We're on our way to Hardship canton to meet up with their leaders. We need to go over our territories and decide what to do about Prideland hunting parties that are moving back and forth between our borders."

She looked up at him. "What is your plan with these hunting parties? Is your plan to just keep harassing them until the Pride leaves you alone?"

He shrugged. "If that's what it takes, then yes. If they suddenly decided tomorrow to stop sending out hunting parties and to stop slaughtering newborn Children, then I would stop all of this."

"Really?" Dina asked. "You seem....."

He cocked his head to study her. "Do you think I'm doing this because I enjoy it? I just want to live my life. I don't ask for much, but no one is going to take that away from me—or from anyone I care about."

"I didn't mean that. It just seems like.....you were made for this. It comes so naturally to you."

"What comes naturally to me is wanting to kill anyone who threatens me or my family." He turned aside and used his claws to tear a piece of raw meat off the haunch in front of Naia.

He stuck it in his mouth and chewed it, but not before she shot him a smirk and then laughed.

He grinned at her and then got serious when he faced Dina. "So tell me what's been happening at Riverbend canton while we've been gone."

"Nothing has been happening. Everything is still the same."

"I mean who's there? Who's on the Council now?"

"Everyone who was there when you left."

He raised his eyebrows. "They said they would abandon that canton and move somewhere else. They said we put them all in danger."

"About half of them did leave after you fought those cats," Dina replied. "Then things settled down and a bunch of them came back. They waited until Riverbend became peaceful again."

"So Link and Troy are still there?" he asked.

"Of course. Link and I are still together. Neither of us would have left as long as the other one wanted to stay."

He stared down into the flames and nodded.

"Why are you surprised that Link and I are still together?" she asked.

"I'm not surprised that you're still together. I thought maybe you coming out here alone meant something might have happened to him. I thought maybe that was the reason you decided to come and find us."

"No, he's fine. He's been waiting to see you again. He goes out searching for you almost every day."

Adrian didn't answer and he didn't look up. Naia listened to their conversation while she worked, but in a second, she took the first skewer off the flames, pushed the roasted meat onto a plate, and handed it to Dina.

"Thank you," Dina exclaimed. "This looks delicious."

"It better be after I grew up watching you do it all those nights," Naia replied.

Dina put a piece of succulent meat in her mouth. It tasted amazing—probably because this was the first time in years that someone had cooked for her instead of the other way around.

Eating it gave her all the time in the world for her to see all the couples comingling around the fire. Their intimacy never escalated to anything sexual, but Dina couldn't deny anymore that they'd all paired off into couples.

Naia set another three loaded skewers over the coals and passed the time by nuzzling up to Adrian. She ran her furry face all over his cheeks and burrowed into the ruff of thick hair along his jawline.

He shut his eyes and growled at her under his breath. Dina forced herself to look away, but that only brought her face to face with the sight of Karim lying behind Iona with his arm around her waist.

Now he was the one burying his face in her neck from behind and Dina heard him muttering into Iona's ear. Iona had her eyes shut, too.

Dina looked down at her plate and concentrated on finishing her food. She didn't know where she would sleep tonight, but she couldn't sleep out here with all the Children tangled up with each other.

Naia pulled away from Adrian, took the skewers off the coals, and slid the meat onto Dina's plate. "I'm going to get you some blankets," Naia told her. "I'll make you a bed in our house. You don't want to sleep on the ground."

Naia vanished into the darkness. Adrian stared into the embers deep in thought and didn't speak.

Dina didn't disturb him. She would probably never know the vast amount of detail and information going through his mind right now.

Naia didn't come back for another half an hour. When she did, she led Dina to the same house with the awning.

Naia disappeared inside and Dina followed her to the corner where Naia had arranged a bundle of blankets on the floor. "Sorry it took so long," Naia murmured. "No one in camp uses blankets. It took me ages to find them."

"Thank you for this," Dina whispered back. "I'm very grateful."

Naia's teeth glimmered in the darkness. "It really is wonderful to have you visit. It would be great if you could stay here all the time...." Her smile faded. "But then you would get lonely to go home to Link. So that wouldn't work. Anyway, good night. I'll see you in the morning. Let me know if you need anything. We'll be right outside."

She left Dina standing there alone in the dark. Dina tried to figure out what Naia meant by saying they'd be right outside, but Dina got her answer when she tiptoed closer to the door and peered out at the fire.

All the Children lay in piles around the flames. Most of them looked like they were already asleep.

Naia sat down next to Adrian, put her arms around him, and started burrowing into the side of his face again. His eyes drifted shut again, but he didn't kiss her.

He pushed her back and curled up on his side with his head in her lap. She ran her fingers through his fur while he shut his eyes again and drifted off.

Dina stood there watching them for a long time. All the Children seemed so happy together—or as happy as they could be in a landscape where everyone wanted them dead.

Chapter 20

D ina woke up to the sound of a deep male voice rumbling right near her head. She stiffened when she thought it might be Renfroe.

She opened her eyes and looked around. She lay in a pile of blankets on the floor of a thatched hut made of branches. She was in the Children's camp and that voice was Adrian's.

"I told you before we won't go down there again until they clear off," he growled. "Tell them if they don't want to cooperate, we'll leave them unprotected and they can take their chances with the cats themselves."

"I've already told them a dozen times," Leroy replied. "You've given them too many warnings as it is. If you don't make good on your threat now, they'll just keep pushing you and pushing you until you either give in and defend them or throw them to the wolves."

"To hell with them," Amir added. "Let them die. They don't support our campaign and they refuse to acknowledge your authority, Adrian. We don't have any more time to waste on them."

"Fine," Adrian snarled. "Pull all our scouts back from the valley and leave them to take care of themselves."

"It's about time," Riggs muttered. "You never should have given them so many chances to throw it in your face."

"I think I can decide for myself how many chances to give them," Adrian fired back. "They have resources we need. They would be much more useful to us alive than dead."

"Maybe the cats will give them a good scare and the Black Warren Children will change their tune," Leroy suggested.

"Amir is right. We can't waste any more time waiting for them to come to their senses," Adrian replied. "Send out an advanced scout to rendezvous with the Brookhollow Children. Tell them we'll be delayed while we take Dina home to Riverbend canton."

"What about having the Brookhollow Children come out to meet us halfway?" Riggs suggested. "That will cut the trip in half and we won't have to worry about anyone from Brookhollow giving us grief about camping so close to their canton."

"Good idea," Adrian replied. "You can do that."

Riggs laughed. "I was hoping you'd say that." A scuffle followed. It ended with a rustle in the branches overhead as Riggs took off into the treetops.

Dina sat up, folded her blankets into a neat pile, and went outside. Naia rushed up to Dina instantly. "Oh, you're awake! That's great. Here's the leftover food from last night. You can eat that for breakfast. We'll be moving out soon to take you back to Riverbend."

"Right now?" Dina countered.

Naia nodded. "We would have left sooner, but we wanted to wait for you to wake up."

Dina put a piece of the meat in her mouth to stop herself from answering. She didn't expect the Children to make such an effort on her behalf.

Based on what she just heard from Adrian, he would be delaying an important negotiation between him and another canton so he could travel slowly enough to accompany her back home.

She ate as quickly as possible while the rest of the Children worked to pack their supplies. Each member of the traveling group carried a bundle and they stayed walking upright on the ground. They didn't shoot away into the treetops.

"Let's go," Adrian finally decided after Dina finished eating. "We have some miles to cover before we get there."

He wasn't kidding. The party walked all day, climbed out of the gorge, and traversed miles of rough country, slogged up mountains and down into valleys before they made it back to territory Dina started to recognize.

The party topped a high ridge toward noon and started to follow it north. They made it to the far end where a treacherous, rocky path plunged into another steep valley.

They were just about to descend when branches crashed and snapped in the jungle below. Riggs shot up the mountain at high speed, vaulted off another branch, swung around a third, and landed in a crouch in front of Adrian.

"There's another hunting party moving this way!" he panted. "They're coming up the Crooked Fork from Moonlight canton and they're coming fast! It looks like they're on their way toward Brookhollow. The Brookhollow Children are already on their way over, but they might not get here in time."

Adrian dropped his bundle. "Everybody get into position and flank the Fork valley! Riggs, you take the Black and the Auroras on the south side. Kaiser, you take everyone else on the north side. Riyadh, Israel, and Cairo, come with me. Stay here, Dina. Don't leave this ridge no matter what happens. Understand?"

He hesitated just long enough for her to nod before they all exploded down the mountain. Adrian took a running jump off the high rocks, landed in the canopy below him, and rocketed away in a split second.

The other Children split into two flanks. Dina followed their progress as the branches rippled and tossed from the Children's passage.

They divided onto the two sides of a steep valley. The Children plunged to the bottom and then each group fractured as all the Children spread out to cover more ground.

Dina paced down the ridge trying to keep track of them all. She finally found an outcropping where she could see a river winding up the valley far below.

She couldn't see the Children in the undergrowth, but she did see another hunting party of cats making its way up the valley from the east.

The Pride wasn't playing games anymore. They'd once again sent out big, strong, heavy cats—thirty of them, this time.

Dina's stomach tightened in knots when she realized what was about to happen—and what was already happening. The Children were hunting again. They were hunting the hunting party.

Adrian wasn't just defending his territory anymore. He was using his scouts to scour the countryside for any cat the Pride dared to send after him. Adrian was going out of his way to defy the cats' rule. This could only end one way.

The cats raced up the riverbed winding their way deeper into the mountains. They leapt fallen logs, swerved around trees, and glided over the landscape moving as fast as Riggs said.

They didn't look right or left to see if anyone was moving in on them. Link had been right about them. They didn't think strategically—not even after all the times Adrian and his people attacked and slaughtered cats in this jungle.

The cats climbed higher up the steep valley. The riverbed became rougher and the valley walls steeper. Dina couldn't see any of the Children now—not even the branches moving to show where the Children were hiding.

The valley walls closed tighter into a bottleneck—the most perfect place for an ambush. The cats didn't see it coming until it was too late.

They broke cover into an open place, and out of nowhere, Adrian, Riyadh, Israel, and Cairo dropped down in front of the cats to block their way.

The cats must have been expecting to run into Children up here. The cats might even have been hoping for a scenario just like this.

They didn't stop running. They picked up speed and gathered their bodies to spring on the four Children.

Adrian and his three comrades sped up, too. They bounded down the rocky defile covering the ground easily. Adrian adjusted his trajectory to target the biggest, heaviest jaguar. The Pride didn't send out any tigers this time.

The jaguar coiled his hind legs and propelled himself off the ground in a flying leap to close with Adrian. Adrian jumped at the same instant. All the other cats leapt, too. No way could four Children defeat thirty cats.

At the last second before the cats pounced and finished off the four Children, the rest of Adrian's hidden party plummeted out of the trees.

They landed on top of the cats en masse and smashed all the cats to the ground. The cats still outnumbered the Children almost two to one, but the sudden surprise attack tipped the balance in the Children's favor.

The Children attacked impossibly fast, killed seven cats, and snapped the leg bones of six more. The Children sprang away from their targets and hurtled for those cats still in fighting condition.

Kenji landed on top of the jaguar that had been about to close with Adrian. Kenji went down under the jaguar's weight and then Adrian jumped in to help Kenji put the jaguar down.

The Children whizzed from one cat to another, injuring them here, blinding them there, and killing any cat not fast enough or strong enough to defend themselves.

In less than a minute, the Children reduced the hunting party to five. Then the Children ganged up on the survivors and finished them off with brutal precision.

Dina watched the whole gory procedure with her heart in her mouth. She actually started to feel sorry for the cats. They'd ruled Prideland for centuries using their teeth and claws and pure chilling fear, but they would never be able to match the Children's ferocity.

She cringed when she saw the Children—her Children—going through the hunting party and slaughtering the last injured survivors. The Children showed no mercy. They didn't let even a single cat walk away.

She would have liked to tell her Children to show a little compassion for the cats, but that would never work.

For one thing, the Children had grown beyond listening to a word she said. Adrian would conduct this campaign his own way. The slightest word from her would only turn the Children against her.

In a way, he was right about all of this. The cats only understood an enemy that was stronger than themselves. They lorded it over their human helpers and subsidiaries. The cats had hunted slags in the jungle whenever it suited them to do so.

Even after more than a year of repeated defeat at the Children's hands, the cats still hadn't learned their lesson. They would never stop hunting Children until the Children delivered a telling defeat that broke the cats' dominance once and for all.

Maybe, when too many hunting parties didn't come back alive, the Pride would finally wake up to the fact that this planet had evolved a species stronger than the cats. The cats would have to face up to the harsh reality that they weren't the dominant predators on this planet anymore.

Dina summoned all her resolve not to say a word when the Children climbed back up to the ridge. They left all the dead cats lying where they'd fallen. Any cats that came out looking for their friends would find the bodies torn to shreds and rotting in the open.

Adrian panted, "Let's go," when he rejoined Dina and she fell in line with the rest of the group.

They continued on their journey as though nothing had happened, but Riggs and a few others kept breaking off, taking to the treetops, and ranging over the countryside before they came back to deliver their reports to Adrian.

Chapter 21

A drian halted under the trees five miles from Riverbend canton. "We'll stop here and wait for the Brookhollow Children to come out to meet us. You can make your way home from here, Dina. No one will bother you, but we won't go any closer."

"Are you sure you don't want to come home and see Link and Troy?" Dina glanced around at Leroy, Devon, Franco, and their sisters. "I'm sure your dad would love to see you."

"No, we won't go back to Riverbend," Adrian replied. "You can tell either of them that they're welcome to come out and visit us if they want to. We'll stay here for a few days, so they won't have any problem finding us. Tell them both they'd be welcome, but you can understand why we don't want to go back to the canton."

"Yeah, I can understand." Dina shifted her weight. She wanted to hug her Children and make a fuss over them, but some unbridgeable divide stopped her from doing it.

They didn't need that affection from her anymore. They got it from each other now. She would only drive a wedge between herself and them if she tried.

"I guess I'll.....see you soon," she mumbled.

"Travel safely, Dina," Amir told her.

"Come back and visit us soon," Naia added.

She smiled at them all. "I will. It's so wonderful to see how well you're all doing. I'm proud of you all and I know Link is proud of you, too. I won't tell you to be safe because I know you won't be. Just....you're all going to do well for yourselves. I know it."

She cast one last glowing smile around the group and they all looked back at her. Her heart overflowed with pride for all of them, especially Adrian, but she didn't tell him that. He didn't need to hear that from his mother.

She started to turn away when Iona called out, "Dina!"

Dina turned around. Iona came toward her.

Iona had grown up, too. She wasn't as tall as Karim, but she was taller than Dina now. Iona's body had developed into a curvy, muscular, statuesque picture of glowing health and strength.

She radiated all of Adrian's charisma in a purely feminine way. She was intoxicatingly attractive and as wild and untamed as all the other Children.

She stopped in front of Dina and Dina suffered another dizzying wave of disorientation. This was her daughter—the little girl Dina had spoken to in the forest. Iona was a woman now—a magnificent woman with a husband as powerful and determined as herself.

Without warning, Iona put her arms around Dina and hugged her. That hug only lasted a minute, but it meant the world.

Iona leaned back and smiled down into Dina's eyes. "Bye," Iona murmured.

"Bye, sweetheart," Dina choked and tore herself away. She didn't look back as she made her way back to Riverbend canton.

She knew this part of the country. She could find her way to the Children's camp if she needed to, but she didn't want to be around when the Brookhollow Children showed up for their meeting with Adrian.

The alarm and tension of the last two days caught up with her on the walk back to the canton. She'd held herself together while she was with the Children.

Getting upset or acting shocked by their behavior obviously offended them, especially Adrian. She buried it around them.

Now it all came to the surface with a vengeance. How could she explain this to....well, anybody?

She spotted Troy the minute she got near the gate, but he was over by his own house. He didn't see her until she'd already entered and veered toward her own house.

Link sat on the steps in the sun sharpening one of his hunting knives. He looked up and his expression changed when he saw her. "Where have you been? You were gone when I got back yesterday. I thought something must have happened to you."

She waved her hand at nothing, but that didn't help her put everything she'd seen into words. "I.....uh....I went out to see the Children."

"Are they here?" He glanced toward the gate. "Where are they?"

"They're out there." She waved toward the gate.

He stood up. "Good. You can show me where they are. I want to see them."

"Wait." She stepped in front of him. "They're......"

He waited for her to say something. "They're what? Are they okay?"

"They're fine. They're just.....different."

"What do you mean?"

"Well.....for a start......they're married."

His eyes popped wide open. "They're what?"

Dina scrambled for some way to explain all this, but before she could do that, Troy came over. "Did you find the Children, Dina?"

"Yeah, I found them," she mumbled.

"What are they doing?"

She shuffled her feet. "You know.....fighting cats......"

"You mean like they were before?"

Dina heaved an almighty sigh. Why sugar-coat it? "No. Not like they were before. They're hunting cats in about as different a way from before as you can possibly imagine."

"What do you mean?" Link asked.

"They're.....the Children are hunting down Prideland hunting parties......and annihilating them."

Both men gaped at her in mute shock. She knew they would react like this.

"Are you saying.....?" Troy began, but just then, another group of parents showed up.

Half of them belonged to the Council. The other half had been hostile to the Children from the beginning.

"You went out into the jungle to see the Children again, didn't you, Dina?" Salman demanded.

"Yes, I did," she grumbled. "The last time I checked, there was no law against me moving about the countryside to visit my Children."

"Are they nearby?" Meredith demanded.

Dina's patience stretched to the breaking point and threatened to snap. "Where they are is none of your business. You might have your head so far up in the clouds that you actually think you have the authority to stop someone from entering this canton, but you don't have the right to dictate where the Children go or where they're allowed to be."

"If they're near enough to our canton to put us in danger, then we have a right to know," Fitch interjected.

"Well, you're in luck because I won't tell you where they are." Dina turned her back on them. "So you can all go back to your business because you'll never interfere with the Children again."

"What are they doing out there?" Nicholas asked. "My Children are out there, too. I'm worried about them."

"You don't have to worry about the Children," Dina told him. "The Children are just fine."

"At least tell me what they're doing. Are they still hunting cats?"

She squirmed. "In a manner of speaking."

"Do the Children have a permanent base somewhere?" Paul Frasier asked.

Dina hesitated and then said, "Yes." These parents couldn't possibly do anything with that.

"How are they defending themselves if they aren't hunting cats?" Salman asked.

"She said they *are* hunting cats," Nicholas reminded him.

"You might as well just tell them the truth," Link chimed in. "Get it all out in the open. Heaven knows the Children don't need you protecting them."

Dina glanced over at him. He hadn't moved from the step.

If she trusted anyone here to advise her on how to deal with these people, she trusted Link.

She took a deep breath and faced the other parents. "All right. I'll tell you everything except where their permanent base is. The Children are hunting Prideland hunting parties, wiping out the cats, and leaving none alive. Adrian is using scouts to gather intelligence on all these hunting parties, where they're going, which cantons the cats are approaching, and then laying ambushes for them. The Children's plan is to send a message to the Pride that hunting and killing Children is a losing proposition......and since you really want to know, the Children are camped about five miles from here. They're meeting representatives from Brookhollow canton so they can all coordinate their efforts into a unified fighting force and accomplish more. They're already working together and Adrian is sending out his messengers to warn the other cantons when hunting parties get too close. Then he's giving orders about when the other Children should attack, where they should attack, and how." She hesitated and then blurted out, "And the Children have established an advanced social structure amongst themselves. Most of them are married to each other."

Dead silence fell over the group. Dina cringed when she saw all the parents' shocked expressions. They really were not expecting any of that at all.

Link broke the tension by chuckling under his breath. "Good for them. I'm proud of them."

"So....." Troy stammered. "They're within walking distance of here. That's good. I want to see my kids."

"I wouldn't do that if I was you," Dina interrupted. "They won't be happy if you show up in the middle of their negotiation. Wait a few days until it's over. Adrian said they would stick around that long in case you or Link wanted to go out and visit them."

"But not the rest of us?!" Fitch snapped. "Link and Troy are welcome to visit their Children but we aren't?! That's outrageous."

Dina groaned. "How many times did I warn you that this would happen? You all voted that the Children should be banned from entering the canton at all. What did you think was going to happen? You made it clear that you didn't want to see them as long as they were arming to fight back. Now they don't want to see you, either. Get used to it."

"That's easy for you to say when you've just seen your own Children," Meredith countered. "Tell us where they are. We're going out there to see them."

Dina hesitated. She could easily avert this disaster by keeping the information to herself. Then again, like Link said, the Children didn't need her to protect them—from anything.

She pointed toward the south. "They're in a clearing between the draw and that big stand of rocks west of the underground channel in the river's southern fork."

Meredith instantly turned to Fitch. "It's too late to go out there now. We'll leave first thing in the morning. If we have to, we'll bring all the Children back to the canton. We'll make sure they don't go out again."

"That won't work," Dina told them, but no one listened.

The parents started talking fast and shooting ideas back and forth.

"There must be some incentive we can offer the Children to get them to come back," Salman suggested.

"We could offer them seats on the Council," Richard Shriver chimed in. "Maybe they just want more of a voice in community decisions."

"We'll have to make accommodation for their......their partners," Fitch put an extra emphasis on the last word. He couldn't even say the words to acknowledge that the Children had spouses instead of partners.

Dina stared at them all coming up with every wild idea in the book to win the Children over. Were these parents completely out of their minds?

It never once entered their heads to give the Children the one thing they really needed—the one thing they already had—their freedom.

A lot of different things came to her to convince these people to just let the Children live their lives, but she discarded each of those suggestions. The parents wouldn't listen to her. She'd already tried too many times.

Meredith, Nicholas, Fitch, Salman, Richard, Paul, and Lucy Callaghan went off together to make their plans to go out in the morning to bring the Children in.

A minute later, Troy walked off by himself.

Dina didn't want to be around when the parents and Children met up again, especially not under these circumstances.

She got a shock when Link stood up, dusted off his hands, and said, "The sun will be going down soon. We'll wait for dark and then go out to find the Children."

"Are you nuts?" she countered. "You can't go out there now!"

"We have to warn them that the parents plan to come out and make a stink. If the Brookhollow Children are there and Adrian is negotiating with them to fight the cats, then he'll need us to warn him that these people plan to roll up on him and disrupt the negotiation. We can't let the parents spring this on him." He climbed three steps to enter the house and stopped. "Are you coming or not?"

She heaved another massive sigh and mounted the steps. "I guess so."

Chapter 22

"This is so fantastic!" Link breathed on the way south toward the Children's camp. "If you're right about what the Children are doing, it could be the greatest thing that has ever happened to Prideland."

"I am right about what they're doing," Dina replied. "They had two hunts when I was there—one yesterday and one today. They both ended with all the cats getting wiped out and the Children walking away scott free."

He chuckled under his breath. "That is so great! It's better than I ever could have imagined. I wish I could see it!"

"I'm sure they would love it if you did," she murmured. "Adrian took all your ideas about thinking strategically and exploiting the cats' weaknesses. He's combined them all into a completely unique fighting style. The Children can take on large groups of cats—groups that outnumber the Children—and the Children still put them down."

He stopped walking to stare at her in the dark. Then he shook his head and kept walking. "He's a military genius. He's better than I ever dared to hope."

"I'm pretty sure he knows it, too."

"What did you mean when you said they're married?"

"You'll see," she muttered.

He didn't ask any more questions. They made their way through the dark jungle using only the moon to light their way.

They traveled down the river, but when they got nearer, they didn't need any light to find the Children's camp.

The noise of dozens of voices and the flicker of firelight guided Link and Dina to the Children's camp. They'd built three huge bonfires and a bunch of strange Children crowded around.

All the Children talked and socialized with each other. They didn't appear to be in the middle of a sensitive military or political negotiation, but maybe this was how the Children negotiated.

One of the strange Children noticed Link and Dina first. He was a tall, muscular man with grey-brown tortoise-shell fur.

He sprang away from them with a fearful snarl. "What are they doing here?! Go back to your canton where you belong!!"

Adrian stepped between them. "Wait a minute." He turned back to Link and Dina. "What are you doing here, Link? You shouldn't have come—not tonight. I thought Dina would have explained to you that we were meeting our friends from Brookhollow."

"She told me," Link replied. "Some of the parents from Riverbend want to come out here and confront you tomorrow. I had to warn you. That's the only reason we came tonight." He glanced at the strangers standing behind Adrian. "I'm sorry we had to interrupt. We wouldn't have done it unless it was absolutely necessary."

"What do the parents want now?" Leroy snarled.

"They want the same things they've always wanted—which is to stop you from doing everything you're doing," Dina replied. "And your father isn't involved, Leroy. He still supports you. I'm certain of it."

"He better," Leroy growled.

"We'll leave now," Link told Adrian. "I just wanted you to know so you could prepare. The parents don't plan to leave the canton until morning. You can finish your negotiation tonight and your friends can return to Brookhollow before the parents show up." He took hold of Dina's elbow. "Come on, Dina. We can make it back to the canton before morning and no one has to know we were here."

"Wait, Link!" Adrian interjected. "Don't go yet. Stay here. Spend the night with us. We haven't seen you in months."

Link glanced over at the Brookhollow Children again. "Are you sure? I don't want to intrude."

"You won't be intruding," Riggs told him. "We already finished the negotiation. We were just hanging out."

Adrian turned to the Brookhollow Children. "These are my parents. They've support-ed our campaign from the beginning. We wouldn't be where we are now without them. Help us welcome them. It will be all right. They can help us. They're our allies. I swear it."

The tall man who'd first noticed Link and Dina curled his upper lip at them. "I do not associate with humans."

"You might have to if it comes to open war against the cats," Adrian told him. "We can't afford to turn away anyone who wants to help us. There are good people in Prideland—people who want to defeat the cats as much as we do. Stay. Don't leave. Tonight has gone so well. Don't let this spoil what could have been a perfect evening."

The man from Brookhollow growled at Link and Dina again, turned his back on them, and shoved his way through the crowd toward the back where he wouldn't see them again.

Adrian burst into a grin and grabbed Link's arm. "Come sit down. I want to talk to you about everything."

He led Link to one of the bonfires and pulled Link down onto the ground. Adrian sat down next to him and Dina took a seat on Link's other side.

Adrian launched into a detailed and elaborate explanation of all his scouting teams, his attack parties going after Prideland cats tracking down the Children, and all the different groups of Children Adrian had organized from a dozen different cantons.

"The Pride just keeps sending out more and more hunting parties," Adrian finished. "I don't know what you think, but it looks to me like we need to escalate to the next level."

"What is that?" Link asked. "What is the next level?"

"Taking the fight to them, of course," Adrian replied. "The next level means not waiting for them to send parties into the jungle. We would go into Prideland and engage them head-on in open warfare."

"That's a big step," Link remarked. "You would need a lot of power to accomplish that."

"By power, do you mean weapons?" Adrian asked. "We don't have artillery we can use to bombard their cities the way you bombarded us at the canton."

"No, you can't do that. There are too many civilians living in the cities. Bombarding them would wipe out millions of people. There has to be a better way."

"What would you do?" Adrian asked. "How would you do it if you were in my situation?"

Dina remained silent through this conversation. She tried not to resent that Adrian was asking Link's opinion on military matters. Adrian would never ask her about any of this.

Link stared into the flames while he thought it over. Before he could answer, Naia came over with a platter of chopped meat and started skewering and roasting it for Link and Dina the way she did before.

She distracted both Link and Adrian. Adrian took some of the raw meat off her plate, ate it, and got another wicked grin from her.

Adrian waited for Naia to serve both Link and Dina before he brought up the subject again. "What were you about to say about how to attack the cats without hurting any of the civilians?"

"It seems like you're heading that way now with this campaign of yours."

"What do you mean?" Adrian asked.

"If you keep going the way you are, the Pride will send out bigger and bigger parties to come after you. All you would have to do is go out to meet them between the jungle and the cities. The cats will leave their human helpers behind and come after you themselves. Then you don't have to worry about it. You can kill as many cats as you please. If it's open warfare you want, you're bound to get it. All you have to do is keep defying them. They'll do anything to stop you from doing that."

"And you....." Adrian glanced back and forth between Link and Dina. "You think that's what I should do? You think I should go for open warfare?"

Link shrugged. "You know the situation better than I do. What possible advantage can you gain by avoiding it?"

Now it was Adrian's turn to stare into the flames. "It's like you said. Maybe we don't have the power to accomplish it."

"I find that hard to believe," Dina interjected for the first time. "You said you had five hundred Children at your camp. You must have thousands more all over the planet at different cantons. If war breaks out, all of them will fight the cats. The cats won't let them NOT fight."

Link spun around. "That many?!" He turned the other way to stare at Adrian. "You have that many?"

"Only at our camp," Adrian replied. "Most of the other Children stay at or near their home cantons. Only those that can't go home come to us."

Link gulped visibly. "How many do you think you could call up if you needed to? How many total?"

Adrian shifted in his seat. "I don't know. Maybe five thousand if I really had to."

Link's jaw dropped. Dina stared at Adrian in flabbergasted shock.

"Do you think that's enough?" Adrian asked. "That's the only reason I would hold off—because we didn't have enough Children to take on all the cats at once."

Link picked his jaw up off the ground and bent over the meat that Naia had given him. "I'd say it's enough."

"Then.....you think I should do it?" Adrian asked again. "You think I should go on the offensive—like all-out war? It seems like.....I don't know.....It seems like a step too far."

"I'd say you're already in a war, pal," Link croaked. "The only question is how it's going to end. It can only end one of two ways. Either you win or the cats win. That's all you really need to think about."

Adrian's expression hardened and he turned aside to stare into the flames. "You're right. That makes it pretty clear what I have to do, doesn't it?"

"Anything you need us to do, you only have to ask," Link told him. "We'll do anything to help you. I don't know what we *can* do that you can't do for yourselves, but if there is anything, we're prepared to support you in any way we can."

Adrian looked up and smiled. "Thank you for coming out. I really needed to talk to you."

"Of course." Link squeezed Adrian's shoulder. "I'm proud of you. You're doing something great out here. You're becoming the leader you were born to be. You're becoming everything I saw in you when you first asked me to train you."

Adrian lowered his eyes and half-whispered, "Thanks."

Link put his arm down. "So what's the first job?"

"The first job is communicating my intention to the other cantons," Adrian replied. "The Children in the other cantons, I mean."

Link smirked at him. "I got that."

"Do you remember when you told me about getting humans to fight the cats, too?" Adrian asked. "Did you mean it?"

"Of course!" Link countered. "Look at me and Dina—and Troy. We would fight for you if we thought it would do any good. You Children are so much better at fighting the cats than we are."

"I didn't mean fighting the cats. I meant fighting the helpers."

Link opened his mouth to argue, but no sound came out. He blinked once and then his shoulders slumped. "I didn't think of that."

"You said it, not me," Adrian reminded him. "You were the one who said the Pride would recruit the helpers to fight us if it came to that."

"You're right. I did say that."

"It doesn't make sense for us to fight the helpers," Adrian went on. "They'd be defenseless against us. We would need people to fight them."

"I doubt you could recruit enough human beings to fight all the helpers the Pride would bring out against you," Dina interjected. "The Pride could send out a million helpers."

"Not everyone thinks the way the parents at Riverbend canton think," Link told her. "You said that, when you talked to Frank about evacuating the planet, everyone at all the different cantons wanted to leave."

"They said they wanted to leave. They didn't say they wanted to fight the cats."

He shrugged that away. "I bet we could recruit a few."

"A few isn't enough," Adrian told him. "We would need to match their numbers."

"Why are you opposed to fighting helpers?" Link asked. "If they come out against you with weapons, you have to defend yourselves. Them being humans doesn't mean they aren't your enemies."

"It hardly seems fair," Adrian returned. "It hardly seems honorable. It's pathetic."

Link snorted with laughter. "There is no honor in war, my boy. You win or you don't. The helpers are your enemies and they can kill you just as easily with a weapon as you can kill them with your teeth. Kill them and be satisfied that you're upholding your honor by defending your own people."

Adrian looked away. "If you say so."

"So you want me and Dina to go out and kill the helpers for you?" Link asked. "Is that it?"

Adrian looked up and his eyes brightened. "Would you?"

"Of course!" Link exclaimed. "Show me the helpers and I'll kill them all for you."

Adrian split in a grin. "Great! Thanks."

Link chuckled again and put another piece of meat in his mouth. "This is delicious. You got yourself a keeper there."

Naia giggled. "Don't get used to it, Link. I'm not here to put Dina out of a job."

Link beamed at her and then at Adrian. "I'm happy for you. You deserve each other."

"Thanks," Adrian murmured.

Link glanced around the circle and noticed for the first time, now that he wasn't talking to Adrian anymore, what all the other Children were doing.

They'd all paired off the way they did the previous night. They lounged with each other, embraced each other, and curled up with each other in the same couples.

Link's eyes darted from one pair to another. He couldn't fail to see his own Children—his nieces and nephews that he'd raised from birth—coupled up with the Children they'd grown up with all their lives.

Riyadh had paired up with Nova, Naia's sister. Riyadh and Nova posed a stark contrast to each other because he was so tall, blocky, and muscular and she was so tiny and dainty.

Israel had gotten together with Troy's daughter Sasha and Cairo had gotten together with Amber.

Link's niece Egypt had gotten together with Rome. They were about the same size except that he was so much burlier and more powerfully built. Link's other niece India had gotten together with Brock.

Dina looked down at her plate so she wouldn't see Karim and Iona kissing across the circle. Dina would probably never get used to that.

The silence stretched out longer and longer. No one picked up the conversation again.

The fire cracked and Naia leaned against Adrian's side. He put his arms around her shoulders and she slipped hers around his waist.

Dina didn't want to think about how far it would have gone right in front of her, but after a few minutes, one of the Brookhollow men came over and asked Adrian to follow him so he could show Adrian something.

Adrian got up and left. Naia started cleaning up all the gear she'd used to cook Link's and Dina's food. Naia took Link's and Dina's empty plates, disappeared into the darkness, and left Link and Dina sitting there alone.

Dina sighed. She was getting tired and this camp didn't have any houses for her and Link to sleep in. It looked like they would be bedding down right here by the fire with the Children.

Without warning, Link slipped his hand into her lap and threaded his fingers into hers. "Stay here with me," he murmured.

Her head shot up. "What?!"

"Stay here with me—with the Children. We don't have to go back to the canton. We have nothing to stay there for. We could join the Children's war and help them. What else do we have to do? We only stayed at Riverbend so we could be there for the Children. We don't have to go back. We could stay out here."

"Here?" She glanced around the dark jungle.

"You know what I mean," he whispered. "You said you left the *Savannah* the second time so you could free these people from the cats' rule. What better way is there than this?"

"I wasn't thinking *this* when I left the *Savannah,*" she countered.

"You must have been thinking something like it. You might have been thinking about getting the helpers and subsidiaries to rebel or something like that, but it would be something like this."

She didn't answer. She didn't remember what she'd been thinking when she left the *Savannah* or even if she'd been thinking anything at all. All of that seemed so far in the past that it didn't matter anymore.

"What do we have to go back to the canton for?" he persisted. "We have nothing there but a bunch of people who already hate us and blame us for protecting them. Why should we go back?"

"Because it's our home," she suggested. "Because it's the only home I've had since I left Prideland. If we stayed here—with the Children, I mean—"

She broke off when Adrian returned. He sat down next to Link again. "You two should stay with us. You don't have to go back to the canton. We would love to have you. You're both good at fighting cats and we need people like that. We'd be grateful for all the help you can give us."

"We would love it if you had us," Link replied. "We were just talking about that."

"Perfect," Adrian exclaimed.

Naia came back just then and sat down next to him. He put his arm around her and Dina looked away again so she wouldn't see what they were doing.

Link brought her back to reality by squeezing her hand again. She looked up into his eyes and recognized the glow of light in their brown depths. He was thinking about *that* again.

Staying here with the Children meant not going west and starting over, not going somewhere safe from cats, and not having children of their own.

Staying with the Children meant the opposite of all of that. It meant diving straight back into the mouth of the beast—literally.

It meant going back to Prideland and fighting cats again—or close enough to Prideland to fight cats. It meant seeking out cats to fight and then fighting them.

Dina winced at the thought. Why? Why did she pull the wool over her own eyes and let herself think she would never have to fight cats again? Leaving Prideland didn't give her a pass never to fight cats again.

The Children were the ones who made it possible for her to avoid fighting cats all this time. She couldn't avoid it forever.

What was her life worth, anyway? What was her life good for if she didn't help the one group who might actually be able to break the cats' tyranny over this planet?

The helpers and subsidiaries wouldn't be able to do it. Their attachment to the cats and to the status quo stopped them even from thinking about it.

No one but the Children would ever be able to change anything on this planet. The Children wouldn't be able to do it without Adrian's leadership. He was the one who would change things on this planet if they could possibly be changed.

What kind of mother would she be if she didn't help them? She would be no better than the parents at Riverbend canton or the parents at Moonlight canton who drove their Children away.

She couldn't do that. She couldn't let her own Children go into danger and death without doing something, no matter how small.

She still hesitated, though. Going back into any fight against the cats was the absolute last thing in the world she wanted to do.

Her every instinct told her to run far, far away—anywhere she could avoid even seeing a cat, much less getting into a fight against one. Even fighting a small house cat scared her half to death.

She couldn't let the Children down, though. They'd grown up listening to her stories about fighting cats. Maybe the other parents were right about her being responsible for the Children's warlike ways.

She couldn't let Link down, either. She felt the same way about him. She couldn't let him get involved in this war without doing something to help him. She couldn't say she cared about him if she let him face that danger without her support.

Chapter 23

D ina sat up and did her best to stretch the kinks out of her body. That was the second night she'd slept on the hard ground. She'd grown soft sleeping in a bed for the last three years.

Grey dawn light streamed through the jungle canopy overhead. The bonfires had all died and the Children didn't relight them.

Half the Children were already walking around doing different jobs. Adrian stood off to one side talking rapidly with three burly men from Brookhollow. They didn't look as angry this morning.

Link was still asleep, but the noise of Children moving around woke him up. He and Dina both stood up, but there were no blankets to fold or any other equipment to organize. They'd left Riverbend canton with nothing but the clothes on their backs.

Dina shrugged that away. What did she really have to go back for, anyway? Everyone she cared about was already here in this camp.

Adrian waved his three friends forward and they approached Link. The Brookhollow Children glared at Link and Dina, but the men didn't act as hostile as they did last night.

"I'm sending my scouts to three other cantons to gather our forces here," Adrian told Link. "We'll assess the country between here and the city to find our most favorable ground for engaging the cats on a large scale. Could you come with us and give us your opinion?"

"Of course—if you want me to," Link replied. "You know the country better than I do. You'll have to explain it to me."

Adrian waved to one of the nearby Children—a younger boy of two years with bright red fur and black spots. He'd been at the Children's camp in the gorge and traveled with the group to this rendezvous with the Brookhollow Children.

He opened his bundle and pulled out all the maps Adrian had been working on at the gorge camp. The boy handed them to Adrian and Adrian rolled them out on the ground.

He traced the landscape with his forefinger. "The Crooked Fork is the cats' favorite way of penetrating into the jungle. They come up the river valley and then spread out following the river's branches north, south, and west. We've used bottlenecks here, here, and here, but I don't see the cats bringing in a large force from there. They'd be more likely to come through this pass here. The country is gentler there and the jungle isn't as thick on both sides of the pass. We could engage them there and attack them at the pass."

"You won't be able to count on them using either of those approaches," Link pointed out. "You'll need to wait and see which approach they use before you decide on your ground."

Adrian nodded. "I know. I'm just trying to explain what their approaches have been in the past and what they might use again. The pass is the only place they could get a large force of cats into the jungle. They would have to travel single file if they used any other approach. That would make them too vulnerable. They won't do that—or if they do, then we wouldn't have to worry about our ground because they would be sitting ducks."

Link shrugged. "Good point."

"The other problem is how we're going to choose our ground once we start attacking them in the open."

Adrian pushed aside the map of the jungle and switched it to a map of Prideland itself. It showed the city in the distance, several of its surrounding villages, and the roads crisscrossing the country in all directions.

"If the cats send out a force as large as we expect, they'll have to use the roads," Adrian began. "We would need to take advantage of any ditches, rivers, or other features of the landscape to flank them and maybe get behind them."

"Interesting idea," Link replied and pointed toward the city. "It would be interesting if you got a body of your people hidden here and here on either side of the city. Then, when the cats send out their numbers to attack you, you engage them on the road.....here. You tie them up in battle and then bring in your second force from behind them."

Adrian nodded. "I like that, but it means positioning our people there before the battle starts. It would mean we would need some advanced warning of when the cats plan to come out against us."

"If you chose the right location, you could keep your people camped there." Link pointed to the map. "This road has trees on either side close to the city. You could hide your people there now—or maybe not now, but closer to the time when you expect the cats to send their numbers out."

Adrian frowned. "I still don't know when that will be."

Link stood up. "The cats aren't ready to send out an attack force that big right now anyway, so you have some time to think about it and plan it."

"You're right and we have more important things to deal with today." Adrian rolled up his maps and handed them back to the boy who'd been carrying them.

The boy stood there watching and listening to Adrian's and Link's conversation. The Brookhollow Children listened, too. They didn't interrupt.

"There are three more hunting parties still at large in the jungle right now," Adrian went on. "We've been waiting for them to move in on one of the cantons or one of our camps, but since we're doing this, we might as well eliminate them now." He turned to the Brookhollow men. "You can tell Ivan to eliminate that hunting party that's been hanging around your canton."

The largest man from Brookhollow nodded. "I sent my scout last night after our conversation. The hunting party should be gone by now."

Adrian turned back to Link. "I sent word last night to three different cantons. They'll be sending us five hundred fighters each. That should get us started with any force the Pride sends out against us."

Link didn't answer. Dina listened in silence. This really was turning into a war—a war as big and destructive as it could possibly be.

She didn't worry about the danger so much when she heard Adrian talking like this.

She highly doubted if the Pride expected the Children to gather a force of one thousand five hundred fighters.

She would have bet any amount of money that the Pride wasn't expecting the Children to be as organized as this or to be planning to wage open warfare against the cats.

The cats still thought of this as a glorified hunt like the way they usually hunted slags. The cats had no clue what they were in for.

She and Link stood back out of the way while Adrian finished negotiating with the Brookhollow men.

"Gather your people over there and get them ready to go out," he told them. "We'll leave as soon as my scouts come in and tell us where the hunting party is."

Then he went through the camp and gave orders to his own people.

"We'll pull back from Riverbend, now that Link and Dina are with us," Adrian decided. "We don't need to stay here. We can set up in more favorable locations closer to the roads leading into Prideland. That will give us easier access to information and a better position to launch any offensive."

He sent different people off in different directions doing different jobs. The rest packed up their bundles getting ready to move out.

They all assembled around the firepits. The Brookhollow Children gathered together at one side. It looked like they would travel with Adrian's group—wherever it was they were going.

Adrian came back. "Our scouts should be coming in any minute. Then we can go."

One of the youngsters from the gorge camp approached him from his other side and started giving Adrian a report on another group of Children coming to meet him from the south.

They were in the middle of their conversation when Adrian spun around to scowl into the trees behind him.

The boy he'd been talking to broke off. "Um.....do you want me to give you my report?"

"Shh!" Adrian hissed. "They're coming!"

"Who?" Link asked.

"The parents. They're coming out from Riverbend."

He turned to face north and the other Children stiffened. Dina didn't hear anything at first, but after five minutes of dead silence, she started to hear footsteps.

Another five minutes of silence passed before the parents appeared. Thirty people from Riverbend canton approached through the trees. Troy was with them as were a dozen people who hadn't been involved in any of the previous conflicts between Children and their parents.

"Whatever you came out here to do or say, you can turn around and go straight back where you came from," Adrian snapped as soon as the parents showed up. "We aren't here to take direction from you. Whatever it is you want, we aren't interested."

Richard opened his mouth to answer, but Troy interrupted by stepping out of line and walking right up to Adrian. "We're with you, Adrian. We want to join you."

"You what?!" Nicholas, Meredith, Fitch, and Paul spun around to gape at Troy. "No, we don't!"

"You don't, but we do," Troy replied over his shoulder and turned back to face Adrian. "Let us come with you. We won't let you down. We want to fight back."

"Who's we?" Adrian asked. "You're the only one here."

Troy waved behind him. Half the Riverbend residents separated from the parents and crossed to stand with Link, Dina, and the other Children.

Troy swiveled backward, planted himself next to Dina, and faced the parents. Adrian watched the Riverbend residents come over to his side. They arranged themselves behind Link, Dina, Adrian, and Troy—right where everyone could see that these people were part of Adrian's force now.

Adrian waited until the shuffling stopped. Then he turned to face the parents, too. "What was that you were about to say?"

The parents stared at him in shock—and then at their friends and neighbors who'd just changed sides in view of everyone.

Adrian waited for someone to say something. "We're going out to war against the cats, so if you want to fall back to somewhere safe, you better do it now. If you aren't with us, you're in our way and I don't have time to stand around arguing with you."

Meredith pulled herself together. "This is unacceptable, Adrian. You can't continue to put us all in danger by harassing the cats and increasing their animosity toward us. They already want to kill us...."

"Actually, they already want to kill *us* and that's the one thing keeping you alive. Now, if you're done talking, we have things we need to....."

Just then, another commotion in the branches made everyone look up. Three younger Children hurtled out of the canopy, bounced off multiple branches, and landed in the middle of Adrian's group.

"They're coming!" a boy with black fur panted. "They're coming.....through the pass right now! A hundred of them—moving fast! They're coming right now!"

Adrian spun away and put the parents out of his mind. "Let's go." He pointed at some of the Children from the gorge camp. "Arm these people and let's move out. Get down to the pass and flank the channel coming up the western river branch. We'll corner them there once they get out of the fields." He craned his head back and yelled over the whole assembly. "Move out!!"

Dozens of Children shot off the ground and took to the treetops. They vanished in seconds and left the humans standing there in stunned shock.

Four of the gorge camp Children rushed over to Link, Dina, Troy, and the others. These Children tore open their bundles and shoved knives, axes, and other homemade weapons into everyone's hands.

The Children emptied their bundles in a rush, armed everyone, and then took off into the trees at high speed to catch up with Adrian's party.

"Let's go," Link told everyone. "We have to move fast if we want to keep up with the Children. Come on."

He broke into a run. Dina, Troy, and the other Riverbend residents followed him. They had to run fast just to keep the Children in sight.

They left the parents standing there with their mouths open, but Dina couldn't think about them anymore.

The Children had given her an axe and a knife. That would have to be enough to fight any cats she came across.

She should have spent the last three years keeping herself strong and fit. She realized her mistake now. She gasped for air long before she and Link caught up with the Children.

Chapter 24

Adrian had selected another narrow ravine to corner the incoming cats. The Brookhollow Children gathered in the canopy on one side of the steep defile while Adrian's party took the other side.

He dropped down onto the ground in front of Link when he and Dina struggled over the mountain and then climbed down the draw at the head of the ravine.

"Stay here," Adrian ordered and pointed to a cluster of trees where the ravine curved eastward. "Confront the cats head on when they come around that corner. They won't be expecting to meet people up here—not people who want to fight them. The cats will slow down as they approach you and we'll attack from the treetops. Understand?"

Link nodded. "You got it. We'll handle our end."

Adrian didn't answer. He blasted off the ground into the canopy and disappeared. Dina couldn't see a single Child up there. They all hid themselves. No one would ever know they were there.

Link turned around and examined everyone in their party. They were all armed and obviously as tense and breathless as Dina. "Is everybody ready?" Link asked.

Dina nodded and so did everyone else. She couldn't tear her eyes away from the trees where Adrian said the cats would come.

This little group of people standing behind her right now—they all seemed so helpless and pathetic compared to what they were about to do. Fifteen people against a hundred cats didn't stand a chance.

Her heart pounded out of her chest and cold sweat broke out on her palms. She was about to fight cats again and she didn't have to wonder which cats they would be.

The Pride wouldn't send house cats or even any Manx to attack the Children. These would be lions, tigers, jaguars, panthers, and pumas. The Pride wouldn't send anything smaller than that.

What if the Children couldn't take a force of cats this big? What if the cats won and killed all the Children?

She didn't have time even to worry about that before the first cats streaked around the corner. They ran as fast as Adrian's scout said.

A big male lion led the pack. Dina thought she recognized him from her time at Hellion House, but she couldn't be sure.

Another forty cats swerved around the corner right behind him before they saw the people blocking their path. Whispers raced through the group of Riverbend residents behind Dina's back.

"That's Kaido Hellion!" one of the women whispered. "He's the patriarch of Hellion House since old Lord Hellion died."

The lion slowed down and all those with him slowed to match his pace. They didn't stop entirely. They just dropped to a walk coming closer to Dina's position.

Her heart stopped. She couldn't breathe as they got nearer. How long would Adrian wait before he attacked?

More and more cats advanced around the corner. They were all running just as fast. They had to crowd together not to trample those in front.

All the cats made sure to stay behind that one big lion. He was fully mature with a thick mane, but he couldn't have been that old. He had a fresh, unsullied appearance like he hadn't been in too many fights in his life.

He definitely didn't have the grizzled, battered look of an older lion and he held himself upright with plenty of authority.

"What are you doing here?" he demanded when he confronted Link's and Dina's group. His eyes dipped to their clothes. "You're slags. You should be in the cantons. You're lucky we're in a hurry or we would reduce you here and now."

Link stepped forward and hefted the axe in his hands. "You aren't going any further. You're stopping here."

"Is that so?" the lion growled. "How will you stop all of us?"

The lion inclined his head slightly to one side to indicate all the cats behind him. Dina couldn't see the back of their group. A third of the cats present still stood behind the corner.

A carpet of feline bodies packed the ravine from one wall to the other. All those cats eyed these people with that predatory intent that made Dina's hair stand on end. The cats were preparing to attack. They were only waiting for the lion to make the first move.

"Stand aside," he rumbled again. "This is your last warning."

"What are you going to do to make us stand aside?" Link countered. "Whatever you're going to do, do it now. We don't have all day."

The lion chuckled. "You're a fool."

"And you're a coward," Link returned. "Are you afraid to attack us? Are you afraid your friends back in Prideland will find out that a handful of slags killed you all in the jungle? That would be a story worth telling. I would love to hear how the helpers whisper when they hear that the great Kaido Hellion went out to hunt Children in the jungle and didn't come back. Come on! Take your best shot."

Kaido curled his lips back from his teeth and growled low, but he still didn't attack. He lowered his head between his shoulders. "You dare?!"

Link lunged forward and raised his axe. He brought it down in a vicious swipe, but Kaido sprang out of the way just in time.

The other cats shrank back and bumped into each other to put more distance between them and this lunatic human.

Dina took a step forward to help Link and that one movement triggered the assault she knew was coming. Kaido leapt off the ground and sailed toward Link to bring him down.

Kaido made it halfway there before Adrian dropped out of nowhere, knocked Kaido out of thin air, and smashed the lion down on the ground. All the other cats charged in for the attack.

A huge jaguar took a flying leap to attack Dina. She crouched and raised her axe to defend herself when another Child plummeted out of the canopy and slammed the jaguar down on the ground.

She took a fraction of a second to realize that the Child wrestling with the jaguar was the big man from Brookhollow—the one who'd reacted so badly to Link and Dina showing up at Adrian's camp.

She froze for a minute as more and more Children plunged out of the treetops and landed on the unsuspecting cats. The whole area erupted into a massive battle with cats and Children wrestling, tearing at each other, and snarling and growling in murderous fury.

The man from Brookhollow yanked the jaguar over to pin the cat down, but the jaguar overpowered the man in seconds. The jaguar mounted the man, threw his weight on top to pin the man down, and dove for his throat.

Dina reacted without thinking. This man saved her life. She couldn't let him die.

She sprinted over to him and hacked her axe down into the back of the jaguar's neck where it met the skull. The cat collapsed on top of the man and she had to drop her axe to seize the cat by the fur.

She hauled him off and pulled the man to his feet, but he didn't stick around long enough to thank her. He leapt away and landed on a panther who had pinned Dexter to the ground.

Dina spotted a tiger standing over Troy not far away. He lay flat on his back holding his axe handle in both hands while the tiger lunged for his face again and again.

Troy shoved the axe handle into the cat's mouth to deflect the tiger's teeth, but Troy couldn't get away.

Dina snatched her axe, ran over to them, and swung her axe in a brutal sweep that hacked the cat's head in half. It toppled and she dragged Troy off the ground. "Get up!" she panted. "Get up!"

She turned one way and he turned the other looking for any cat that might come after them.

What she saw instead were the Children raging through the ravine killing everyone and everything in sight. Adrian had wedged one of his arms under Kaido's chin and pried back the lion's head to expose his throat.

Kaido panicked and roared in fear and frustration. He struggled and kicked out with his hind legs, but Adrian avoided them again.

He pulled the same maneuver on Kaido that Adrian pulled on the tiger at Riverbend canton. He bowled Kaido onto his side, but Kaido's strength saved him.

Adrian dove for Kaido's throat, but Kaido overcame Adrian's grip and squirmed free. Adrian toppled one way and Kaido rolled the rest of the way to his feet.

Both adversaries whipped around and exploded off the ground to collide with each other again. Kaido let out a thunderous roar of savage, murderous rage, and in that moment, Adrian roared back just as loudly.

They both bared their fangs to tear each other apart and they slammed into each other in midair three feet off the ground. Kaido's strength and weight carried him farther and he smashed Adrian backward with unbelievable force.

Kaido didn't count on the Children's speed, agility, and pure tenacious fighting spirit. Adrian took advantage of Kaido's assault, grabbed hold of Kaido, and in a lightning move of mind-blowing brutality, he shoved one elbow into Kaido's neck and forced his chin up.

Kaido had been lunging for Adrian's throat, too. Kaido never saw Adrian's maneuver coming. In a fraction of a second, Adrian dove under his own arm and clamped his teeth in the vulnerable skin between Kaido's mane and his chest.

Kaido gave another ground-shaking roar—of fear this time, but he couldn't stop what was about to happen. His weight fell on top of Adrian and slammed Adrian down on his back.

Kaido panicked again and tried to wrench himself out of Adrian's grip. Adrian used Kaido's own strength against him, flung the lion sideways, and ripped his teeth out of Kaido's neck taking the jugular with him.

Kaido tried to roar again and choked on his own blood. He flipped onto his back, tried to get to his feet, and collapsed thrashing and spasming.

Adrian rolled upright with blood all over his face and running down his chin. He bared his fangs and his eyes flashed with deadly savagery as he looked around the ravine.

Dozens of Children smothered the cats in brutal attacks. Three women from River-bend canton whom Dina had always considered rather useless had cornered a large, muscular puma against a stand of trees.

He yowled and swiped his claws at them, but they closed around him from all sides so he couldn't get away. Only one of the women was armed with a knife. The three women had no other weapon between them, but they didn't back off.

The puma lunged for the woman on the far left and the woman on the far right rushed him, grabbed him with both arms around his neck, and brought him down. He screeched and struggled, but the other two women pounced on him just as fast.

The second woman added her efforts to the first. The first woman threw her weight on top of him and pinned his forelimbs.

The second woman tackled his hind legs and the third woman landed on the cat's head. She hooked her elbow under his chin, pried his head back, and slashed his throat before all three women sprang clear and left him bleeding to death.

Chapter 25

Adrian strode through the ravine surveying the dead cats. Two men from Brookhollow and one of the young Children from Adrian's gorge camp had also fallen in the battle.

He stopped and stared down at the three dead Children. "Take your dead home, tend to your wounded, and then meet me on the ridge west of the Crooked Fork tomorrow morning," he told the Brookhollow Children. "Bring as many fighters as you can muster."

The Brookhollow Children gathered the bodies of their dead and disappeared into the undergrowth without a word.

Adrian went down on one knee next to the boy from the gorge camp who'd lost his life. Adrian ran his hand down the side of the boy's furry face. "He has no family. He came to the gorge camp because he was alone. His own family threw him out because he wasn't human enough."

He straightened up, cast a hard glare around the group, and pointed out two of his own scouts. "Dutton and Enoch—take him home to the gorge camp, bury him, and then bring everyone we have up to the ridge west of the Crooked Fork tomorrow morning. Tell them it's time to stop playing games."

Adrian left the two boys to gather their young comrade and carry him away. Most of the other Children were bleeding and Troy had suffered some deep scratches and bites to his arms when he'd been trying to hold the tiger off.

Adrian nodded at the Riverbend residents who'd come out to join his campaign. "You all did very well. I'm proud to have you with us. Tomorrow will be harder, but we'll win in the end. I know it. Now we have some miles to cover. We'll camp on the ridge tonight. That will give us a perfect launching point for tomorrow's campaign."

Dina would have liked to ask what he had in mind for the next day, but no one else asked, so she didn't, either.

The Children stayed there over the bodies of their dead victims while Naia and some of the other Children put Vaga sap on everyone's wounds.

The tiger had slashed Troy's arm down the bicep and she ended up putting his arm in a sling. "Do you think you can fight again tomorrow?" Adrian asked him. "If not, we can send you back to the gorge."

"Like hell you will," Troy countered. "I didn't come out here to sit on the sidelines. I'm going with you. I can still fight."

"Good," Adrian replied. "Let's go. We can find you all some more weapons, now that we know our plans for tomorrow."

He didn't share his plans for tomorrow, and in a few minutes, the Children started to leave.

The Brookhollow Children didn't wait around. They took off through the branches heading in a different direction.

Most of Adrian's people did the same thing. They blasted into the canopy and evaporated into the jungle in seconds.

Adrian and a dozen other Riverbend Children walked in company with Link, Dina, Troy, and the other humans who'd joined them.

Dina was starting to understand how much these Children considered it a sign of respect to walk slowly along the ground, plodding over mountains and fording streams, to keep pace with these people.

The Children could have leapt through the branches and made it to their destination in a few minutes. Instead, they traveled with the human party and never left them alone.

It took the rest of the day to toil up another heavily forested mountainside to the ridge overlooking the Crooked Fork. The party didn't find the Children's camp until dark.

The group walked in on a scene of celebration unlike anything she'd ever witnessed. The Children had built five huge bonfires and hundreds of new Children gathered on the ridgetop.

Dina recognized a few Brookhollow Children who had been involved in this morning's assault.

All the rest were new to her. Some wore more human-style garments than others. Some wore no clothes at all.

Their clothes acted as a kind of uniform that identified their affiliation to different groups associated with different cantons, but all those Children came together in a deafening wall of noise as they shouted, cheered, laughed, and recounted today's exploits.

None of the Children showed any hostility to the humans joining their celebration. In fact, the big guy from Brookhollow whom Dina had helped during the battle came over to her, grinned at her, shook her hand, and then hugged her.

He yelled something into her ear, but she couldn't understand him over the noise. She just smiled at him and he moved off to rejoin his friends.

The celebration went on late into the night. Strange Children kept showing up out of the shadows, bringing in the bodies of dead animals they'd hunted and killed, and sharing the food with everyone.

Leroy carved the leg off an ox and delivered it to the Riverbend group. Link, Dina, Troy, and the others settled down together to cook it and eat together, but the Children were still celebrating so enthusiastically that they didn't notice or care to notice.

The noise died down toward midnight, but not the infectious excitement running through the camp. The Children remained standing and talking for hours.

"What will we do if we win the war?" Kabir asked.

"We could move into the cities and start keeping humans as helpers," Santos replied and the whole company exploded in laughter and mocking protests.

"We could just go back to the gorge camp and live our lives in peace," Franco suggested. "Then we wouldn't have to go out to fight at all."

"We could go west and start our own country," Nova chimed in. "We could establish our own cities and cantons and towns that are populated by no one but Children."

"What about our parents?" Leroy asked. "What about the people who helped us? The cats might take over Prideland again and our parents would be left to fend for themselves."

"Our parents could come with us," Israel suggested.

"Then the country wouldn't only be for Children, would it?" Aurelio pointed out.

"Let's win the war first before we decide what we do," Adrian interrupted.

"You could become king, Adrian," Kenji told him and the whole crowd exploded in more laughter.

Adrian grinned at them all and didn't answer.

Dina glanced over at Link and he glanced at her at the same moment. What would happen if the Children won the war? No one had thought that far in advance.

Just a few days ago, the idea of the Children taking over Prideland would have seemed too farfetched even to mention. It would have seemed laughable—as laughable as Adrian becoming king.

Now all of those possibilities didn't just seem possible but probable. The Children won today's battle with no planning, no preparation, no additional forces, and no advanced warning.

Now Adrian was calling up his people from all over the countryside to launch an offensive against the Pride. If he won......

Dina couldn't even imagine what Prideland would look like if the Children won. It wouldn't be Prideland anymore. The whole planet would be thrown into upheaval—if it hadn't been already.

Adrian was already the undisputed leader of the Children's army. God only knew how many Children he really commanded or could command if the Children took over the planet.

Who else would rule if not him? What else would they call their undisputed ruler if not a king?

Dina could think of worse fates this planet could suffer than for Adrian to become its king. Him taking over this planet and deciding what happened next couldn't possibly be worse than the way the Pride had been ruling all these years.

Link, Dina, and their Riverbend comrades finished eating and stretched out on the ground near their fires long before the Children settled down. They were all still standing around talking excitedly by the time Dina fell asleep.

She drifted off listening to them speculate about how the war would go, what would happen when the Children went out into open battle against the cats, whether any other humans from the cantons would join them, how many cats the Pride would send out, what their strategy would be, where the Children would meet them, and all the myriad possible angles of attack the Children could use to counter the cats' advantages.

Adrian participated in these conversations, but he kept his plans to himself. He kept his remarks vague as though he didn't have any plans at all and simply intended to improvise everything.

He became progressively more reticent as the night wore on until he barely added anything to the conversations at all. The last thing Dina saw before she faded out was Naia coming over to him, slipping her arms around him, and leading him away into the darkness.

Chapter 26

Footsteps woke Dina from a sound sleep the next morning. She blinked the sleep out of her eyes, but she didn't hear any voices.

She sat up to find all the Children on their feet. They moved through the camp rapidly and silently. None of them spoke at all and she didn't see anyone she knew.

Two young boys from the gorge camp came over to her, knelt down in front of her, and started untying blankets that had been tied into large bundles.

The boys opened their bundles to reveal a stash of weapons. Some were axes, machetes, and large knives like she'd seen before. The boys also included bows and arrows, spears, and a few heavy flails with spikes on their ends.

Dina stared down at the bundles and then at the boys. They made eye contact with her, but neither of them spoke. One of them made a beckoning motion to her with his hand, held his finger to his lips, and pointed toward the east.

All the other Children seemed to be leaving in that direction. They took to the trees one after the other and vanished. The whole camp emptied out in the few minutes Dina had been sitting here.

She glanced around at the other Riverbend residents, but they were all still asleep. She shook Link awake.

He jolted out of his slumber. "Huh? What's happening?"

"Shh!" she whispered. "Be quiet."

He looked around blinking the confusion out of his head. Troy and two of the women sat up.

Dina held her finger to her lips and passed the weapons to everyone. She pointed in the same direction the boys indicated and pulled her companions to their feet.

Everyone got the message real quick, and in a few seconds, they all stood up, gathered their weapons, and filed out of the camp.

Dina didn't dare to ask where they were going or what they were going to do when they got there. She already knew and she preferred to pretend that she didn't.

The party hiked all day down the mountains. The two boys accompanied the Riverbend group all the way. No other Children stuck around long enough even to see what Dina and her comrades were doing.

The boys led the party into another Children's camp that night, but unlike the previous evening, no one spoke or celebrated. No one lit a fire.

Most of the Children slept in the trees. A dozen Riverbend Children curled up on the ground with Dina's party and their two escorts.

The boys pulled another bundle of leather from their luggage, untied it, and spread it on the ground in front of Dina and her comrades. The bundle contained an enormous pile of roasted meat, but it was cold. It was the only food available and Dina didn't see the Children eating at all.

The night got cold fast and the Children didn't provide their human companions with any blankets or any other comforts. Everyone huddled on the ground trying in every possible way to keep warm.

Link wrapped his arms around Dina and held her all night long. She burrowed against his chest, shut her eyes, and blocked out all discomfort. She absolutely refused to complain about any of this. She signed up to help the Children, not to make herself a burden on them.

None of the Children made a sound all night and none of the human party said a word, either. The tension escalated to the breaking point and then got a thousand times worse the next morning.

Dina sat up long before dawn. She couldn't go back to sleep with today's campaign hanging over her head.

It would be something cataclysmic and world-changing. She knew that now. Whatever Adrian was planning for today, Prideland would never be the same after today.

The jungle started to lighten and the Children started moving around in the treetops. Dina couldn't sit still anymore. She and Link stood up, stretched, and started arranging their weapons.

She wanted to hurry up, get to the battlefield, and get the battle started. She didn't want to wait any longer.

The Children and everyone else in the Riverbend party seemed to be thinking the same thing. No one had to wake them up.

Dina's party got to their feet, but the Children didn't take to the treetops this morning. They all descended and gathered around the Riverbend Children who'd stayed with Link and Dina.

More and more Children raced through the branches and dropped to the ground to join their group. The crowd swelled as more and more Children arrived, but still no one spoke.

Naia, Adrian, Iona, and Karim showed up an hour later. By that time, nearly two hundred Children had gathered under the trees. They all stood in silence and the crowd parted to let Adrian walk through them.

He halted next to the human group and turned around to survey his loyal followers. Some of the Children came armed, but most were empty-handed. They all held themselves stiff and tense ready for the coming conflict.

He nodded once in approval and said in a soft undertone, "It's time. Let's go."

He walked off through the jungle and all the Children followed him. None of them launched into the canopy.

The throng streamed through the trees and the human party got swept along with them. Link, Dina, Troy, and their comrades wound up near the back of the crowd, but more and more Children materialized out of nowhere to follow behind them.

Adrian led the way onto a narrow jungle path that wound down the mountain, widened, and eventually joined up with a road heading east.

The sun rose and bathed the day in glorious light—plenty of light for everyone and anyone to see exactly what the Children were doing.

As soon as the Children's army arrived at the road, another two giant hordes of Children emerged from the trees on both sides. They poured onto the road in a mob of hundreds or many even thousands.

Plenty of ordinary human beings came with them. Dina's group wasn't the only group of people who came out to support the Children.

Adrian strode in front with his entourage of closest comrades around him. Link and Dina couldn't get anywhere near him with all these Children around.

None of the Children bounded on all fours. They all walked upright and advanced with deliberate slowness down the road heading closer to the city.

The Children came across a few cats and subsidiaries going about their business. Cats and subsidiaries took one look at the Children's army and bolted.

The Children made it another mile before the Pride sent out their force to stop the army from advancing. A mob of cats streaked out of the city and came up the road to confront Adrian.

He raised his hand and his followers stopped there in full view of everyone. The cats stopped on their side. No one made a sound.

A feeling of glacial calm settled over Dina's mind. In a way, this confrontation put all her doubts to rest. The cats and the Children had been bound for a head-on collision for a long time. At least no one had to wait any longer.

The Children seemed to feel the same thing. The tension drained out of the crowd and everyone relaxed, now that they'd finally come face to face with their enemy.

More cats came out of the city to bolster their side.....and then a large body of helpers showed up. They spread out on both sides of the road.

Dina stiffened again when she saw that the helpers were all armed. The Pride had never allowed the helpers to possess weapons before.

That on its own told her all she needed to know. The Pride was afraid of the Children. The cats must realize by now that they couldn't underestimate the Children's fighting skill. The Children had already killed too many cats.

The Pride had failed to annihilate the Children the way they planned. The Pride tried to eliminate the threat the Children posed to the Pride's rule. How ironic that the Pride's own efforts had created the very threat they were so afraid of.

None of this would have happened if the Pride let the Children live or incorporated the Children into the Pride the way Renfroe suggested.

That would never happen. Now the two sides were about to meet in open combat for the destiny of a whole planet.

Dina didn't recognize any of the cats that came out to stop Adrian's advance.....until Hector strode out of the crowd. She hadn't seen him since that first day when she and the landing team first encountered him and his brother Victor on the road with such disastrous results.

He paced forward to the halfway mark between Adrian's position on one side and the cats on the other. "Turn back to the jungle," he growled. "Don't advance any farther or we'll be forced to attack."

"Why do you think we're here?" Adrian countered. "We didn't come here to run away from you. We came here to fight you. We won't leave until we wipe the floor with your blood."

Hector snarled at him. "You're a fool, boy."

"I might be a fool, but I've tasted enough cat blood in the last year to know you can't defeat us." Adrian sneered at the cats behind Hector's back and then at the helpers. "You must be really desperate if you brought a bunch of maimed, crippled helpers to fight your battles for you. You cats are too pathetic to rule this planet. Do yourselves a favor and step aside for the stronger species to take over."

"We will never step aside!" Hector roared. "We will destroy the Children until none remains."

"You've been trying to do that for four years and you haven't been able to destroy us yet," Adrian replied. "You might be able to kill a few newborn babies, but that's all. You don't dare to set foot in the jungle now. When we finish with you, you won't be able to set foot in your own cities anymore." He raised his head and let his sharp eyes range over the city beyond the cats' barricade. "This whole planet belongs to us. We go where we please and we do as we please. No cat can stop us. If you doubt me, why don't you attack me and drive us back to the jungle? If you want to kill us, we're here. Try it and see how far you get."

Hector's lips shivered back from his fangs and he growled again. Link adjusted his grip on his weapons.

No one could have seen that motion, especially not Adrian who stood at the front of the crowd.

Link tightening his grip set off a chain reaction that rippled through the crowd of Children. It translated all the way to the front of the crowd, and without warning, Adrian rocketed off the ground in a blinding streak of movement.

He slammed into Hector so fast the jaguar didn't have time to brace himself before Adrian grabbed him, tumbled Hector over backward, and they rolled all the way back to the cats' position.

Adrian's sudden attack surprised the cats into springing out of the way to make room for Hector and Adrian to roll into their midst.

In that moment when Hector and Adrian distracted the cats, the rest of the Children launched their own assault with equal speed and ferocity.

The Riverbend Children led the charge, and in seconds, they enveloped the cats in a deadly battle of tooth against tooth and claw against claw.

Chapter 27

Dina's party and all the other humans on the Children's side couldn't get near the front of the battle until half the Children were already engaged with the cats.

The Children surged forward and overran the cats' position. The helpers who'd been standing on either side stayed on the sides. The helpers rushed around the cats to attack from the shoulders on the right and left sides of the road.

Too many Children blocked Dina from getting near the cats, so she veered away to close with the helpers instead.

Most of them were men armed with knives, spears, and some axes. A few women joined the helpers' ranks, but Dina didn't have time to isolate them in the crowd.

A line of men charged her. This moment would be do or die. She couldn't hesitate, so she braced herself and rushed them with all her might.

Two men rushed back at her just as hard. One of them raised an axe to chop her down, but at that moment, the other humans from the Children's side surrounded her and the two armies smashed together in a whirlwind of flying weapons.

One of the men who'd been about to attack her had to turn aside to defend himself against another man Dina had never seen before. He wore the rough, hand-sewn clothes of some canton.

The other helper raised a spear and left the rest of his body exposed. Dina crouched low, grasped her axe handle with both hands, and swung it upward to hack it into his ribs just below his armpit.

He cringed and buckled with a groan, but that one strike exploded her out of her mind. She reared back, yanked the axe free, and chopped it down even harder into his head.

His body toppled sideways and she sprang over him searching for another target. Two women hurtled at her from farther in the back of the crowd. They both carried axes, too, and they converged on Dina from either side.

Her battle rage erupted out of all proportion. She stopped where she was, wound back her axe, and swiped it sideways. It wedged into one woman's head and the body slammed into the other woman.

She staggered and the body of the woman Dina just killed pulled her axe out of her grip. She had to let go of it to confront the woman who was still standing.

The two women came face to face. Seeing her comrade go down made the helper hesitate—but only for a second.

The woman recovered and raised her own axe. Dina was unarmed now. She would have to pull something out of her back pocket to defeat this woman.

More helpers and people from the cantons charged back and forth all around her. Cats and Children covered the road battling, growling, slashing, and killing on all sides.

Two men blundered into Dina from her left. They locked together in a death struggle as both fought to control a knife one of them held in his hand. They trampled Dina out of the way and then both men somersaulted down the embankment still fighting to the death.

The woman took advantage of that moment of distraction to swing her axe at Dina. Dina ducked the weapon and lunged for the woman. Dina had to disarm this woman fast.

She tackled the woman backward and grabbed the axe, but the woman outweighed her and Dina couldn't knock her over fast enough.

The woman might have won in the end, but both women tripped over another cluster of three helpers all piled on top of a different man from Moonlight canton.

The woman pitched onto her back and Dina roared in fury. She jerked the axe sideways, but the woman's grip held. She didn't let go, so Dina used every ounce of her strength to smash the axe head's blunt back edge into the woman's face.

The woman's nose cracked and Dina struck without mercy. She ripped the axe out of the woman's hands, but Dina didn't take the time to turn the axe itself on its owner.

Dina slammed the axe handle into the woman's face again and again until she reduced the woman's head to a pulp.

Dina tore the axe out of the woman's hands and looked around in wild confusion. The three helpers were about to overcome the man from Moonlight canton. Two of them restrained him while the third crushed a spear shaft against his neck to choke him.

Dina sprang to her feet, hacked her axe down into the third helper's head, and then went to work on the other two. She freed the man, helped him to his feet, and retrieved her first weapon before she looked around a second time.

She and the man from Moonlight canton stood side by side for an instant surveying the scene of carnage and destruction.

Adrian and Hector remained locked in a death struggle on the road. Dina couldn't tell from here which of them was winning—if either of them was.

Cats and Children occupied a hundred yards of the road with another hundred cats still standing behind the cats' original position, but these cats didn't attack.

The Children's furious assault and the sheer madness of their fighting style made the cats retreat to avoid getting involved in the conflict. Some even turned around and trotted back to the city to abandon the battle entirely.

Adrian and Hector didn't notice this. They were too busy tumbling over each other, slashing at each other, and swiping each other with their claws.

In that split second when Dina and the man from Moonlight canton paused to survey the battle, Adrian overcame Hector's weight, threw the jaguar on the ground, and clambered on top of him to mount the cat.

Hector pitched and fought harder than ever, but he couldn't hit Adrian with his hind claws like this. Adrian used every advantage of his human shape to grab Hector by his forepaws and slam both paws to the ground on either side of Hector's head so Hector couldn't harm Adrian with them, either.

None of the other Children noticed the helpers. The Children completely ignored the helpers on both sides of the road.

Dina turned in the opposite direction to see if any of her own people needed help. That was the moment when she saw one man charge through the battle from the helpers' ranks.

This man ran well. He must not have been given the House of Man, or maybe the scars hadn't cut deeply enough to damage him as badly as the other helpers.

He rushed the road from the side, arched back his arm, and flung a spear at Adrian, who was just bending over to dive for Hector's throat.

The spear whistled through the air. Adrian didn't see it. Dina was too far away to stop the spear from impaling him through the body.

She choked out his name one last time. "ADRIAN!!"

He looked up, but he couldn't move fast enough to avoid it. At that moment, Link charged down the shoulder running parallel to the road, plunged into the spear's path, and it impaled him through the chest hard enough to burst out through his back.

"LINK!!" Dina shrieked, but it was too late.

He teetered and looked down at the spear in surprise. Then he tilted backward and slammed down on the ground hard enough for the spear to slide all the way back out through his chest.

"NO!!!" Dina screamed and would have rushed him, but the man from Moonlight canton grabbed her and held her back.

He yanked her away. She struggled to break his grip and only realized a fraction of a second later that he was holding her with one arm while he fought off three more helpers with his free arm.

Adrian stared at Link in horror. He sat frozen on top of Hector still gripping the jaguar's forelimbs in both hands.

Hector gave another fearful roar and writhed under Adrian's weight. That movement snapped Adrian out of his trance. He plunged in to tear Hector's life out and then climbed off the jaguar's dead body.

Adrian cast a terrible glance over the battle. The Children had overcome enough cats that the Children made another rush at those cats waiting in the back of the cats' position. Most of them ran from the Children.

The helpers turned out to be braver. They stayed behind and engaged with the Children's human supporters. The helpers stayed long after the cats fled. The Children finished off the last cats and then turned on the helpers.

Adrian took a few steps down the shoulder and stopped there to stare down at Link's body.

Dina struggled against the man holding her. She heard herself screaming, "NO!! NO!!" again and again, but her position and the angle with which he held her gave her a perfect line of sight to see that yes, Link was dead with the spear shaft still sticking out of his sternum.

Enough helpers kept fighting and she fought so hard that she eventually broke the man's grip. She charged across the grass to Link, but once she got there, she couldn't decide what to do.

She attacked him trying to pick him up. "LINK!!" she screamed. This broken place in her heart would never heal—not ever. "LINK!! NO!! LINK!!"

His body felt impossibly heavy. He'd never felt this heavy when he'd been alive.

"LINK!!" She choked on his name and then the sobs started. "LINK—NO!!"

The noise of battle faded, but her screams didn't. Her broken shrieks made the Children stop what they were doing and they all saw.

"LINK!!" she screeched. "LINK!!"

He couldn't hear her and he didn't see her. He stared straight up at the sky. What a fool she'd been not to give herself to him when she had the chance.

She could have had human children with him. She could have had everything with him if only she'd overcome this stupid idea about them already having enough Children.

She would never get over the shame of that. She would never forgive herself for holding anything back from him.

Her sobs became so excruciating that she couldn't even say his name anymore. She kept tugging at his shoulders trying to pick him up, but he was too heavy.

The spearhead might have gotten jammed into the soil for all she knew. It might have skewered him to the ground.

Someone came up behind her, took hold of her shoulders, and tried to pull her away. She didn't see who it was.

She shook them off and went back to trying to pick him up. She had to make him stand up.

She had to make him walk and talk and go back to the way he was just a few minutes ago. He couldn't be gone.

Someone said, "Dina...." in her ear, but she still didn't recognize the voice. She couldn't hear anything over her own racking sobs.

Some distant part of her brain became aware of the Children gathering around. They all stared down at Link's body and Adrian said, "Pick him up and take him home."

"NO!!" Dina screamed and tried one more time to hold onto Link.

Whoever was touching her used a little more force, and when she still wouldn't leave Link alone, strong hands clamped on her arms and pulled her away.

"NO!!" she shrieked, but the Children were already moving in. Adrian pulled the spear out of Link's chest, threw it aside, and Kaiser, Riyadh, Israel, and Aries picked up Link's body.

Dina burst into a hysterical fit of screaming and struggling, but whoever was holding her wouldn't let her go. They pulled her out of the way while the four Children carried Link back up the road toward the jungle.

Dina couldn't watch anymore. If they carried him away like that, it must mean he really was dead. He would never let them carry him anywhere unless he really was dead. He wasn't coming back.

She fought to break out of the hands holding her. She jerked hard to her right and whirled all the way around. Whoever had been holding her let her do it just far enough to face him and then he closed both arms around her. It was Karim.

She couldn't stand that. The smell and feel of his fur on her skin and face broke the dam of all this tortured emotion and she broke down in pieces right there on his chest.

He clamped his arms around her in a crushing grip. He didn't follow the other Children carrying Link's body out of sight. Karim stayed there holding Dina while she buckled in tearing, life-destroying sobs that would never, ever stop.

Chapter 28

Dina halted under the trees and stared out of the shadows of Riverbend canton. Was it just last night that Link asked her never to come back to this god-forsaken place?

The journey back here had taken all day. The sun had gone down long ago and now deep, dark night hung heavy over the jungle.

Karim, Kaiser, and Kenji had stayed with Dina all the way. The rest of the Children had gone ahead to take Link's body home.

Lamplight flooded from her house beyond the fence. She could see straight into the house through the open gate.

The Children had laid out his body on the floor where he used to sit and talk to them. They'd covered his body with a blanket and left his head out where everyone could see him.

The Children sat around in their usual places. She could see them holding each other and some of them rocking with sobs.

Tears poured from her eyes exactly the way they'd been pouring from her eyes the whole way here. Link wouldn't be waiting for her when she got home. He would never come back to that house from his hunting trips. He was gone.

She really didn't want to go in there. She wanted to turn around and disappear into the jungle. She wanted to go somewhere—anywhere else where she wouldn't have to deal with this.

She didn't see or care what happened to Troy and the other people who'd fought side by side with the Children out on the road. All those people had vanished out of her life. Now nothing remained but her and the Children.

She hated herself for loving Link and not being able to share everything with him. She should have gone west with him before this war ever started. She should have come up with some solution to stop him from fighting. He would be alive right now if she'd only thought of it soon enough.

Karim put his arm behind Dina's back and touched her to signal her to keep moving. They'd already spent too much time traveling here.

She started forward, but the repulsive force pushing her away from the house got stronger as she got nearer. She could make out individual Children now and see everything they were doing.

Link's nieces and nephews sat nearest him. Egypt and India bawled their eyes out while Brock and Rome did their best to comfort them, but tears streamed down both boys' cheeks, too.

Riyadh, Link's oldest nephew, sat by Link's body staring into space in stunned shock. Nova sat next to him with her arms around him, but Riyadh didn't even see or notice the woman he loved.

Israel sat farther away with his head turned so he wouldn't see Link's body. Sasha sat next to him facing the opposite way facing Link and she sobbed openly.

Cairo and Amber sat together in the opposite corner with their arms around each other in a deep embrace. They didn't separate, not even when Dina halted at the top of the steps outside the threshold.

Adrian sat with his arm around Naia's shoulder while she shook with sobs. She covered her mouth with both hands, but Adrian just stared down at Link with the same blank expression Adrian had when Link first got hit.

Iona sat on Naia's other side. Iona was all alone until Dina came back. Then Iona shot to her feet, rushed across the room, and threw her arms around Karim howling with sobs.

Karim and his brothers left Dina standing there, made their way into the room, and sat down with the others. Iona collapsed in Karim's arms and broke down in a fresh bout of sobs.

Dina's face hurt from crying so hard for so long. She didn't want to enter that room and deal with all these Children's grief. Her own grief hurt too much.

All of this happened because she and Link committed themselves to the Children's cause. She couldn't back out on that now.

She stumbled into the room and buckled on the floor. The only place left where she could fit was five feet away from Link's body, but she didn't care. She didn't want to see his body anyway.

The Children had closed his eyes. He looked like he was asleep on the floor there, but he wasn't. He'd never slept on the floor in this house—not even once. He'd always slept in the bedroom he shared with Dina.

She couldn't look at that room anymore, either. She would never sleep in that bed ever again. She would really like to burn this house to the ground so she wouldn't have to remember how much she loved him.

She loved him more than she'd ever loved Tom. She couldn't remember anymore if she loved Renfroe, but if she did—if she could call that love—it never came close to the way she felt about Link.

She couldn't cry anymore. The Children's sobs expressed her grief enough. She could let them express it for her.

Now she just felt raw, bruised, and completely destroyed. She had no life left. She had nothing left—nothing at all. Even her very self had died on that roadside.

What was the point of any of this? What was the point of trying to accomplish anything or trying to do the right thing—or anything? What was the point of living if she had to suffer agony like this?

Part of her wished that she'd never met or fallen in love with Link. She wouldn't be feeling this misery right now if she'd never loved him.

She couldn't wish that, though. Loving him had been one of the greatest privileges of her life. She'd shared her greatest challenges with him.

They'd raised twenty-nine Children together, seen them grow up and get married, and seen their Children become adults any parents would be proud of.

She and Link had heard Adrian tell people that Link was his father. Adrian had treated Link that way and respected and admired him as a father. Link had given his life to save Adrian.

Link did all that because he knew how important Adrian was. The Children's war would go on because Adrian was still alive. The Children didn't need Link, but they did need Adrian. The planet's whole future hinged on Adrian.

Dina's life hinged on Link and now he was gone. She never would have gotten involved in the Children's war if not for Link.

Maybe she would have, but now his driving energy no longer pushed her forward. What was the point? Her Children didn't need her anymore. She would only slow them down. She saw that today.

She sat on the floor for hours. She felt too shattered even to think straight.

Sometime in the night, Dexter got the blankets out of the cupboard and passed them around to everyone. A few people curled up and went to sleep. Most stayed awake and kept silent vigil over Link's body.

Dexter stopped in front of Dina, draped a blanket around her shoulders, and pushed her sideways. "Lie down and go to sleep," he told her.

She lacked the energy even to resist that. She wrapped the blanket around herself and curled up on the floor, but she couldn't shut her eyes. At least she wasn't trying to sleep in that bedroom.

She was still lying there staring at nothing when the sky started to get light outside. The Children came and went from the house, and when the sun came up, Troy came in and delivered a butchered ox for the Children to eat.

They moved out of the way for him to set it on the floor, but he didn't stay. He vanished without a word to anyone.

The floor got too hard and uncomfortable, so Dina sat up, but she couldn't bring herself to go anywhere or do anything. Link's body still lay in the same place. She refused even to think about what she ought to do with him.

As soon as she sat up, she noticed more Children from other cantons sitting around on the grass outside. They surrounded her house on all sides. She even recognized the man from Moonlight canton she'd fought with during the battle.

She didn't notice what the Children around her were doing until Riggs came over to her. He set a bucket of water in front of her, squatted on the floor, soaked a rag in the water, and started wiping down her face, neck, hands, and hair.

He scowled at her with a kind of tortured fury that did nothing to hide the grief underneath. The sight of his face twisted in rage and the feel of the cool cloth passing over her face made the tears spring to her eyes again. She couldn't survive this, but she had to.

He finished washing her down and took his bucket away. Then Naia showed up, took Dina's hand, and took her into her own bedroom.

Dina didn't understand why until she got there and found a set of clean clothes laid out on the bed. Dina didn't recognize them. They were brand new.

Naia took hold of the buttons on Dina's shirt. "We need to change your clothes. You're covered in blood from the battle."

Dina glanced down at her clothes and realized for the first time that Naia was right. Splattered blood and random gore covered Dina all over. No wonder Riggs had to clean her up. She must have had it all over her face and hair, too.

Dina woke up enough to change her clothes. She had to or Naia would have done it for her. Dina never doubted that.

"Come out to the main room and get something to eat," Naia told her in a forceful undertone as soon as Dina finished changing. "You need to eat something before we leave."

"Where are we going?" Dina asked.

"We're taking Link to the gorge camp to bury him with our dead. We can't bury him here." Naia crossed to the door. "Come on, Dina. You have to come with us."

Naia slipped out of the room. When Dina got back out to the main room, the Children had already taken Link's body outside.

Osiris's daughter Emerald sat on the floor where Link and Dina used to sit. Emerald held a skewer of meat over a clay pot full of glowing embers to roast the food for Dina.

Dina stumbled over to Emerald, slumped onto the floor, and ate the food that Emerald put in front of her. The Children were taking over her life, but she didn't care. She obviously couldn't function well enough on her own. She couldn't even think about what to do with herself.

She ate a few mouthfuls before Emerald finished, put the rest of the meat in a bowl, and then left to put the pot somewhere. The Children went through the house cleaning up and putting everything away.

Emerald came back a few minutes later, took the bowl with half the meat still in it, and said, "Come on, Dina. It's time to go."

She would have pulled Dina to her feet if Dina didn't get up by herself. They walked outside to find all the other Children on their feet, including the Children from other cantons.

They'd constructed a stretcher to carry Link's body. Riyadh, Israel, Cairo, and Aries carried the stretcher's four corners.

The Children started filing out of the canton as soon as Dina stepped outside. They formed a procession in no particular order. Adrian walked somewhere in the middle. He wasn't in charge today.

The others paired off in couples and Dina got swept into the crowd. She didn't pay attention enough to tell if any particular people were supposed to be guarding her or keeping an eye on her. Maybe all of them were.

They began the long, hard, slow, agonizing hike all the way back to the gorge camp. No one raced ahead and no one leapt through the treetops. The Children stayed on the ground plodding at the same deliberate torturous pace.

They didn't make it to the gorge until after dark. The four pallbearers put Link's body in Adrian's and Naia's house. Then the Children built bonfires and everyone sat around staring silently into the flames until they fell asleep on the ground.

Dina fell asleep on the ground, too. She just didn't care anymore about anything, not even her own comfort. None of this meant anything.

No one talked the following morning, either. The Children sat up, went about their morning chores, and then, at some unspoken signal, the same four men took Link's body out of the house and set off down the gorge.

Dina didn't know where they were going. Not even that mattered.

The Children filed down the steep canyons and through another treacherous defile to a place deep, deep in the jungle wilderness.

The canyons snaked back and forth around sharp corners and eventually ended in a wide, flat, sandy opening surrounded on all sides by vertical cliffs rising to the sky. No one could see this place except from directly above.

Twenty mounds of rocks sat in rows one next to the other. The four pallbearers set Link's stretcher at the end of the line lying parallel to the other mounds.

Then Riyadh placed a round river stone in the center of Link's chest and backed away. Israel and Cairo did the same thing.

Egypt and India both burst into tears again when they approached Link's body. Egypt knelt down next to him, kissed him on the cheek and hugged him, and then put a round stone in his hand where it lay next to his side.

Rome pulled her away and she buried her face in his chest sobbing hard. Her sobs were the only sound in the intense quiet.

India placed her stone next to Link's head and stood there with tears streaming down her cheeks until Brock came forward, put his own stone next to hers, and then wrapped his arm around her shoulders to lead her away.

Adrian approached next, placed another stone next to Riyadh's in the middle of Link's chest, and then the rest of the Children followed one after the other.

Each person placed a rock on or next to Link's body. So many stones piled up that they formed a mound over him and he vanished underneath them. He became one of the honored dead in the one place in Prideland where he would finally be safe.

Dina watched the whole funeral in blank torment. Her insides ached with grief. She hurt too much even to go near Link's body—not even to say goodbye.

She stood back out of the way and watched from the sidewall as the rocks mounded higher and higher. They eventually covered his face until no part of him remained visible. He became another grave in this Children's graveyard.

Even that gave mute testimony to the honor they were doing to him. He was the only human being lying in this graveyard. He would always be the only human being who ever lay in this graveyard. He was the only person who would ever be worthy of that honor.

Even the Children from other cantons placed rocks on the mound to pay their respects. Adrian was still alive to carry on this war because of Link's sacrifice.

The Children who'd placed their rocks first retreated out of the way to let the others come forward. In the end, enough of the mourners finished and left the canyon on their way back up the gorge.

They didn't stay in the camp. They filed through it with the last mourners bringing up the rear as they finished placing their rocks on Link's grave and leaving him there.

Dina followed her Children out of the canyon and they all just kept on walking all the way back to Riverbend canton.

Chapter 29

Dina entered Riverbend canton for the second time and didn't feel the slightest bit of surprise when she saw lamplight streaming from her own doorway.

Two dozen Children sat around in there and they had another fresh ox carcass waiting to share with everyone. Dina didn't ask where they got it.

Conversation restarted, now that Link's body wasn't here anymore, but everyone kept their voices subdued. The Children from other cantons camped outside. Only Link's and Dina's own Children stayed in the house.

"When are we going back out?" Dexter asked Adrian.

"I don't know," Adrian mumbled. "Maybe tomorrow. We'll see how things go."

"What things?" Riggs asked.

"Our scouts are watching the roads," Adrian replied. "They'll let us know if the cats make another move. We have no reason to go back out until they do."

"Aren't we patrolling the jungle anymore?" Kenji asked. "What about all the hunting parties that are still out here?"

"Any hunting parties that are still out here are small fry compared to the force the Pride will bring out against us in the future," Adrian replied. "We don't need to care about hunting parties anymore. We're fishing for something much bigger now."

"What's that?" Israel asked. "What are we fishing for?"

"The whole Pride," Adrian replied.

That killed the conversation. People still talked, but they talked about other things and avoided asking any more questions about the war itself.

Dina didn't want to hear about the war—or anything else. The sound of voices in this house offended her. Anyone living in this house offended her, including herself. The simple fact that she was still alive at all offended her.

Emerald started a fire in the alcove in Dina's kitchen counter and brought over a pot of glowing coals to cook some food for Dina, but the sight of someone doing this for her pushed her over the edge.

She took the skewers out of Emerald's hands. "I'll do that. You don't have to take care of me anymore."

"I want to," Emerald replied. "I want to make it easier for you."

"You'll be making it easier for me by letting me do it for myself. You don't have to baby me. I'll get over Link's death and I'll be all right."

Emerald frowned and studied her. "Are you sure? I don't mind."

Dina did her best to smile, but she didn't feel like it. "I'm sure. You should eat."

Emerald turned over all the cooking supplies to Dina, but Emerald didn't leave Dina's side. Emerald stayed sitting there and Keith handed Emerald pieces of the raw meat to eat.

Dina saw the Children taking turns spending time with her and taking care of her. She had to get them to stop doing that. They were adults....and she was an adult.

The only way to get them to stop doing it was to start taking care of herself. She had to make them believe she *could* take care of herself.

Thinking that made her come out of the trance she'd been in since Link's death. She slipped into a numb stupor where she allowed herself to feel the full devastation of losing him.

Now she looked around the house as if for the first time. Coming out of her trance and taking care of herself meant living in this house again. It meant cooking for herself, bringing in water, washing the sheets.....

Imagining herself doing all of that made her sick. All those little details she used to do with Link and for Link—she would never be able to do any of them again without thinking of him.

Taking care of herself would make her think of him and miss him. It would slap her in the face every day that he wasn't here. He died under the worst possible circumstances. He died saving Adrian's life so Adrian could continue to wage war against the Pride.

She didn't want to eat, but she forced herself to do it anyway so the Children wouldn't see her falling apart all over again. How long would this horror go on? How long would she live like this—entombed in grief and devastation? She might be like this forever.

She finished eating, stood up, and went through her old routine of putting the coals away and cleaning up after herself. The Children were still eating their dead ox. The

Children out on the grass had brought in a different dead animal to share amongst themselves.

She was just grabbing a bucket to go fetch some water for everyone. She bent down to pull a towel out from under her kitchen counter, but it got stuck. She had to sit down on the floor to unhook it from the splinter that held it in place.

Her head shot up when she heard voices outside. They didn't sound happy or subdued at all. They were yelling at each other.

Those voices brought up memories of the Council members arguing with her and Link. Those arguments seemed like they'd happened a thousand years in the past. Now they were happening again.

She went to the open doorway, but Adrian got there first. She stopped next to him and looked down.

The usual Council members stood in the middle of the yard. They'd obviously been coming from the house they used for Council meetings, but they only made it halfway before they came face to face with Troy and the three women who'd fought with the Children on the way down to the city.

"You are NOT going over there, Meredith," Troy snapped in her face. "Just leave them alone. They've been through enough."

"I won't leave anyone alone," Meredith fired back. "This is the last straw. We all knew something like this would happen and now a man is dead because of this nonsense. Someone has to do something to put a stop to this."

She tried to dodge around him, but he sidestepped in front of her and actually shoved her to make her back off. "I swear to God, Meredith, if you take one more step toward that house, I'll have to use violence to stop you. It's bad enough she's lost Link. They all have. I won't let you make it worse by interfering, especially not like this."

"Get out of my way, Troy," Meredith snarled. "We still have the authority to throw you out of the canton, too."

"I don't give a damn what you do to me," he countered. "You and the other parents drove a wedge between me and my own Children with this attitude of yours. I won't let you do it again. The Children have been through enough..."

"*They've* been through enough!" Fitch spat. "They haven't been through anything! We're the ones......"

Adrian sprang off the steps without touching them. He did it in a very catlike way, landed on the grass, and then strutted over there standing straight upright. "What's going on?"

"Nothing," Troy barked over his shoulder. "It's nothing you need to worry about. These people were just leaving."

Adrian didn't stop walking. He halted right next to Troy. "Do you people have something you want to say to me?"

Meredith looked down her nose at him. "We've said it before and we'll say it again. You and these strangers aren't welcome in this village, especially not after Link's death. This is your fault, Adrian. Putting people at risk who have deliberately chosen to put themselves at risk is one thing. Now a man is dead—and not just any man, but our friend, our neighbor—a valued member of our community."

"Link deliberately chose to put himself at risk," Troy interjected. "He made a conscious decision to join the Children's war because he believed in this cause. We all did. The same thing could have happened to any of us. It's a risk we all took and he....."

Adrian silenced him by laying his hand on Troy's arm.

Troy spun around to stare at him, but Adrian didn't look at him. Adrian gazed back at the Council members. "Is that all you have to say—that I'm the reason Link is dead—that his death is my fault? Is that what you came over here to say?"

Meredith tried her best to square her shoulders, but she wound up squirming instead. "Essentially.....and that the Council calls you to our meeting tonight. As long as you and the other Children are in this village, you answer to the Council. We have some questions we'd like to ask you about yesterday's events—and about your plans in general."

"Is that all?" Adrian asked again.

"Isn't that enough?" Fitch cut in.

Adrian dipped his chin one last time. "Now you'll hear what I have to say. I'll come to address your Council tonight.....and you will all stay away from that house over there." He inclined his head sideways to indicate Dina's house. "I will personally kill anyone who crosses that line and comes near my mother's house. I will personally kill any of you who even speaks to any of my people, especially Dina. Is that clear? I won't warn you again."

Dead silence answered him. The Council members stared at him in slack-jawed shock. None of them could even summon the voice to gasp at his audacity.

None of the Children sitting around on the grass moved, either. They all sat frozen in silence listening to this. His words rang through the canton.

All the Children heard what he said. They would obey him to the letter. Any of them would kill the Council members or anyone else who intruded on Dina's privacy—if Adrian didn't get to them first.

He waited just long enough for those words to sink in. Then he glanced once at Troy, turned on his heel, strode back through the assembled Children, and climbed the steps to reenter the house.

He had to walk past Dina to get inside. He made eye contact with her and then disappeared behind her back. She heard him sit down with the other Children and he went back to eating.

Troy stayed where he was standing face to face against the Council and then he stormed off back to his own house.

The Council members remained staring down at all the Children on the grass. They stared straight back up at the Council members in open challenge to see if anyone had the nerve to cross into their domain.

The Council members fidgeted for a minute and then returned to the house where they held meetings. They went inside, shut the door, and they didn't come out again.

The same tense hush fell over the canton. The Children on the grass talked in low tones, but no other Riverbend residents came out of their houses, not even to fetch water from the river. Everyone huddled in their houses waiting for the Children to leave.

Dina waited for a long time before she got her bucket and went out to the river to bring in water for the Children. The canton never sounded this quiet. Only the Children dared to speak.

Chapter 30

D ina finished cleaning the main room and throwing the ox bones into a pile behind the house. Night had fallen and most of the Children on the grass outside had already curled up together to go to sleep.

Dina's Children still sat on the floor talking and combing their fingers through each other's fur.

Dina sat down next to Adrian. "Are you really going to address the Council."

"I might as well," he drawled. "I'm already here. Addressing them won't make any difference except to make them angrier and more upset than they already are. I might as well enjoy myself by pestering them. This might be my last chance to have some fun with them."

"Would you mind if I come with you?" she asked.

His head shot up. "Why do you want to come? You've heard it all before."

"I just want to be there. You're my son and I want to support you. I promise I won't say anything," she blurted out. "I'll stand in the very back so no one knows I'm there. I promise I won't interject myself into the meeting. I promise."

"You said that already. You don't have to keep saying it."

"Oh. Okay. Well.....can I come?"

He narrowed his eyes to scowl at her and then shrugged. "I guess I can't think of any reason why you shouldn't. Just don't say anything. I'm sure Troy and the others will be saying enough."

"I won't," she promised again.

He frowned at her again and then went back to what he was doing.

She would have liked to question him further. Maybe that's why she wanted to go to the Council meeting—to hear how he answered their questions and demands that he explain himself.

She shouldn't have needed those answers. She already knew why he was doing what he was doing. Maybe she just needed to hear him say it out loud.

He'd never expressed any doubt about what he was doing—except once. He'd only ever expressed that doubt to Link. Link was the only person Adrian would ever have turned to for advice. Now that was gone, too.

Adrian sat around doing a whole lot of nothing for hours. God only knew what state of hysteria and anxiety the Council members were in waiting for him to show up.

None of the other Children showed any sign that him going to face the Council meant anything. They all pretended that the Council hadn't challenged Adrian in front of everyone, but they all knew it.

Hours later, he stood up and brushed the dust off his fur. The Black stood up, too, and so did the Pygmies, Iona, and the Manx brothers.

They closed into a pack. This was it. They were going out to war against the Council this time.

Dina followed them as far as the threshold, but Adrian didn't leave the house. He stopped there and looked down at the Children on the grass. If any of them had been asleep before, they were all wide awake now.

They looked up at him and all their eyes glowed in the lamplight coming from behind him.

He dropped his voice deep into his chest and it rumbled out of him in a low, growling flow that twisted Dina's stomach into knots.

"Link is dead," he boomed. "Our last tie to humankind died yesterday. The last barrier separating us from our destiny fell with him.

"We'll leave here tomorrow morning, and when we do, all of Prideland will tremble before us.

"We go out to open warfare against the Pride—for Link, for ourselves, and for all those with the courage to fight with us. His sacrifice shows us the way.

"Link wanted us to fight. Link taught us to fight so we could make a stand against the Pride and that's what we're going to do.

"Starting tonight, there is no force on this planet that can rule us. We make our own road and our own law. We forge our own destiny and our own future without regard to Councils or Senates or any understanding with the Pride.

"Starting tonight, everyone will feel our might and we won't stop until we defeat everyone who stands in our way—no matter what species they belong to. Starting tonight, there will only be two races on this planet—those who stand with the Children and those who stand against us.

"Those who stand against us will tremble in fear—but only as long as we allow them to live. Those who stand with us will rule with us and we'll inherit this planet from those who aren't strong enough to keep it from us."

A murmur of excitement shivered through the Children listening to him. They didn't burst into cheers the way humans would have. These Children didn't act like humans at all.

The resemblance between them and their human relatives kept fading and becoming less significant with every passing day—or maybe it wasn't the days that did it.

Every threat, every insult, every battle changed them. All those assaults forged the Children into something completely unique and utterly untamed.

Adrian paused there at the top of the steps to make sure everyone heard him, including whatever forces governed this planet that might be listening to him.

Then he strode down the steps with his entourage of close companions. They crossed the yard to the house the Council used for meetings.

Dina slipped in behind them. Half the canton's residents were already in there, but they didn't yell and argue and wave their arms around. They just stood in silence waiting for the Children to show up.

They drew back when Adrian and his people entered the house. The canton residents held their breath.

Troy and the others who'd fought alongside the Children stood at the front of the room, but they hadn't been yelling at the Council, either.

Troy nodded at Adrian and then backed away to give Adrian the floor. An aura of danger surrounded the Children.

Dina flattened herself against the back wall—not because she promised Adrian she would. She didn't want anyone to see her or think about including her in this confrontation.

It would be a confrontation. Everyone knew that ahead of time. The tension in the room made it inevitable.

Adrian had been younger and less experienced the last time he came here to confront these people. He hadn't even addressed the Council. He'd addressed the other residents.

He didn't even look at the residents this time. He barely looked at Troy and those who'd fought alongside the Children.

Adrian stopped in front of the Council table and stared down at them from above.

"Thank you for coming, Adrian," Nicholas began. "We all share your sorrow over Link's death."

"I'm sure that isn't what you called me here to say to me," Adrian returned in a perfectly neutral tone of voice.

Fitch cleared his throat. "We understand you plan to wage war against the Pride. Is that true?"

"I don't plan to. I already am waging war against the Pride. Link told me that. Did you know that? He was the one who made it clear to me that I'm already in a war against the Pride. I have been since the day I was born and this war can only end one way. Either the Children win or the cats win. If the cats win, all the Children on the whole planet will die and all of *you* will either be killed or thrown back into slavery. Do you understand that? The Children's total victory is the only thing that will prevent it. Link taught me that and that's what I'm going to do with your support or without it. There is nothing you can say or do that will stop me from waging war against the Pride and using all my resources to win. You might not like it, but I owe Link and all the Children my best effort to win."

"You still don't recognize our authority to determine how far you can put our people in danger....." Fitch went on.

"I don't recognize your authority to do anything," Adrian returned. "I don't answer to you. I don't believe I ever did."

"You put yourself under our authority when you entered this canton," Nicholas replied. "You grew up here. You know how the canton works. As long as you and the other Children are here...."

"Don't worry. We're leaving first thing in the morning," Adrian interrupted. "Then you won't have to worry about us anymore and it will be thanks to us that you can live in safety or live at all."

"The Pride knows about you now," Nicholas went on. "They'll never rest until they wipe you out."

Adrian only hesitated for an instant to sweep his gaze down the table. He made eye contact with each Council member and then growled low under his breath, "Bring it on," and walked out of the house.

Chapter 31

S ilence followed the Children out of the house where the Council sat in shock over Adrian's speech. None of the Riverbend residents spoke or even shuffled their feet.

The door banged shut behind the Children. A few of the canton residents exchanged uncomfortable glances and then Troy and the other fighters left.

Dina stayed where she was. She didn't know why she was even still in here, but she didn't seem to be able to leave.

More people filed out of the house. The Council members turned to each other, but none of them spoke above a whisper. Their voices didn't disturb everything Adrian just said.

He didn't say anything she didn't already know. He'd been right about that, too.

She didn't know where she was or what she was doing with her life or even who she was anymore. She never would have believed her very being could have become so intertwined with Link.

She only found out now that he was gone. Now her whole life and being were at sea with no direction and no anchor.

She finally ducked outside, but she didn't return to her own house. She couldn't go back there. The very lamplight spilling from the open doorway repelled her. She already knew everything that would happen in there.

The Children on the grass were relaxing again. They'd all heard Adrian, both when he addressed them and when he addressed the Council—as if he ever had to explain himself to the Children.

None of them would ever question his authority ever again—if they ever did. He'd been telling them what to do since his earliest childhood. They followed him like no humans ever followed a human leader. The Children didn't operate that way.

She turned in the only direction left and strode out through the gate toward the river. The moonlight flickered on the water spilling over stones. The waterfall sprayed a silver eerie mist into the darkness.

The moon refracted in the spray and created a million stars flashing and twinkling right here in front of her.

She stared out into the jungle. She knew everything that would happen out there, too.

Nothing in this world held any appeal or interest for her anymore. Everything she once valued was gone and dead.

She didn't even care when she heard footsteps coming up behind her. "Isn't there any way to reason with the Children, Dina?" Nicholas asked.

She turned around to find him, Richard Shriver, and Lucy Callaghan standing there in the dim moonlight. Those three had been slightly more rational about the Children's situation, but these people still hadn't supported the Children outright—not like Troy and the others did.

Dina didn't remind these people of Adrian's threat to kill them if they ever spoke to her again. "Reason with them how?" she asked.

"Convince them to give up this war," Richard replied. "There has to be another way to come to an understanding with the Pride."

Dina raised her eyebrows. "You did not just say those words."

"You know what I mean," he exclaimed. "The Children have killed enough cats to make their point. They don't have to put us all in danger by going to all-out war."

"Didn't you hear a word Adrian said? He's doing this to protect you from the danger you're already in—and the even bigger danger you would be in if he *didn't* wage this war."

"Can't they negotiate with the Pride?" Nicholas asked. "The Children are in a position to bargain, now that the Pride realizes they can't just push the Children around. The Children listen to you. You could at least bring it up with Adrian."

Dina let out a heavy sigh. "I'm quite certain that won't work. He wouldn't listen even to me."

"Won't you at least try?" Richard asked. "For all our sakes?"

Dina would have liked to turn her back on them. She had more important things to think about and these people were intruding on her solitude.

She didn't turn her back on them. She couldn't imagine why she even dignified them with her time. "I might be convinced to try if I thought for an instant that the Children would change their minds, but they won't. You've been trying for two years to convince the Children to see things your way. It didn't work and it definitely won't work now. Adrian is more entrenched in his own way of thinking now than when he was younger. If you're smart, you'll take my advice and drop it. The Children will leave this canton in the morning and fight their war somewhere else. You won't have to think about it ever again."

"Are you sure there isn't something we can do or say to convince you to at least try?" Richard asked again.

"I'm sure. There's nothing you can do or say to convince me to try."

This time, she really did turn her back on them. She walked away down the river just to make sure they got the message loud and clear. She didn't want to talk to anyone, especially not about that.

She stopped by the waterfall and watched the moonlight wink in a million tiny droplets. The beauty didn't touch her. It did nothing to move her out of this dull feeling of living death.

The noise of the waterfall prevented her from hearing anything else. She stiffened when she heard a different voice behind her.

Then she relaxed when she recognized the voice. It was Troy. "Are you going to be okay?" he murmured. "I'm sorry you had to hear all that—Meredith blaming Adrian for Link's death and all that. I tried to keep them away from you."

"I'm all right," she replied over her shoulder even though she wasn't. He must have realized she was lying. "I'll be okay. I guess I'm still just in shock."

He swiveled around to stand next to her. "You have every reason to be proud of Adrian—and all your Children. You and Link did an incredible job of raising them. They're all fine people with strong integrity to do the right thing. They learned that from you—from both of you."

She mumbled, "Thanks," but she really wished he'd leave, too.

"I mean it," he breathed. "You took all those Children in when they had no one—even when Tania abandoned her sons on your doorstep. You didn't have to take on all that responsibility, but you did. You gave all those Children a home and a family they never would have had otherwise. They're the people they are today because of you."

She looked back up at the waterfall. She didn't want to talk anymore. She just wanted to be alone.

"I know this is all still fresh and everything...." he went on, "but I'd like to help you....if you'll let me." Without warning, he slipped his hand into hers and squeezed. "Let me make it better for you. You know I've always liked you and admired you, even before you got together with Link."

His hand radiated heat up her arm. It threatened to thaw this block of ice in the middle of her chest.

She would have liked to yank her hand away so she wouldn't feel that melting sensation. She managed to withdraw her hand without making him see how disgusting she found his proposal.

"I can't," she told him. "If I was going to love anyone besides Renfroe, it would be Link and now he's gone." She turned back to the waterfall and addressed herself only to it. No one and nothing else made any difference anymore. "Everyone I care about dies. First, it was Frank and now Link is gone, too."

He opened his mouth to answer—maybe to try again to convince her. Everyone always tried to convince her.

The block of ice spread its cold, dull feeling to her outer skin. Whatever he was about to say would bounce right off her the way the Council's arguments would bounce off Adrian.

Troy thought better of it and walked away, too. Finally.

Dina stayed outside in the darkness for a long time before she wandered back through the gate and reentered her house. All the lamps were still lit and all the Children were still awake.

She didn't sit down with them. She went through the house putting things in order and organizing the few possessions she owned.

Nearly everything in this house belonged to the canton. She'd simply been using the tools and implements to maintain her household and her family since she came to live here.

"You should go to sleep, Dina," Adrian told her. "You have a long way to hike tomorrow to get back to the ridgetop. We'll rendezvous with the other Children there before we go back down to the road for our next battle."

"I'm not going with you," she told him.

His head shot up. "Of course you are. You said you would help us with the war."

"That was before. I can't go back now."

Iona sat up. "Why can't you? You can't stay here. We'll be leaving in the morning. You're coming back out into the jungle with us."

"No," Dina replied. "I changed my mind."

"You changed your mind!" Adrian snapped. "You changed your mind about supporting our fight against the Pride?! Is that what you want us to believe?"

"I didn't change my mind about supporting you. I just changed my mind about going back out into the jungle."

"Why did you change your mind?" Riyadh asked and he didn't try at all to keep the iron out of his voice.

"Because Link is dead," she replied.

"You supported us because of Link?!" Adrian snapped even more harshly.

"No!" she exclaimed. "I still support you."

"Then what's stopping you from coming out to the jungle with us?" Iona asked. "You know we need people to fight the helpers. Everyone follows you. You have to come."

"Troy or one of the others can organize any people that go with you. You don't need me."

"Don't tell me you plan to stay *here*," Adrian sneered. "That would be ridiculous."

"No, I can't stay here. This place reminds me too much of Link."

"Where are you going to go, then?" Karim asked. "If you don't stay here and you don't come out to the jungle with us, where else is there?"

"I'm going back to the city," Dina replied. "I promised Renfroe before I left that I would go back to him when you were all old enough to take care of yourselves......"

A dozen voices cut her off. "No way!" Riggs snapped. "You aren't going back. We won't let you!"

"That's out of the question, Dina," Adrian interrupted. "You already risked your life three times leaving Prideland. You can't go back."

"I've already made up my mind," she replied. "You have your road and I have mine."

"Are you serious?!" Iona fired back. "Whose side are you on?"

"Yours, of course," Dina replied. "I can help you more from inside the city...."

"You're lying," Adrian spat. "You're going back for *him*. Just admit it."

"You're still a slave," Iona snarled. "All those stories you told us about fighting back—they're all meaningless. One thing goes wrong and you go running back to Renfroe."

"You don't need me," Dina went on. "You stay away for weeks at a time and you won't even let me help you. I don't know your plans. Sometimes I feel like I don't even know you anymore."

"We just said we do need you," Adrian countered. "You could go to another canton if this place reminds you too much of Link—or you could go to the gorge camp. You never have to see anything that reminds you of Link. You're dishonoring his memory by turning your back on the war. He would have wanted you to keep fighting.

"Well, I don't want to keep fighting," she muttered. "I lost something when Link died."

"That's just another way for you to run away and hide," Iona growled. "You're just like the other parents."

"That isn't fair," Dina fired back. "It isn't like that at all."

"Really?" Adrian replied. "That line about being able to help us from inside the city is just an excuse."

She turned around to confront him and saw for the first time that he, Iona, and half the Children in the room were on their feet facing her.

Iona glared at Dina in livid fury. "You're a slave," Iona snapped again. "You've always been a slave. You never came back from the *Savannah* to free anybody. You came back so you could give yourself to Renfroe. You were free. You escaped from Prideland and you came back willingly to make yourself a slave—his slave. You're doing the same thing right now."

"I'll just have to prove it to you. I'm not turning my back on your cause."

"How will you prove it to us when you *are* turning your back on our cause?" Adrian returned. "We need you out here even if you don't fight. We need you a hell of lot more than Renfroe does."

"I told you I made a promise."

"That promise doesn't mean a thing," Iona fired back. "He threatened your life. You gave that promise to save us and yourself. You don't owe him anything." Iona threw up her hands and spun away. "Oh, what's the use in even talking to you? You're one of them. You're a helper to your core. You belong with him if you could do something like this."

She stormed out of the house, and a second later, Karim and some of the others left, too. They didn't come back.

Dina turned to face the rest of her Children, but she saw the same mistrust and betrayed rage in all their eyes.

She finally summoned the courage to face Adrian. He didn't look at her with betrayed rage. Instead, his eyes went cold—even colder than they'd been these last few days. A wall of solid granite separated her from him—a wall that hadn't been there before.

"Don't think the worst of me," she told him. "I don't belong out here anymore. I don't belong anywhere. I don't know who I am or what I'm doing."

He inclined his head to one side to study her, but his eyes didn't soften at all. "The nice cats who treat humans well are more dangerous than the ones who treat people badly. It's easy to hate the ones who treat people badly."

"What do you mean?" she asked. "Renfroe is the only reason I'm here now. He's the only reason I survived to bring you and Iona and the Black and the Auroras out of the city."

"Renfroe is not your friend," Adrian snapped so harshly that Dina cringed. "You have to get rid of this idea that nice cats can be your friends. Renfroe is our enemy as much as any other cat. He's as much or enemy as Hector or Kaido or Khalid or any other cat that you hate so much."

"You can't put him in the same category with them," she argued. "He's been trying to help the Children from the beginning. I told you that."

"He might treat you better than another master would, but he's still a master and you're still a slave. If you don't see that, then Iona is right and everything you've been trying to teach us these last three years doesn't mean a thing."

This time, he was the one who walked out. The other Children stared up at Dina for a minute and then they each got to their feet and walked out one after the other. They left her standing there alone and too stunned even to think straight about anything they said.

Chapter 32

D ina hefted her bundle onto her shoulder and cast one last look around her house. This was the last time she'd ever see it, but she felt nothing but relief that she was finally leaving it.

She was leaving behind all the memories of herself and Link—all the evenings she sat on this floor and cooked his food for him—all the nights he watched her tuck in their Children and kiss them good night—all the nights she spent with him in that bedroom over there—all the days she sat out on the steps and felt that soaring feeling when she saw him come back from hunting—all the conversations they shared—all the dreams they discussed about starting over somewhere else......

She pushed those memories out of her mind and walked out of the house. The Children crowded on the grass outside her house, but they weren't waiting for her.

Adrian, the Black, Naia, Dexter, Cairo, and Aries waited for her at the bottom of the steps. None of her other Children stayed in the canton to wish her goodbye or even to take their leave from her.

Dina winced when she saw that Iona was already gone. She hadn't spoken to Dina once since Dina announced that she was going back to Renfroe.

Dina stopped at the bottom of the steps and drew herself up in front of Adrian. He stood five inches taller than she did. Why didn't she notice how much bigger and more ferocious he'd become?

This last break seemed to have made him even bigger than he'd been at the Council meeting last night.

Maybe Dina only saw him that way because of the impassable divide that separated her from all her Children now.

Adrian leveled her with a hard stare. He didn't speak to her to start the conversation. She winced again when she realized that he would let her walk away without a word if that's what she wanted.

"I'm sorry we couldn't agree on this," she began.

He dipped his chin once. "You've made it clear where your loyalties lie."

"I'm still as loyal to you as I ever was. I'll prove it to you."

"Don't think about it," he told her. "You're going back, so you must belong there. Your loyalty lies with the cats, not with us or our war."

"Let me prove myself to you. I can give you information about what the cats are doing. I can help you from the inside."

"How will you do that when you're in the city and we're in the jungle?" Kaiser cut in. "You're cooking up this fantasy to gloss over what you're really doing."

"Give me a little credit," she countered. "I wouldn't have gone to all this trouble for you, only to throw it away now. I'm doing this because I think this is the best thing for all of us—me and you."

"You're lying," Adrian replied. "I might believe that you were so out of your mind with grief over Link's death that you were lying to yourself, but you've spent all these years teaching us the opposite. I have to believe you lied to us all along."

"No!" she exclaimed. "I didn't! You have to believe me."

"Well, I can't. I can never believe a word you say ever again. I can never trust you about anything. None of us can." Adrian turned away and steered the other Children toward the gate. "Have a safe trip. I hope you find what you're looking for."

They all walked out and left her standing there. The rest of the canton's residents stood aside and watched the Children leave. Maybe these people didn't really believe Adrian when he said the Children would leave today.

The Children walked upright until they got as far as the gate. Then they sprang forward on their hands and feet, sprinted into the jungle, and vanished.

Troy and the other people who'd committed themselves to the Children's cause filed out of the canton following the Children much more slowly.

Each of those people carried a heavy pack and numerous weapons. They would follow the Children to their camp on the ridge before they all went out to war.

That left the rest of the canton's residents....and Dina. Iona's words rang in Dina's ears. The Children considered her as cowardly as the other canton residents—or worse.

Staying here was no longer an option and she couldn't rejoin the Children, either. She had nowhere left to go, especially not after the argument last night and now Adrian's comments.

She threw back her shoulders and took a deep breath. She would just have to show the Children that they could still trust her. She didn't have a clue how she would do that, but the road before her had never been clearer.

She set off walking and didn't look back. Troy's party headed southeast. Dina followed them at a distance for a while and then turned downhill going straight east.

The journey back to the city she knew took a lot longer. The survivors of the last massacre had traveled for three days over rough country to get to Riverbend canton where they would be safe.

She couldn't go back to Moonlight canton—not with so many of Adrian's allies living near there.

She camped in the open that night and followed the Children's example by not lighting a fire. She wrapped a blanket around herself, ate some cold roasted meat she'd brought from Riverbend, and curled up to sleep on the ground.

She consoled herself with the certainty that tonight would be the last night she ever slept on the ground like this. By tomorrow, she would make it back to Renfroe's house where all the old luxuries waited for her.

She found some familiar landmarks the next day and steered clear of Moonlight canton. She returned to the road by noon and stopped there when she saw a colossal army of Children engaged in a catastrophic battle against hundreds of cats.

She never dreamed the war could escalate this far this fast. Adrian had said he would regroup all the Children on the ridge, but he must have received reports of the Pride's force coming out and changed his mind.

Dozens of people battled helpers. They got all mixed up with cats and Children flaying each other to pieces right there in the open road. The battle covered most of a mile of territory blocking all access between Prideland and the jungle.

Dina surveyed the scene from a distance. She didn't see any Children she knew, but the battle became so chaotic and violent that she couldn't really make out anyone of any species.

The noise coming out of the battle sent a shiver up her spine. Cats yowled and roared. Children bellowed and snarled. The screams and cries drifting to her ears sounded like cats, people, and Children all being torn limb from limb right here in front of her.

She cut a wide circle away from the road and struck out over open farmland heading east. She didn't want to get caught in the fighting.

She made it another mile and still didn't put the battle behind her. She searched the horizon for a clear path to get back to the road. The subsidiaries' village occupied its usual spot at the intersection of multiple roads going in different directions.

She didn't see any subsidiaries there. They must all have been out there in the battle helping the cats.

She faced front to survey the city. What would she find when she got there?

At that moment, the noise of death and mayhem erupted even louder than before. She spun around just in time to see the battle spilling over into the countryside. She didn't see what caused the shift.

In seconds, cats, Children, helpers, and people poured into the fields streaming straight for her position. She froze for a second and then burst into a dead run trying to get as close to the city as possible, but the battle was coming too fast.

Cats and Children tumbled over each other in her direction. They threw each other off and lunged for each other before they rolled over and over on the ground, but somehow, they always worked themselves closer to her no matter how far she ran.

A deafening bellow of some stricken animal burst out right behind her. She didn't see what caused that noise, but it electrified her nerves.

She shot forward running with all her might. She had to find somewhere to get away from all this chaos and upheaval, so she bolted for the one refuge available.

She charged into the village, but the battle overran that, too. She swerved around a random house and almost ran straight into four cats charging straight for her.

She skidded back behind the house only to realize a second later that a pack of seven Children were running these cats down from behind.

The Children were all big, muscular, burly men with dark fur. They ran on all fours, overtook the cats, pounced on them, and all of them smashed into a different house hard enough to crack the mud walls.

The whole group went down snarling, slashing, biting, and tearing. Dina dashed away in a different direction, but the battle surrounded her on all sides.

Four people in canton clothes hounded a group of helpers out of the fields and onto the road. The helpers spun backward to confront their attackers and the two sides rushed each other right in front of Dina.

Everywhere she turned, she ran almost under the feet of some attacking force bent on killing anyone in their path.

She charged back the way she came, and in her last act of desperation, she raced toward a barn on the very outskirts of the village.

She had a flashback of Frank telling her how he'd hidden in a barn when the cats were hunting for him. The smell of animal manure masked his scent until the cats went away.

This might not work, but she had to try it. She ripped the door open, dove inside, and then cast around for somewhere to hide.

The screaming, howling, snarling, tearing sounds coming from outside triggered another instinctive reaction. She sprang for the nearest stall, tore it open, and rushed into it, only to freeze all over again.

A woman huddled in the straw clutching five human children around her. Dina had to stop there and blink at them. She'd spent the last three years around Children. She wasn't used to seeing regular human children without fur and fangs.

Her brain took another five seconds to recognize them. The woman was Darcy Mathus and she crouched in the corner with one arm around her daughter Sonya.

Chapter 33

"What's happening out there?" Darcy whispered to Dina.

Dina crouched against the wall next to Sonya and listened to the sounds of roaring, yowling, bellowing, and thumping coming from outside the barn. "The Children are out there. They're fighting the Pride."

"They'll kill us all," one of the younger boys murmured.

"No, they won't," Dina replied. "The Children won't, I mean. They don't want to hurt anyone. They just want......"

She trailed off. She couldn't explain the Children to these people.

She could just imagine what the Pride had been telling everyone about the Children. She would have an uphill battle to overcome that if she could overcome it at all.

"Father's out there," the younger girl added. "The Children will kill him."

"If he's trying to kill them, then you're right," Dina replied. "You can't expect the Children to just stand around waiting for someone to come along and kill them. They have a right to defend themselves against anyone who threatens them no matter who it is. That's why they're fighting. They're fighting for their right to live—which the Pride is trying to take away from them."

Darcy looked up at Dina with huge eyes. "Have you seen them? Have you seen the Children in person—I mean, up close?"

Dina looked away. "Yes, I've seen them."

"The factors say the Children are going to kill us all," the older boy told her. "They say the Children want to wipe out everyone and take the planet for themselves."

Dina snorted. "You should know better than to believe anything the factors tell you. If the factors said it, you can believe the opposite is true."

Darcy gasped. "You could get visited for saying that!"

"I don't care if I do," Dina countered. "No one can stop me from saying what's true. The Children don't want to kill anyone, especially not the helpers and subsidiaries. The Children just want to live their lives in peace. The cats are the ones who have decided to wipe out all the Children. The Children were just helpless babies when the Pride started killing every Child they could find. They would do the same thing now if the Children didn't fight back."

"You're a liar," the older boy fired back. "Father is a factor. He wouldn't tell us something that wasn't true. He's the one who's out there protecting us from the Children."

"We're safer from the Children than we are from the Pride," Dina replied and let the subject drop.

She should have expected that no one in Prideland would listen to reason when it came to the Children. Everyone would believe whatever the factors told them.

The noise outside faded. "It sounds like they're getting farther away," Darcy murmured. "Maybe they'll leave."

"I'm hungry," one of the younger boys complained.

"Just a little longer, sweetheart," Darcy told him and turned back to Dina. "What are you doing here? You shouldn't have left the city again. Your benefactor won't be happy."

"Don't worry. I had his permission to leave and I'm on my way back to him right now." Dina spun around to stare at Darcy when she remembered.

Darcy and Sonya had helped Dina and Tania escape from Prideland with Dina's Children. Did Darcy even remember that?

Maybe Darcy thought Dina delivered the Children to the canton and then returned to the city afterward. Darcy didn't know that Dina had been out in the jungle all this time—with the Children.

Dina looked away and rested her head against the hard boards behind her. None of these people knew anything about what she'd been doing for the last three years. None of them knew about Link.....or the war......or Tania.....or anything.

It didn't seem possible that an entire society could exist that didn't know about Adrian and Iona and Karim and Riyadh and all the Children.

They formed such a massive part of who she was. They *were* her whole world—they *were*. They had been, but they weren't her whole world now.

The noise faded entirely and silence fell over the barn....and then the rest of the village. "How long do we have to wait?" the older boy asked.

Darcy opened her mouth to answer when the outer barn door burst open and footsteps thumped on the dirt floor outside. "Darcy!" a man called.

The stall door flew open and Alexander Mathus staggered in. Blood coated his shirt from his elbow to his wrist and ran from his scalp to cover his cheek. He limped badly on his left leg.

Darcy shot off the floor and left her children sitting there. They followed more slowly while she grabbed Alexander, helped him back out of the stall, and lowered him onto a bench against the wall.

"Oh, what did they do to you?" Darcy moaned. "Those Children are devils! I knew it!"

"The Children didn't do this," Alexander growled. "We never got anywhere near the Children. They have hundreds of people fighting for them. Their people take the helpers and subsidiaries. The Children only fight the cats."

"Then Dina is right," Sonya interjected from behind her mother's back. "The Children aren't interested in fighting people."

Alexander shot his daughter a death glare and then noticed Dina standing behind the other children. "What are you doing here?"

"I got caught in the battle," Dina replied. "I only hid in here to get out of danger. I'll leave now."

"You aren't going anywhere," he snapped. "Did you run away again? Is that it? You're as much a slag as you ever were."

"I didn't run away and I'm going back to my benefactor now. I had his permission to leave the city. You can ask him if you want to. He'll tell you the same thing."

Alexander glared at her. "You better not be lying."

Dina turned away, but Darcy grabbed Dina's arm to stop her. "Wait! Don't leave yet. It might still be dangerous out there. Stay. You can catch a wagon to the city in the morning. If you leave now, you could get caught in another spat of fighting. You don't want that."

"Yeah," Sonya chimed in. "Stay, Dina. We haven't seen you in so long."

Dina glanced at the girl and Dina's resolve crumbled.

She hadn't seen Sonya in three years. The girl had grown, but not as much as the Children did. She'd been eleven or twelve when she got the House of Man.

Now she's grown into a young woman of eighteen and she was as tall as her mother with a willowy, curvaceous figure.

Her oldest two brothers couldn't have been much younger than she was. The oldest looked about seventeen and he had shot up, too. He was as tall as his father and still growing.

The youngest boy looked about thirteen or fourteen—just old enough to get the House of Man. The younger girl looked about twelve at the most.

Darcy must have seen Dina looking at them. "You remember my other children, don't you? This is Christian....." She indicated the older boy. "These two are Peter and Jared and this is Alva."

Dina forced herself to nod. "I remember."

Darcy went back to fussing over Alexander's injuries. "Come to the house," she told him. "We can dress these there."

She helped him up and supported him while he hobbled to the end of the barn. Alexander scanned the village outside before he threw the door open.

Dina followed the family outside. The dead bodies of cats, helpers, and subsidiaries covered the road and the surrounding fields. A few village men were already working to load the bodies onto wagons to take them out of town.

"I don't see any dead Children," Dina remarked.

"They took all their dead with them," Alexander growled over his shoulder. "They took dead humans and Children alike. They didn't leave anyone behind."

Dina paused and turned around to gaze toward the jungle. The Children would take their dead up to the gorge camp and bury them there with Link.

More human beings would lie in that graveyard—the human beings who made the ultimate sacrifice for the Children's cause.

Dina would never be one of those people, but she didn't regret her decision. Her path led elsewhere. She didn't know where it did lead. She just had to find out.

Darcy and Alexander made their way back to their house. The children followed them inside.

Darcy lowered Alexander onto the floor by the fire, built it up to warm the house, and the children settled down opposite their parents. Darcy kept hovering around Alexander, cleaned the blood off his face, and then took his shirt off to examine the wound in his shoulder.

"One of those rotten slags stabbed me," he growled. "They're as ferocious as the Children. You would think the slags are half wild themselves. They're barely human."

Sonya saved the day by turning to Dina. "Where have you been all this time? How do you know so much about the Children? Did Senator Renfroe tell you about them?"

Dina almost told the truth, but she changed her mind when she noticed the rest of the family watching and listening.

"Senator Renfroe thinks the Pride should let the Children live," Dina finally told her. "He thinks we should integrate the Children into the Pride and make them an asset instead of trying to eliminate them."

Alexander snorted. "That is never going to happen."

"I know it's never going to happen because he's the only cat who thinks so—or rather, he's the only cat who has the courage to say so publicly."

"What is that supposed to mean?" Alexander fired back. "He's crazy if he thinks the Children could ever be an asset. They're the greatest threat Prideland has ever faced. You didn't see the way they fought out there. You don't know what you're talking about."

Dina didn't answer. She didn't tell him that she knew more about the Children than he did or that she'd seen them fighting up close and personal.

She also didn't tell him that she knew at least two senators who agreed with Renfroe about keeping the Children alive. Osiris and Elyse had both risked their lives to make sure their Children survived.

Now all their Children were out there fighting the war—and leading the war. The ironies just kept piling up all over the place. The Mathus family would never understand any of this and Dina didn't try to explain it to them.

Why was she here? Why exactly did she come back to Prideland?

She couldn't explain it to herself, but some part of her sensed that her role in the war lay in Prideland—not in the jungle or the canton or the gorge camp.

She wouldn't have been able to do anything there. She didn't know what she would be able to do in the city, but she had to at least go there. She would find out why once she got there.

Darcy finally finished tending to Alexander's wounds, sat down, and started heating water over the fire. "You can travel back to the city with Sonya and Alger tomorrow," she told Dina. "You don't have to walk."

Dina's head shot up and she looked back and forth between Darcy and Sonya. "You're going to the city? Why?"

"She's becoming a helper," Alexander replied.

Dina gulped down a wave of nausea. "You're.....becoming a helper?"

"She's going to Amaryllis's house," Darcy added. "It's a very good placement. We couldn't be happier. Amaryllis is a good benefactor. Everyone says so."

Sonya stared back at Dina, but the girl kept her expression flat. Dina couldn't read Sonya's reaction if she had one at all.

The news that Sonya was going to the city to become a helper made Dina sick—and to a benefactor like Amaryllis of all cats. Dina couldn't imagine a worse fate—except maybe going to Khalid.

At least Fallon was dead now. Sonya wouldn't have to deal with him, but from Dina's brief encounter with Amaryllis and Dina's later dealings with Anoushka, Amaryllis was likely to be as hard and cruel as Fallon himself.

Dina didn't say any of that out loud. The subsidiaries shipped their young people to the city to serve the cats all the time. Why should Sonya be any different? She wasn't.

Dina made up her mind to talk to Sonya privately before they went back to the city, but Dina couldn't do that here.

Darcy made some soup and served it to everyone. The more time passed since the Children left, the more everyone calmed down and went back to their normal activities.

A few other factors stopped by the house to discuss the battle. Alexander left with them, but they all agreed that the Children were no longer in the area. They'd retreated back to the jungle.

No one talked about the outcome of the battle itself. Alexander changed the subject whenever Christian tried to ask if the cats had defeated the Children. The Children must have won again.

Alexander and the other factors complained loudly about how many helpers the slags killed. "It's bad enough that the Children are waging war against the Pride. We would be able to help the cats defeat the Children if they didn't have so many people attacking us."

So Adrian had been right about that, too. The people who fought alongside the Children were an integral part of the Children's offensive. The Children really did need these people to fight on their side.

Dina couldn't bring herself to wish she was one of them. Troy would do a good job of organizing and leading those people. They would help the Children better than she could—or in a different way than she could.

She couldn't find any flaw in her own logic for going back to Prideland. The Children just didn't understand why she needed to do this. She would just have to find a way to make them understand—whatever that was.

She could have walked back to the city by now, but the prospect of talking to Sonya made Dina stay. She kept watch for hours for any opening where she could talk to Sonya alone, but the family never left anyone alone.

They stayed together in the house. Jared asked if he could go outside and play, but his mother stopped him. "You don't want to get caught by the Children, do you?"

"That's why I want to go outside—to play with the other children," he grumbled.

"You know what I mean," she chided. "It's for your own protection."

Dina finally gave up on talking to Sonya, and by then, it was already getting late in the afternoon. She didn't even care when Darcy handed her a blanket. "I'm sorry we don't have any beds. You'll have to sleep on the floor by the fire."

"I don't mind," Dina replied. "Thank you for your hospitality."

She wrapped the blanket around herself and curled up by the fire. All her agony about Link slipped farther away as she left the jungle and the canton behind. The relief lulled her into a sound sleep.

Chapter 34

D ina squinted when she stepped out of Alexander Mathus's dim house into the blazing sunshine. A wagon waited outside the door.

Alexander, Darcy, and their children gathered around to say goodbye to Sonya. Darcy petted Sonya's hair and a mist of tears glistened in the mother's eyes. "I know you'll be all right."

"I will be," Sonya replied.

"Make us proud," Alexander told her. "Serve your benefactor and come to a good understanding with the Pride."

"I will," Sonya repeated.

"Have a safe journey, then." He stepped back and Sonya climbed into the wagon.

Dina waited for one of them to show some kind of affection toward their daughter—or for one of the younger children to at least hug their older sister.

No one stepped out of line, not even to smile at her. She didn't seem to treat this behavior as anything strange, either. She didn't act at all distressed about leaving her family, possibly forever.

A man and a boy stood by the wagon, too. The boy was Sonya's age and he resembled the man so closely that they had to be father and son.

"You remember Porter Wainwright, don't you?" Darcy began. "This is his son, Alger. He took the House of Man at the same time Sonya did. You remember."

Dina nodded at Porter and Alger. She remembered. How could she forget? "Thank you for giving me a ride," she told Porter.

"It's my pleasure. Climb up and we'll get going. It isn't that long a drive."

Dina turned to Darcy and Alexander. Dina really hoped this would be the last time she saw them, too, but she didn't hold out much hope for that.

"Thank you again for your hospitality." She raised her hand to offer it to them and then changed her mind. She let it drop. "I wish you all the best."

"You, too." Darcy managed a watery smile. "I'm sure you'll be fine once you go back to your benefactor."

"I'm sure I will be, too. Goodbye."

Dina climbed into the wagon and Alger got into the bed with her and Sonya. Porter sat in the driver's seat and took the reins.

Darcy and Alexander thanked Porter for driving Sonya and everyone waved goodbye, but the younger three Mathus children were already turning away to go do something else.

Dina was still watching them retreat into the distance when Sonya grabbed her arm. "You know all about the Children, don't you?" she blurted out. "Tell me everything. You couldn't tell me with my parents around. Tell me now."

Dina glanced over at Alger. He sat there staring straight at her.

"Don't worry about him," Sonya went on. "Alger and Porter want to help the Children's rebellion as much as I do. Tell us about them. What are their plans? Will they invade the city once they get past the villages?"

"Hold it. Slow down a second," Dina exclaimed. "I can't tell you all that. I don't even know the Children's plans."

"You know more than we do," Sonya insisted. "When did you see them? Did you talk to one of them? You had some of them with you when you came through here before. What did you see?"

Dina looked away. "I did a lot more than see them. I raised them. I've been in the jungle with them all this time. They're.....they're my Children. My son is their leader. My Children are the ones fighting this war."

Sonya gasped. "They are?! Why didn't you stay with them?! Why didn't you help them?! I would give anything to fight with them."

"They wanted me to," Dina murmured. "Some other things happened....I don't know. I guess I feel like my way lies in the city."

Sonya blinked at her and then the girl's features hardened. "I'm going to help them, too. I don't care if I'm a helper. I'm going to help the Children in any way I can. You can help me, too. We can work together. We can give the Children information...or whatever they need."

Dina found herself smiling at the girl. "Be careful that you don't make Amaryllis mad. The Manx can be vicious toward anyone who steps out of line."

"I don't care," Sonya fired back. "The Children are the only ones who can stop all this. They're the only ones who can change anything. I'm going to help them. I don't care what it takes."

"You don't know what you're getting yourself into. Being a helper isn't what you think it is. Helpers do things you wouldn't want to do."

"Like what?" Sonya asked. "I can cook and clean. That's easy."

Dina squirmed. How much should she tell these young people about what the helpers actually had to do? "I'm just telling you that being a helper isn't always about cooking and cleaning, especially when you have a benefactor like Amaryllis. Not all benefactors are kind and caring. In fact, very few of them are. The subsidiaries don't want to admit what it's really like. Your benefactor will expect you to do certain things whether you want to or not."

"I understand all that," Sonya replied. "But you'll be in the city, too. We can communicate and arrange how we're going to help the Children. Right?"

Dina shrugged. "Maybe."

"You aren't going to the city to turn your back on the Children's war, are you?" Sonya insisted. "You're going back to help them. I know you are. The Children's war is the only way any of these people will ever be free. You know that as well as I do. You're the one who taught me that."

Dina shrugged. "I guess so."

"Whatever my benefactor wants me to do, it can't be any worse than the House of Man, can it? I've already suffered the worst that can happen to any person in Prideland. I have nothing left to lose."

"Don't be too sure about that. There are some things that can happen to a person that are worse than the House of Man. Sometimes the scars are on the inside instead of on the outside. They hurt worse than the House of Man ever could and those scars don't heal."

"I thought you would want me to go to the city to be a helper," Sonya went on. "I thought you would be happy about me doing whatever I can to help the Children. *You're* doing it. We can do it together."

"I'm just worried about you," Dina replied. "I don't want to see you get hurt. I mean, I don't want to see you get any more hurt than you already have been."

"I won't." Sonya straightened up and her expression cleared. "This is going to work. I just know it. The Children are going to win and bring down the Pride. Then all of us will be free and no one ever has to take the House of Man again."

"I hope you're right," Dina murmured and turned her eyes to the city getting closer on the horizon.

It breathed with all the possibilities she knew lay within its borders. She knew all about what went on in there, but now a new possibility raised its head—a possibility no one ever anticipated.

The Pride had managed to keep the Children and their war isolated in the jungle for the last three years. Now all of that was changing and the Children's war would be coming right into the heart of the city—right onto the Pride's doorstep where no one would be able to ignore it or deny it any longer.

End of Book 3.

Keep Reading

Prideland Series: Book 4: The Pride Unvanquished

No one can keep out of the war for Prideland or avoid taking sides as the conflict reaches its epic conclusion. The human helpers who have served the cats for so long will have to choose between life and death as the Children of the Pride take over the planet and leave nowhere for the cats to hide.

With Lieutenant Dina Dyer caught in the crossfire and her life in turmoil, she'll have to use all her resources to protect her family's survival and give them the one thing they need most—a place for next generation to grow up in safety from the cats' threat.

Loyalties will be tested to the breaking point and those she thought were her enemies just might be her most valuable allies. The final battle will bring Prideland to its knees and leave the planet's future in jeopardy.

You can find it at your favorite book retailer.

Sign Up Once--Get all Theo Mann's free books including brand new releases

S ign Up Once--Get all Theo Mann's free books including brand new releases

Humanity on the brink of annihilation.

A mysterious package, a corrupt officer, and a conspiracy that goes all the way to the top? What could possibly go wrong?

When a routine mission goes horribly wrong, Warrant Officer Ewing Archer and a handful of faithful friends get trapped in a battle to save the last survivors of Earth.

The human race has abandoned the ecological disaster of Earth. Now all that remains is a network of interconnected ships, stations, and satellites surrounding the planet.

But when war breaks out, Archer becomes a firebrand that could destroy it all....or save it.

Sign up at www.theomann.com to read it for free

About Theo Mann

I write 70 books per year—and yes, before you ask, all these books are my original creative work. Nothing written under my name is AI-generated or ghostwritten because I write better than AI and any ghostwriter out there.

People don't read fiction for entertainment or to escape from reality. People read fiction to see their humanity reflected in another person's character and story.

This is my promise to you. When you read my books, you'll see your own humanity reflected in the characters and stories. I take this commitment to my readers very seriously. My books are an intimate form of communication between us. I would never disrespect my readers by turning that over to a machine or another writer. This is my bond between me and you as my reader.

I write 20,000 words per day as my daily work output. If anyone with a public platform would like to challenge me to prove this in a controlled environment, feel free to contact me on this website's contact page.

I worked as a professional ghostwriter for fifteen years. Now I'm on a mission to set a Guinness World Record by writing 700 books over the next ten years and 1400 books over the next twenty years, all originally written by me. See my website for the full book list.

I'm also the author of *Proof for the Existence of God* and the *Crimes Against Fiction* blog. You can find all my nonfiction work at www.crimes-against-fiction.com.

If you have a story idea, or if you would like me to explore a series in more depth, or if you'd like me to explore a character by writing a spinoff series about that character or world, leave me a message on my website's contact page. I answer all reader emails, so ask me anything, tell me what you liked and didn't like, and let me know where you'd like your favorite series to go. I would love to hear your ideas and find out what you'd like to read next.

Find out more at www.theomann.com.

Also by Theo Mann (so far)

www.ingramcontent.com/pod-product-compliance
Lightning Source LLC
Chambersburg PA
CBHW052028020726
47501CB00004B/1297